THE
DEATH
OF
GOLDIE'S
MISTRESS

THE
DEATH
OF
GOLDIE'S
MISTRESS

A LIZA and
MRS. WILKENS
MYSTERY

LINDA NORLANDER

LEVEL
BEST BOOKS

Author Photo Credit: Jerry Mathiason

First edition

ISBN: 978-1-68512-571-4

Cover art by Level Best Designs

This book was professionally typeset on Reedsy.
Find out more at reedsy.com

To Jerome

Praise for The Death of Goldie's Mistress

"In Linda Norlander's engaging novel, *The Death of Goldie's Mistress,* intrepid sleuth Liza Johnson—with some help from a delightfully persistent octogenarian, a cat named Goldie, and a voice from within—unravels the mystery behind a suspicious death in a shady church congregation. An excellent start to a new series!"—Alan Orloff, Anthony, Agatha, Derringer, and two-time Thriller Award Winning Author of *Sanctuary Motel*

"Prompted by her irrepressible 84-year-old neighbor, Liza agrees to investigate the death of a former student. Haunted by her own childhood trauma, Liza finds help and inspiration in Charlee, the voice of her dead sister, who appears intermittently to guide her pursuit of a killer. Rounding out Liza's unlikely band of co-conspirators is Goldie, a cat whose personality is rendered in comedic detail... With an abundance of red herrings, a host of well-placed clues, and a satisfying conclusion, *The Death of Goldie's Mistress* is a must-read for mystery fans."—Lori Robbins, award-winning author of the On Pointe mysteries

"*The Death of Goldie's Mistress* by Linda Norlander is a true cozy with modern motivations and clues. Norlander takes us on amateur sleuth Liza's reluctant journey to discover who really killed a recovering drug addict that Liza had befriended. Along the way, a tenacious octogenarian, religious charlatans, drug dealers, and recovering addicts fill Liza's days as she investigates. An unexpected attraction to one of her sources keeps Liza busy, along with the pushy adorable cat, Goldie."—Lou Kemp, author of the cross-genre Celwyn series

Chapter One

Mrs. Wilkens, my eighty-four-year-old upstairs neighbor, barged through my doorway while I was in the middle of season five of *NCIS* reruns. I was in recline mode, lounging about, feeling sorry for myself because of my unintended summer off from teaching. She startled me out of my binge-watching-induced stupor.

"Remember Ramona? Well, Grace said her work called, and she hasn't been in, and she's in a quandary about what to do. You know she can't get around much since they put in those new knees." Mrs. Wilkens stood over me and pointed to her phone.

"What? Ramona has new knees?" This didn't make sense. Ramona was in her late thirties, and the last time I'd seen her, she seemed to be walking just fine.

"No," Mrs. Wilkens shook her head with an impatient expression, "Grace has new knees, and Ramona is missing."

Because I was bathed in the heat of the summer and the lethargy that comes from not doing anything constructive, I simply stared at Mrs. Wilkens. She wore a T-shirt that said *Resist*, baggy cargo shorts, and her day-glow orange tennis shoes.

"Ramona hasn't been at work?" I finally responded.

Mrs. Wilkens frowned. "Not for a couple of days, and she isn't answering her phone."

Ramona had a long history of drug addiction but had been clean for over a year. When I tutored her last fall to help her pass her GED, she'd been open about her past and optimistic that she was on the right track.

"It doesn't sound like her." Ramona had never missed an appointment with me.

I clicked off the television in the middle of the dramatic ending of episode five of *NCIS*. "Maybe we should check in on her. Maybe she's sick or something." What I didn't say was, maybe she slipped back into using.

Mrs. Wilkens was up and heading to the door. "Yes, let's go. You drive."

"Of course, I'll drive." I'd been in a car with her once and felt like if I ever rode with her again, I was going to have to write a will first.

It was one of those muggy midsummer days in Minneapolis that caused moneyed people to retreat to their cabins by the lake. The rest of us relied on air conditioning, which, in my case, hardly worked.

You could have baked bread in my fifteen-year-old Toyota Corolla. When I opened the door, the heat blasted out and nearly took my breath away. Mrs. Wilkens wasn't bothered at all by it—perhaps one of the joys of old age.

"Tell me about Ramona. I haven't seen her since last spring." I turned on my barely functional air conditioning and felt it spit out hot air.

Ramona, I knew, was Mrs. Wilkens's sister Grace's niece-in-law or something like that. She was widowed and had two daughters who had grown up mostly in the foster care system. When I had tutored her, she was working hard to make amends with her daughters.

Mrs. Wilkens buckled herself in, "Grace said something changed a couple of months ago. She got involved with a church, and Grace sort of lost contact with her."

I'd talked with Ramona in the spring at Mrs. Wilkens's eighty-fourth birthday party. She'd just passed her GED exam and said she was going to enroll in community college to study nursing. "Please tell me the church wasn't some kind of a cult."

"Oh no," Mrs. Wilkens' voice was emphatic. "Ramona wouldn't do that."

I wondered what bubble Mrs. Wilkens lived in. She should have a conversation with my mother about wacky church involvement. I said nothing, however, as an SUV skidded through a red light and almost hit us.

"Whoa." I hit the brakes. Several people honked at the SUV—unusual in

Minnesota, where people were so polite.

Mrs. Wilkens hardly noticed as she busily tapped out something on her phone. "I'm texting Grace to let her know we'll check on Ramona."

It took a while to get to Ramona's building because of summer road repair. I had to take several detours and nearly ended up going the wrong way on a one-way street.

Ramona lived in an apartment in a questionable neighborhood near downtown. Gentrification had not met this part of Minneapolis. When we finally arrived at the tired-looking red-brick building, I was drenched in sweat thanks to the tepid air conditioning. A police car was parked near the entrance, with its cherry top blinking, and a red fire rescue truck blocked one lane of the street. I had to park a block away in front of a rubble and trash-strewn vacant lot.

"Must be a fire," I said, sliding out of the car. Mrs. Wilkens was already striding down the sidewalk before I had the car locked. I wondered how she could have so much vigor when I, the youngster, felt so dragged down by the heat and humidity. Maybe I needed to pull myself away from binge-watching and get some exercise.

Several people milled outside the building. As we approached, I heard one say, "You can't imagine what the smell was like."

I finally caught up with Mrs. Wilkens as she marched up the steps. She was stopped by a uniformed policeman. "Sorry. I can't let you in until they've finished the investigation."

I joined her. "What investigation?"

He shrugged.

"But who?"

"Some lady on the third floor."

His voice was quiet enough that I didn't think Mrs. Wilkens heard him, but my knees weakened. Ramona lived on the third floor.

A woman wearing a long skirt and a bright red head scarf stood on the bottom step, wringing her hands. I recognized her as the building manager from one of my visits to Ramona.

"Do you know what is going on? We're here to check on Ramona." I pointed up. "She hasn't been answering her phone."

The woman's eyes, a beautiful soft brown, widened. "Oh, police are there now."

"At Ramona's?"

"The neighbors complain about smell." She hugged herself. "I call police and let them in. She die in there, they say."

This was not turning out to be a good day. To make it worse, Mrs. Wilkens's voice rose as she interrogated the policeman. "Young man, I'm here to see my niece. You need to let me by."

I grabbed her by the elbow and pulled her away before she got arrested.

"Listen," I said. "I think this is bad news."

Mrs. Wilkens was no dummy. When she saw the expression on my face, she simply shook her head. "She's dead, isn't she?"

I pointed to the woman with the head scarf. "The caretaker called the police and let them in. They found her."

I stood on the hot sidewalk outside the shabby building and remembered Ramona sitting at her kitchen table with books and a study guide. She had long, thick, brown hair and eyes that told the story of someone who had survived prostitution, addiction, and unspeakable abuse. It was the eyes, though—dark and filled with excitement, like she had been born again.

My thoughts were interrupted as Mrs. Wilkens gripped my arm. Two attendants pulled a gurney through the front door. The gurney clattered as it bumped over the threshold. A body bag was strapped to it.

We were not allowed into her apartment, and after thirty minutes of standing around outside, I finally convinced Mrs. Wilkens we couldn't do anything for her at this point. It was late afternoon by the time we got back from Ramona's.

On the way home, she kept repeating, "They said a drug overdose. I don't believe it. Ramona wasn't using, and she wouldn't kill herself."

I'd known a number of people, mainly friends of my mother's, who had done the rehab thing, gone straight, and then relapsed. In my mind, you couldn't predict what might send someone back to using or drinking. "I'm sure the police will sort it out."

Mrs. Wilkens's blue eyes filled with tears. "She wouldn't do this. Someone murdered her."

That night I crawled into bed in my too-warm apartment and tried not to think about the dark-haired woman who was trying to turn her life around. Every time I closed my eyes, I saw the body bag and heard the voice of the bystander talk about the smell. I tried not to imagine what Ramona looked like after three days in a hot apartment, and at that point, I felt tears rolling down my cheeks. Tears for Ramona, for her daughters, and for Mrs. Wilkens's odd extended family.

I tossed and turned, kicking the sheets away, pulling them back over me, and kicking them away until I was exhausted. I should have gotten up, fixed myself a cup of tea, and watched something stupid on television. Instead, it was as if I was locked onto the bed with only a hint of air coming through the bedroom window. I fell into a fitful sleep.

Charlee came to me in the middle of the night. In the dream, she called out. *Liza, I'm here.*

Charlee?

You have to find out what really happened to Ramona.

I do not. It's none of my business.

Liza, you know you do.

I woke up with a start, gasping for breath. "Damn it!" I coughed. "I thought I got rid of you after years of therapy!"

Charlee, the twin that died when I was four but still talked to me, was back. What more could happen this week?

Chapter Two

Three days later, I sat glassy-eyed in front of the television, watching the Hallmark Channel. After seeing the body bag, I had lost interest in crime shows. Just as the heroine of the Hallmark story returned to her small town after a disastrous marriage, Mrs. Wilkens pushed her way through my doorway. She held a cat carrier in one hand and a cell phone in the other,

She set the carrier down on the couch beside me. "Here, Liza. You have to take the cat. I can't have her, and neither can Ramona's girls. They live in a rooming house, you know."

I cleared my throat. "Excuse me?" As soon as I opened my mouth, I was sure I heard the cat hiss.

"It's only for a couple of days, until we can find a good home." She stood over me, her feet planted firmly on my worn carpet. "Please?"

It was more a command than a request. I looked up at her. "What? No. I don't want a cat."

She didn't know that when I was in fifth grade, I'd taken Foskie, the classroom gerbil, home for Christmas vacation and accidentally let him out of his cage. Foskie found his way into the heating duct work and never found his way out. After that, I vowed never, ever to have a pet.

As I searched for a nicer way to tell her to take her cat to the cat shelter, the determined look on her face suddenly melted.

"Ramona. She loved this cat." Her voice cracked. "I know Ramona didn't kill herself." Mrs. Wilkens started to pace in a little circle in front of me, waving her phone as she talked. "We have to do something about this."

I sighed and thought, you and Charlee. Why can't people leave me alone to wallow in my crime shows and maudlin romances? Can't a person be depressed in peace? I patted the couch and motioned for Mrs. Wilkens to sit down. Beside me, the cat hissed from her cage.

"Let's talk." I switched off the television as the star-crossed lovers embraced.

"They said she planned it, but I don't believe it." Mrs. Wilkens's eyes misted behind her thick glasses. "Ramona would never abandon her cat or her girls."

Outside my garden-level apartment, a gas lawnmower sputtered and then roared to life. Mr. Diaz, our caretaker, was mowing once again.

I reached over and took Mrs. Wilkens's hand. "Tell me what you know."

She faced me. "Ramona was doing so well since she came out of rehab. Getting her life together." She pressed her finger into the mesh of the cat carrier. A little pink tongue lapped at it from behind the mesh. "I don't understand what happened."

I patted her hand, feeling a little silly about it. Mrs. Wilkens was generally not the pat-the-hand kind of octogenarian, and I wasn't the hand-holding kind of thirty-something.

"Don't move. I'll be back." I stood up. It was time for a little happy hour— or, in this case, an unhappy hour.

In my apartment kitchen, I quickly mixed a gin and tonic for each of us. I was out of limes, so I sliced a limp, nearly moldy cucumber and hoped my neighbor wouldn't mind. Considering her state, I doubted she would notice.

Meanwhile, Mrs. Wilkens had taken the cat out of the carrier and was raking her fingers through its fur as if she was brushing snarls out of its hair. The cat purred, loving the abuse.

I remembered the cat from when I'd sat in Ramona's kitchen while she struggled with math problems. The cat had a scrappy look, a torn right ear, and a muddy orange coat. This was not the cutesy kind of cat who could go viral on YouTube—another reason not to have it in my apartment, even temporarily. Who wants an ugly cat?

When I handed her the drink, the cat didn't bother to look up at me. "Now, tell me what you think is going on."

In my mind, Ramona had probably relapsed and gotten hold of a bad batch of whatever she'd injected. I hated to feel so cynical because I truly liked Ramona and thought she had straightened herself out.

"It was that church. My sister Grace told me something changed with Ramona when she got mixed up with them late in the spring."

I thought about my experience as a teenager in Josiah's Household of Love and shuddered. If Ramona was seeking a new life, I could see her falling prey to a cult just like my mother had.

"Tell me about the church."

Mrs. Wilkens took a sip of her gin and tonic and grimaced. "This is awful. Where's the lime?"

I shrugged. "Ran out. I had to use a cucumber."

Normally, Mrs. Wilkens would berate me about not keeping enough fresh fruit in my kitchen. Today, she was too distraught.

"Where was I? Oh yes, the church over by Minnehaha Falls. Claims to have a multicultural congregation."

Josiah didn't have a congregation. He had a household of women and children. Maybe Ramona's church was legitimate.

The lawn mower roared by my open window, blasting us with noise and the smell of gasoline. I closed it and switched on the air conditioner. It rattled and eked out a stream of warmish air. The cat continued to purr on Mrs. Wilkens' lap.

Ode to Joy on Mrs. Wilkens' phone interrupted us. She handed me the cat before answering. The cat stiffened as I set her on my lap. I felt little claws digging into my shorts. Apparently, cat-purring time was over. I patted her like you would burp a baby, and she responded by digging her claws in deeper.

After listening to a few snippets of the conversation, including, "It all started after she joined that church," I set the cat down on the floor.

"Sorry," I whispered to her. "But I think you are drawing blood."

Goldie looked at me, blinked, lifted her tail high, and sauntered towards my bedroom. Maybe she'd note all the dirty laundry and beg to be let free.

Charlee whispered in my head. *A cat, eh? Good choice.*

Honestly, the voice in my brain was teasing me.

"Can't you leave me alone?" I headed for the kitchen, hoping Mrs. Wilkens wouldn't notice me talking to the thin air.

It's hard to describe Charlee, especially to sane people. Yes, she was a voice in my head, just like we all have that ongoing dialogue in our heads. Yet, she was different from the regular chatter. I'd tried to banish her from my life, but she was good at showing up in times of stress, claiming I needed her. Right now, I was a little rusty dealing with her because, after the Josiah's Household of Love incident, she'd only made rare appearances.

Poor Mrs. Wilkens.

"Why are you here?"

You need me.

"No, I don't. I'm perfectly fine. I'm not in danger, and you are a figment of my imagination. Or at least that's what the therapist said." Dr. Slack, the nice middle-aged therapist who helped me through the Household of Love "incident," suggested Charlee was the result of imprinting in utero with my identical twin Charlotte Lee, who died when I was four. The sane side of me thought Dr. Slack was full of baloney—or worse.

Don't believe everything you hear.

Charlee might have been a figment of my imagination, but she could be persistent.

"How can I get you to go away? Come on, it's been over twenty years since that pedophile who called himself a 'shepherd of the flock' tried to shepherd me."

You care about your students. Ramona was a student.

This stopped me cold as I mixed another gin and tonic. I am a schoolteacher, and teaching is my passion. I'd do just about anything to keep my students safe. "What do you mean?"

Find out who killed Ramona.

I took a sip of my second gin and tonic and poured it down the sink. The gin was cheap, and the tonic was flat. And Charlee's insistence that I *do something* gave me both a headache and a stomach ache. "Can't you just go away?" I hissed.

Help Mrs. Wilkens. You two make a good team.

"What? Holmes and Watson or Laurel and Hardy?"

Who's being snarky now?

While I was arguing with a voice inside my head and the cat was exploring and possibly peeing on my dirty laundry, I heard Mrs. Wilkens say, "Liza will help us get to the truth. She got fired from her summer teaching job, you know."

I hurried back to the living room to glare at her. I did *not* get fired. For the past four years, I'd spent my summers working with the fifth graders that no other teacher wanted. I loved the challenge. This year, though, I was outbid at the last moment by a teacher with far more seniority. Outbid and left in the dust.

"What am I going to help you with?" My voice rose in concern.

Help her.

I squeezed my eyes shut to wish Charlee away.

Mrs. Wilkens was about to say more when *Ode to Joy* interrupted us again. As I watched her answer the phone, I decided I needed to find her a new ringtone. This was not an occasion for joy.

Goldie sashayed back into the living room, oblivious to the fact that I was talking to myself. I looked at the cat and said to her, "I hear voices, you know. Best if you found a different home."

Hey, don't you forget I saved you.

"Once. Mostly, you nagged me."

Pah!

I might have gone on arguing with myself, except that I heard Mrs. Wilkens say, "Liza will bring me. No, I'll be fine." Her voice had a tremor to it as she put the cell phone away.

"She said it's ten o'clock tomorrow morning, and they won't have lunch afterward because the church doesn't have a working kitchen."

"What?"

"The Welcome Congregation by Minnehaha Park." Mrs. Wilkens headed toward the door. "We can leave at 9:15."

"We what?"

She turned to me with an exasperated look, as if I hadn't been paying attention. "The funeral, of course. I've got to arrange for the flowers."

"Wait." I pointed to the cat, who was sidling towards the door. "What about her?"

"Well, you'll need to get some food and a cat box."

"But," My voice rose to a near squeak.

"Oh yes, her name is Goldie."

After she left, I turned to the empty couch and asked. "Do you think someone at the church is involved in this?"

Charlee didn't respond, and the tingling in my head disappeared. Goldie stared at me and coughed up a hairball on my carpet.

"The cat shelter isn't too far away. I'd watch my attitude if I were you."

I sat back on the couch and wondered if I had just dreamed this whole scene—Mrs. Wilkens, the cat, and Charlee. What stuck with me, however, was the suggestion that someone had harmed one of my students. That was something I couldn't let go.

Chapter Three

I brewed a pot of coffee and sat at the kitchen table, staring at the steam rising from the mug. Charlee had been mostly gone from my life for years. Why had she suddenly reappeared? Was I losing my mind?

Goldie sniffed the air while I drank the coffee and headed back into the bedroom. I wondered what was of such interest to her. I had no catnip or anything resembling something a cat would want. I followed her into the bedroom and found her settling next to an old ratty slipper in the closet. For some reason, it made me sad. The poor cat had been taken from her loving home and dumped with Liza, the anti-pet woman. She meowed loudly at me with an expression that said, "Leave me alone."

"I guess you won't qualify as my therapy cat, will you? If you are going to live here for the next couple of days, you might as well enjoy the slipper."

I sensed the irritating buzz in my head.

Take care of the cat.

"I don't like cats."

You need her.

"No, I need a summer job to pay off my student loans." But I knew I also needed to find out more about Ramona and the church and what might have happened there.

That night, after a trip to Pet Smart to buy food and kitty litter, I sat on my bed and talked to the cat in the closet. "Listen, I am sorry you are stuck with me, and I'm sorry about Charlee. I don't know if she's real or my imagination, but she saved me from something really bad when I was fourteen."

Charlee had been by my side for almost as long as I could remember as a kid. She was the one who whispered in my ear when I had the impulse to do something naughty. She'd tell me not to, and I'd do it anyway, and then I'd get punished, and she'd tell me, *I told you so.*

"Listen, cat. I mean Goldie. I'm going to open a can of cat food. If you're hungry, you'll ignore any spirits that haunt me."

I walked into the kitchen and dished out a half a can of something labeled "Liver Treats." It smelled like raw meat left in the trunk of my car for two hot summer days. Goldie sauntered out and delicately ate it.

"You know, Goldie, I sort of remember Charlee, my twin, when she was alive. She was the quiet one. Never got into trouble. When I got into Mother's lipstick and decided to create art on the wall, I remember my mother with her arms on her hips saying, 'Why can't you be more like Charlee? And then, one day, Charlee was gone.'"

Goldie didn't care right now about me or Charlee. She was too busy filling her belly with meat and grain by-products. I hoped she wouldn't throw up on the rug.

"I found out later that Charlee was so quiet and gentle because she had a congenital heart condition. She died when I was four, but she stayed with me."

At least, that's how Dr. Slack presented it. "Liza, that voice in your head isn't really someone else. It's a different half of you."

I'd wanted to spit out, "Like Jekyll and Hyde?" But even as a fourteen-year-old, I had the sense to keep my mouth shut—especially if I wanted out of the adolescent psych ward. My twin with the voice that whispered in my ear became a secret.

After Goldie finished her dinner, she wandered back to the bedroom and left me with my thoughts about Charlee and Ramona and this mysterious church. I decided I needed a walk in the twilight to clear my head.

It was a warm, languid Minnesota summer night that held in the odors of the day. As I walked down the block, I smelled the faint scent of roses from the neighbor's yard. What should I do about Ramona's death? Mrs. Wilkens thought it was murder. I thought the poor woman had relapsed.

But Charlee was insistent I do something.

Which opened up the next question. What should I do about Charlee showing up so persistently after all these years? "I guess I'll have to call Dr. Slack, assuming she's still practicing," I mumbled.

A shimmer built in my head. *I'm real. Or maybe sort of real. You can't wish me away.*

"You always were such a pain."

Someone had to keep you out of trouble.

"If you are so real. Or 'sort of real' why did you go away for all those years."

You didn't need me.

"Well, I sure don't need you now."

Says the woman who spends these beautiful summer days watching reruns on television instead of going with your friends on the Superior Hiking Trail.

"I would have gone with them, except I thought I had a summer job."

Harumph! You never liked hiking.

A woman pushing a baby carriage and walking a little dog approached me. The dog immediately started to yip.

"Buttons! Behave!" She spoke as if you could reason with a yappy little dog. The woman tugged on the leash.

I passed her with a little wave. As soon as we got by her, Buttons stopped whining.

See, even the animals know how much you don't like them.

I opened my mouth to retort, but she was right. I loved the kids and all my students. Pets—not so much. Good thing Goldie was a temporary cat.

When I reached my apartment building, set between two older South Minneapolis houses, I stopped. My school colleagues sometimes teased me about living in "The Elderly Arms" because most of the residents were over age seventy. Many of them had moved in long before I was born.

I watched as the light in the second-floor corner apartment snapped off. Mrs. Wilkens had finally gone to bed.

When I let myself in, Goldie made a dash to escape. She almost got by me before I grabbed her by the scruff of her neck.

"Hey," I closed the door behind me and glared at the cat. "I bought you food and some of that disgusting kitty litter. You'd better appreciate it while you can. You've got three days with me, and if they don't find you a home, Cat Haven is your next stop."

As soon as I set her down, she scrambled for the bedroom.

In her wake, I surveyed my living room. It had the ambiance of an undergraduate student apartment, complete with a brick-and-board bookshelf. The coffee table was littered with several overturned paperback books, an empty coffee mug, and a juice glass with orange sludge in the bottom.

"See? I don't need a cat. I need a housekeeper," I muttered, cleaning the dirty dishes off the coffee table.

That night, my dreams were filled with images of Ramona lying crookedly on the floor with a giant needle sticking out of her arm. As I approached her, the room filled with dark smoke. Something evil licked at the back of my legs. If I could reach her, I could save her. I tried to call out, and the sound came out like the cawing of a crow. I woke up with a start and looked over to see two cat eyes staring at me from the extra pillow next to my head.

I sat up, panting from the fear I'd felt in the dream. Goldie jumped off the bed, landing on the floor with a soft thud. As I watched her slip into the closet, it occurred to me that Goldie was the only witness to the death of her mistress. I wished she could tell me what happened, just like I wished someone could tell me why Charlee had suddenly shown up.

My head pounded, telling me I hadn't hydrated enough after drinking gin and following it up with coffee. I stumbled to the bathroom for some ibuprofen, trying to shake off the dream.

I groped in the dark for the bottle because I didn't want to see my face in the mirror. After fumbling around and knocking the plastic drinking glass onto the floor, I relented and pulled the cord on the light over the sink.

As blobs of light floated in front of my eyes, the person who stared back at me wasn't a pretty sight. Her short blond hair stood up in little cowlicks in the back, like the pointy-haired boss in the Dilbert comic strip. Worse, she had bags under her eyes and looked to be about the same age as Mrs. Wilkens. The face was too thin, and the eyes too puffy.

"Thirty-something going on eighty, I guess. No wonder you scared the cat," I growled, swallowing the pills.

Chapter Four

The next morning, Mrs. Wilkens met me in the parking lot behind our building. She wore a pink, flowered shirtwaist dress that was probably in style in 1961, and she carried a big white purse in the crook of her elbow. If she'd put on a hat and white gloves, she could have been the late Queen Elizabeth. I dressed in the only pair of summer slacks that didn't have ink or coffee stains.

After we were buckled into my old Corolla with the bald rear tires, I turned to her. "Where is it we're going?"

She gave me the address for the Welcome Congregation Church and said nothing more. I was surprised she didn't ask me about the cat. Did I get a cat box and food? How did Goldie handle being in the new setting? Instead, she sat silently beside me.

As we drove, I recalled reading or hearing something about the Welcome Congregation but couldn't remember the details. I knew the congregation was made up mainly of new immigrants, and it was a Christian church with no affiliation with any major denomination. I assumed it was probably rooted in ecumenical philosophy and embraced a variety of beliefs. It turned out I was very wrong about that.

In the three miles between my apartment and the church, our only conversation focused on the best way to get there. I chose Minnehaha Avenue, even though she thought Hiawatha would be faster. Of course, she was right. Minnehaha was all torn up due to gas line replacement, and even the detours had detours. Mrs. Wilkens sat with her arms folded and a stony, I-told-you-so expression on her face. I felt a certain sympathy for the late

Mr. Wilkens as I finally gave up and turned onto Hiawatha.

The church stood on the corner with a small parking lot in the back, which was full, of course. I had to drive a block down the street to find a place for my Corolla.

"I can drop you off," I said as Mrs. Wilkens tapped on her watch.

She frowned. "I can walk."

As we headed for the church at a near jog, I noticed a scarlet red BMW convertible parked at the corner. It was shined to perfection with custom license plates that read DTOX123.

"Pretty high class for this neighborhood," I commented.

Mrs. Wilkens didn't reply.

It promised to be another muggy, mosquito-breeding day. Summer in Minneapolis could be wonderful—clear, dry, and filled with the smells of newly mown lawns. Or it could be hot, humid, and oily. Today, it felt like we had been transported to the jungles of Central America. For emphasis, a mosquito landed on my cheek. When I slapped it, my hand came away with a smear of blood. I once read that, while we spend our time fearing large animals like bears, we should actually be more afraid of the insects. I hoped I wouldn't end up with West Nile virus.

Mrs. Wilkens pulled me out of my musing by finally talking to me.

"See?" she pointed to the church as we approached it. "They haven't been taking care of it."

As usual, I had no idea what she was talking about, but I did note the paint on the outside of the clapboard church was peeling, and one of the front gutters sagged as wet leaves spilled out of it. A sign in front painted in simple lettering said Welcome Congregation. Services on Sunday at 10 a.m. Reverend Albert Jennings, Senior Pastor.

By the looks of the outside of the church, including the ragged lawn filled with dandelions, this was not a wealthy congregation.

I took Mrs. Wilkens by the elbow and guided her up the steps. We were joined by a number of mourners, many of them with Hispanic features. Inside, the church was about a third full. It smelled damp and moldy. I wondered if it sat on a rotted foundation.

18

A man in a wrinkled suit and a sheen of sweat on his forehead handed me a program.

"Seat yourself," he said in an unusually high voice. His accent hinted at Eastern European. He scowled as he dropped one of the programs on the floor.

"Not very welcoming," I whispered to Mrs. Wilkens. She focused on the front of the church and did not reply.

We walked up the aisle to the closed casket for the viewing. A spray of roses at the head of the casket gave out a sweet fragrance that contrasted with the moldy smell of the church. A small photo of Ramona stood on a stand on top of the coffin. In it, she looked almost surprised, as if she hadn't been expecting the camera to capture her. You could see that she had once been pretty, but the wrinkles around her eyes and a tension around her mouth indicated a hard life and premature aging.

Beside me, Mrs. Wilkens sniffled, then turned to the people in the front row. Two of the mourners were the young women. "Her girls. Good kids. The oldest is first-year law." Both girls had guarded expressions. I sensed they were working hard to hold back their emotions.

Next to them sat a younger version of Mrs. Wilkens. She nodded at us as we walked back to our pew. "How is your sister Grace?" I whispered.

Mrs. Wilkens didn't answer.

We slid into a pew midway between the back of the church and the altar. The organ sounded a wheezy chord, and two ministers emerged from a side door by the altar. The older one was rail thin with a pasty white complexion. The younger was my age, mid-thirties, with sandy hair and a blank expression on his face. At the older one's signal, we all stood and sang a hymn that was so musically complicated it made the "Star-Spangled Banner" sound as simple as "Twinkle, Twinkle, Little Star." The organist's voice soared above the congregation. She sang in a trained operatic soprano that seemed out of place in this damp, dismal church.

Halfway through the third excruciating verse, I heard a commotion in the back of the church. I looked back to see a young dark-skinned girl wheeling in a woman wrapped in a shawl, wearing a knit cap on her head.

Considering that it must have been at least 90 degrees in the church and the young woman was so bundled up, I surmised she was quite sick. Mrs. Wilkens glanced back, too.

"Jennifer," she whispered to me. "The minister's wife. Ramona used to sit with her."

I glanced up at Reverend Jennings and whispered back, "She's awfully young for him."

"No," she hissed. "Pastor Jacob, his son."

The service was more of a dirge than Mozart's Requiem. It was hard for me to think of this as a church with a multi-cultural congregation. I saw no evidence of the standard tributes to diversity—banners, colors, translated materials. Instead, the stained-glass windows were covered with years of grime, and the pews were barren except for tattered hymnals and Bibles.

The younger man, Pastor Jacob, gave a sermon that could have come out of "Generic Funeral Services for Dummies." Honestly, I thought he simply did a fill-in-the-blank whenever he mentioned Ramona. He spoke in a monotone, and I wondered if he'd taken too many tranquilizers before the service. Meanwhile, Reverend Jennings sat behind his son and stared straight ahead, frowning from time to time when Jacob stumbled over some of the words.

As Pastor Jacob droned on, I grew more and more creeped out by the heat, the mold, and the dourness. This funeral service gave funeral services a bad name. Where were the tributes to Ramona? Where were the humorous little anecdotes? If the minister said one more thing about "Death is the ultimate enemy," I swore I was going to leave.

The day was saved near the end when the young dark-skinned girl who had wheeled Jennifer into the church stepped out in a white choir robe. She looked to be about sixteen, slender, with large brown eyes and short, nappy hair. The program listed her as Hannah LeCuyer.

With a nod from the Reverend Jennings, she began an a cappella version of "Amazing Grace." Her voice was clear and rich and did not fit the small body of the girl in the choir robe. She sang in a slow and heart-wrenching soprano. Around me, the tears began to flow. Mrs. Wilkens dabbed her eyes, and I have to admit I developed quite an ache in the back of my throat as I listened.

At last, I felt some humanity for poor Ramona.

Hannah sat down, and the ministers led the pallbearers and the casket out of the church. I watched for Mrs. Wilkens's sister as the family followed the casket out. She stood about six inches taller than my neighbor and, despite the purple-gray hair, couldn't have been more than sixty-five. Mrs. Wilkens had once explained the difference in age by calling her sister a "change-of-life" baby. "Mother was eighteen when I was born and nearly forty when she had my sister."

The sister looked shaken but still managed a little wave to Mrs. Wilkens as she walked by.

I stood in line to express my condolences to the daughters. Behind me, a man in his early forties, wearing jeans and a sports coat, caught my eye. I nodded to him.

"Did you work with Ramona?" he asked. His dark hair was peppered with gray and carefully coifed. If it hadn't been for the blow-dry look of the eighties, I might have thought him to be good-looking.

"I tutored her when she was studying for her GED." I pictured Ramona concentrating on the worksheets I'd given her and felt an overwhelming sadness.

The man must have sensed it. He held out his hand. "I'm David Gray. I was Ramona's counselor. It's a terrible loss—for her daughters and our community." His grip was firm.

When we reached the front of the receiving line, one of Ramona's daughters greeted me with a look I couldn't read. After she shook my hand, she smiled at David Gray. I backed away, figuring they needed some private time.

The family and the mourners milled outside as they loaded the casket into the hearse. The younger minister stood behind his father as if he didn't want to meet the line of mourners. Instead, the organist stood close to Reverend Jennings and shook hands as people came out of the church.

Mrs. Wilkens spoke with her sister while I waited a discreet distance away.

She was using a lot of hand gestures and speaking with more animation than I'd seen in a while.

A small voice at the door of the church called out, "Can you help me?"

I turned to see Jennifer struggling to push herself in the wheelchair. Her face was pale and damp with sweat. I hurried up the steps to her.

"Would you like to go down?"

She nodded, and I carefully maneuvered the wheelchair down the rickety wooden ramp by the steps.

Once down, she looked up at me and smiled wanly. "Thank you. Are you—were you a friend of Ramona's?"

"I helped her work on passing her GED. She was a good student."

Jennifer nodded. "I liked her. She was nice."

We made a little small talk about Ramona's sad passing. A distressed expression crossed Jennifer's face. "She was so full of life. I can't imagine why she would go that way. You know, the overdose." A tear trickled down her thin cheek. Suddenly, her expression changed, and her eyes grew narrow. "But Jacob would know."

We were interrupted by Hannah, who came hurrying out from the church. She wore a beige shift-type dress that came down to midcalf. She looked like a waif from a 1930s orphanage.

"I am so sorry to be late, Mrs. Jennifer. Would you like to go back?" Hannah had an accent that took me a minute to place. I remembered one of my students who spoke English the same way.

"You're from Haiti?"

An expression of fright crossed Hannah's face. I'd seen the look on a number of my students. It usually meant, "I can't talk about where I came from because I'm not supposed to be here." Quickly, I changed the subject.

"You have an exceptional voice. It was a beautiful tribute to Ramona."

The girl gazed at her feet and did not reply.

"Ramona used to read to me," Jennifer interrupted. Her voice rose, "She suspected, you know."

"Excuse me. What did Ramona suspect?" I stared at Jennifer.

She turned her head away. "Doesn't matter now, does it?"

Help her.

"I will," I whispered. What made Charlee think she had to be my conscience?

"Did you say something?" Jennifer frowned in confusion. If Charlee was back, I had to remember to stop talking out loud to her. The one time I spent as a teenager in the adolescent psych unit was enough for me.

"I have some free time this summer. Would you like me to come over and read to you?"

"Oh, would you? That's so nice. Everyone else is busy."

"What would be nice?" Pastor Jacob joined us. He still wore his robes, and his forehead was beaded with sweat.

Jennifer nodded at me and said, "Jacob, this is a friend of Ramona's, and she said she'd like to read to me. Remember how good Ramona was at keeping me company?" Jennifer's voice had an edge to it that didn't fit with her sickly features.

Though Pastor Jacob offered me a limp hand and murmured, "Nice to meet you," the look on his face said he'd rather be anywhere than right here. So much for the warm embrace of the church. From what I could see, the Welcome Congregation Church was not a cult but definitely lacked a feeling of community spirit.

I wrote down my name and phone number on the back of the funeral program and handed it to him. If I spent a little time with her, maybe I could discover why Ramona had become so involved with this church.

Jennifer waved as Hannah rolled her back to the parish house next to the church.

As Mrs. Wilkens and I walked to the car, I told her I had offered to read to Jennifer. Mrs. Wilkens did not reply. Her gaze was fixed on Pastor Jacob, who had joined David Gray and appeared to be in an intense discussion. At one point, Pastor Jacob grabbed his arm.

"Looks like a fight is brewing," I commented to Mrs. Wilkens.

She ignored me and kept a fast pace to the car. "Let's get out of here."

Chapter Five

"That was a godawful service, and they should have had a funeral lunch," Mrs. Wilkens harrumphed as we drove back to our apartment building. "They could have used the kitchen in the parish house."

I wasn't sorry to miss the funeral Jell-O and ham sandwiches, although I did feel the service was a sad farewell for Ramona. I wondered how David Gray, her drug counselor, felt about it. I guessed he'd been to more than one funeral for a client.

Mrs. Wilkens stared straight ahead with a pit bull expression on her face. I knew the anger over the lunch covered for something else.

"Okay," I sighed. "Tell me why you're so angry with the church. Near as I can tell, their only sin is boredom."

A bicycle whizzed by me as I stopped for a light. The rider was not wearing a helmet and appeared to be oblivious to the fact that he'd just gone through a red light. I did the un- Minnesotan thing and honked my horn. The bicyclist ignored me.

"Pay attention!" I honked again as if that would make a difference. I guess I was feeling cranky, too.

Mrs. Wilkens ignored my little outburst and busied herself, brushing a piece of lint off her dress. When she spoke, her voice was subdued. "Ramona told me something wasn't right with the Welcome Congregation. They don't seem to care much about the parishioners, and many people have left the church."

Judging by the lackluster funeral service and the state of the church and grounds, I wasn't surprised. But I also knew churches tended to have a life-cycle, just like a family or a community. Some simply died out.

"She said something fishy was going on in the church, and Jennifer knew about it."

I pictured the ashen color of the minister's wife and remembered her comment. I looked at Mrs. Wilkens. "She did say something odd. She said, 'Ramona suspected' when we talked about her. What do you think she meant?"

Mrs. Wilkens chewed the inside of her cheek. "I need to talk more with my sister. I think she told me Ramona was 'counseling' with Pastor Jacob."

"Interesting. Did you see the guy with the blow-dried hair? He said he was Ramona's counselor. Why would she need him and Pastor Jacob?" I pictured the two men on the church lawn having an animated conversation. Maybe they were each blaming the other for Ramona's death.

She was quiet for a moment before she turned to me with a cunning smile. "Now we'll have a spy in the house to find things out."

"A spy? Who?" It was a stupid question. I wasn't thinking.

"You, of course. Pay attention to what's going on in the parish house when you spend time with Jennifer. That's what Ramona did."

Sure, and Ramona was dead.

My cell phone rang as I parked the car in our gravel lot behind the apartment building.

I looked at the caller ID. "Mother," I answered.

"Liza?" She sounded so surprised.

Mrs. Wilkens pointed to the staircase as we entered the building and mouthed, "See you later."

Meanwhile, Mother skipped all the niceties like How are you? and What's the weather like? Instead, she stated in an abrupt tone, "The news is bad."

"Yes?" I let myself into the apartment ready to catch the cat. She was nowhere to be seen. The kitchen reeked of old garbage. Had I forgotten to take it out? Poor raggedy-eared Goldie having to put up with my sloth. I quickly opened the window over the sink in my kitchen, the phone still plastered to my ear. Mother was cutting in and out.

"Well, at first, they said it was a back problem. You know, a pinched nerve from jogging."

I interrupted Mother. "Who are you talking about?"

"Chester, of course."

Chester was the love of Mother's life. God knows how the two of them got together. While Mother still wore long earth mother skirts and bangles, Chester dressed in Ralph Lauren polos and pressed khakis. When I first met him, I thought he'd gotten lost on the way to a golf tournament. He turned out to be both kind and good. I was happy for Mother.

She kept talking. "It was the physical therapist who said things weren't quite right. So, he went to a neurologist, and they said he had that baseball player thing."

It took me a few moments to understand what she was saying. "You mean he has Lou Gehrig's Disease?"

"Yes, that's the one." Her voice broke, and I heard quiet weeping sounds on the phone.

The news about Chester saddened me. After all these years, Mother deserved a decent man.

"Mother, do you want me to come?" She lived near Grass Valley in California among the redwoods and the poison oak.

"No," she hiccuped. "We have a couple of guests, so I don't have room."

I sighed. Mother always had guests, and most of them were undocumented. They often were women and children fleeing from danger in Central America. She called her log home a sanctuary. I admired her for it but also worried someday she'd get arrested.

"What can I do for you?" I thought about Chester's disease. One of my colleagues, a wonderful sixth-grade teacher, had Lou Gehrig's Disease. I watched him try to live his life to the fullest as the disease took away everything but his wit. He died two years after the diagnosis.

Mother paused. "I was just wondering if you ever saw Jason. Maybe he knows a cure."

Wow. I hadn't thought about Jason in a long time. We'd been engaged during my second year of college.

"I haven't seen Jason in at least ten years, Mother."

"But he's still a doctor, isn't he?"

"I'm sure he is. It's all his father wanted him to be."

Poor Jason was the son of a prominent surgeon. He was destined from the womb to be a doctor. I met him during his one-year rebellion—in fact, I was his rebellion. We spent hours together bemoaning our upbringing. We'd been engaged for about six weeks when Jason's mother cornered me after Thanksgiving dinner that year and wanted me to promise I'd raise the "child" in their tradition. I realized she thought I was pregnant and that's why Jason planned to marry me. This did not bode well for a happy, healthy marriage.

In the end, Jason was his father's son. He married a girl named Rebecca and specialized in neuro-surgery.

"Well, can you ask him about this baseball disease?"

I knew he was still in the Minneapolis area because *Minneapolis-St. Paul Magazine* listed him a couple of years ago in their feature on the best doctors in the Twin Cities. In the photo, he looked trim and smug in his surgical scrubs.

"Please, Liza. Talk to him."

"Sure, I'll see what I can do."

We talked a little longer. So far, it appeared Chester was doing okay. His legs were shaky, and if he got tired, he needed to use a cane.

"He has peace in his heart," Mother said.

"I'm sure you're helping him with that."

After hanging up the phone, I found that I was at a loss. In the span of twenty-four hours, I'd attended the funeral of a woman who shot up for the last time, met another young woman who looked like death warmed over, and now Chester, who probably didn't have long on this earth either. On top of that, Charlee had shown up, urging me to help Mrs. Wilkens and to keep the cat.

Enough of all of that. I needed to clean my apartment.

Goldie meowed from the bedroom. She sounded wretched. I hurried back to find she'd somehow gotten herself stuck in the closet. When I opened the closet door, she scuttled out and made a bee line for the kitty litter box in the hallway. Bless the poor feline's heart; she'd held her pee until she could get out of the closet.

"You just earned one day's reprieve from Cat Haven," I told her as she did her business and carefully covered it up.

The next morning, I called Dr. Jason Epstein's office at nine after walking a mile roundtrip down Lake Street to pick up a Caribou Coffee mocha. I was already hot, and all the sugar, caffeine, and chocolate succeeded in making me jumpy and irritable.

No, I couldn't talk with the doctor unless I was one of his patients. And yes, I could get in to see him. His first available appointment was November fifteenth. Could I give her my insurance information?

I hung up. After scraping the chocolate sludge from the bottom of the coffee mug and eating the chocolate-covered coffee bean, I tried again. This time, I used a little guile.

"Hello, this is Elizabeth Johnson. I'm his ex-fiancé, and I really need to speak with Jason—ah, Dr. Epstein. It's about the ring. He'll know what I'm talking about. Just give him my number."

We had broken up on fairly good terms except for the engagement ring. Mrs. Epstein had made it a point to tell me about it. "This ring has been in our family for three generations. It's never been on a hand like yours, so wear it in pride."

What she meant, of course, was I wasn't of her faith. I looked at her, and I saw my future. The breakup occurred the next week.

I refused to give the ring back even though I thought it was ugly, and I didn't really want it. I think it had something to do with the post-break-up meeting when Jason said, "Mother would like it back. She said it belongs in her family. She said she would be happy to buy it from you."

I was so offended I had taken the ring and shoved it into my sock drawer.

Goldie rubbed her fur on my leg. The receptionist paused, then cleared her throat a couple of times. "Um, well. Uh, Dr. Epstein is in surgery today."

"Please give him the message and have him call when he is available."

The apartment was already heating up. The forecast showed rising temperatures and rising humidity. I could either languish on the couch or I could crank up the air conditioner and finish some cleaning. I was about to opt for the couch when the phone rang.

Chapter Six

"Is this, uh, Elizabeth Johnson?" The voice was familiar, but I couldn't place it.

"Yes?"

He cleared his throat. "Ah, this is Pastor Jacob from the church. I was wondering if you could stay with Jennifer for a couple of hours today. She so enjoyed talking to you yesterday." His voice trailed off.

Considering how ill she appeared at the funeral, I was surprised she remembered me, let alone enjoyed talking to me. Cleaning my apartment or tending the sick? I weighed the two long enough that Pastor Jacob's voice broke the silence. "Uh, hello?"

"Sorry," I mumbled. "Bad connection."

Go.

I felt the internal shimmer. "Honestly, quit creeping up like that."

"Excuse me?" Pastor Jacob sounded puzzled.

"Oh, sorry. I was talking to the cat." Of course, Goldie was nowhere near me.

I agreed to see Jennifer in the afternoon. As soon as I was off the phone, I said, "You are getting pushy, you know."

You need to help her.

"Can you be a little more specific?" My voice rose in irritation.

Pay attention when you are with the girl.

"Do you know something I don't?"

But she was gone—just like that. I felt a little hollowness, a sense of loss, and, yes, a sense of relief. I pictured myself telling this to Dr. Slack and

30

hearing all about real and imagined voices and the concept of disassociation. "Liza, you've had a great trauma, and sometimes this is how the brain works to help you through it." Later, she told me to simply let the voice go, or if it continued, maybe they could try psychotropic drugs to help. I opted to let Charlee go. Or at least not tell anyone about her.

I spent the next hour doing dishes, taking out the garbage, and wiping up the sticky kitchen floor. Boy, I had let things deteriorate in the last couple of weeks.

Goldie watched me warily from a safe distance. "Really," I remarked to her as I mopped the floor. "I don't usually have an extra voice in my head." Goldie was less interested in an explanation of Charlee and more interested in another can of the vile cat food.

It was nearly ninety degrees when I stepped into the Corolla. I was sure you could fry eggs on the dashboard. By the time I arrived at the parish house, I was soaked through my cotton blouse and wishing I'd stayed home with the cat.

The parish house stood next to the church and looked neglected. It was a two-story bungalow with dormers and painted cedar-shake siding. I guessed the last time it had been painted, I had been in grade school. Heavy drapes were pulled shut against the afternoon sun, and when I knocked, no one answered. I tried again, with no result.

Part of me thought, "Oh goody, I can go home now." The other part thought, "This is the right thing to do." Clearly, Charlee had gotten to me.

I tried the front door. It wasn't locked, so I opened it while I continued to knock. I nearly ran into Pastor Jacob as the door swung in. He looked nervous. Sweat stains darkened the underarms of the shirt he was wearing.

"Sorry, the door was open, and no one answered."

"Hannah is supposed to keep it locked." He paused as if he needed to explain. "We've had some burglaries in the neighborhood."

"Oh." Somehow, the parish house didn't strike me as attractive to thieves.

The living room was sparsely furnished with a couch, loveseat, and a couple of straight-backed chairs. The beige carpeting was old and worn down. Offsetting the spare furnishing, however, were walls covered with folk art, including a display of intricately woven baskets. Three large framed photos of teenage boys with smooth, dark skin hung over the couch.

Pastor Jacob noted my gaze and said, "We were on a mission to Haiti after the earthquake. My father, the reverend, took those photos. It was before Jennifer got sick the first time." His voice dropped off.

The sound of breaking glass came from the kitchen just beyond the living room. A small voice cried out, "Ayah!"

Pastor Jacob glanced quickly at his watch and muttered under his breath, "Not now!" He turned quickly, and I hurried behind him.

Hannah squatted by a broken jar of Miracle Whip, holding her hand. Pastor Jacob stood over her, his hand raised as if to either bless her or slap her. I ran to her side and knelt down.

"Are you all right?"

Her soft brown eyes were wide with either pain or fear. A shard of glass was embedded in the palm of her hand.

Accidents like this happen all the time when you are teaching fifth graders. Without looking up, I said to Pastor Jacob, "Get a towel, please, and tweezers. We need to pull the glass out."

The girl continued to stare wordlessly at her hand. She was trembling.

"We're going to fix this," I kept my voice soft. "Let me see your hand."

The shard did not appear to be deeply embedded. A little blood oozed around the wound. I continued to talk to Hannah.

"What happened?"

She rocked back and forth, whispering, "I'm sorry. I'm sorry. Now I be late."

Behind me, the pastor had not moved. I looked up at him and repeated, "Could you get me a towel and some tweezers? I think we can patch this up."

I couldn't read his face beyond seeing that he was frozen in place.

"Please," I said. "If we can get the glass out, we might be able to avoid a trip to the emergency room."

"Oh," The words "emergency room" pulled him out of his trance. He left to find the towel.

While he was gone, I said, "Remember me from yesterday? My name is

Liza."

She nodded. "Mrs. Jennifer told me you come to read to her. She's not good today."

Pastor Jacob came back into the kitchen with a towel and a first aid kit.

"Here." He handed it to me and then stood over us like a sentry as I took out the tweezers.

"Does your hand hurt?"

She did not answer, but her eyes filled with tears.

I guided her to the sink and ran cold water over her hand until I could see the wound more closely. Quickly, I took the tweezers and nipped out the glass. As I suspected, the wound was not deep. I rinsed it and had her press the towel against it.

"Have you had a tetanus shot lately?"

Pastor Jacob answered for her, "Yes. She's had all her shots."

Something in his tone made me think he was talking about a pet. I chose not to comment, however. I wrapped her hand in gauze and told her to keep pressure on it.

Hannah nodded with a panicked expression before looking at the broken glass and Miracle Whip splattered on the floor. "I clean up. I clean up."

"No time now. They're waiting for you outside." Pastor Jacob nudged her toward the front door. He turned to me. "She helps out some of our parishioners in the afternoons."

Hannah slipped out the door to the sound of a horn honking. I wondered what she helped them with.

Pastor Jacob led me to the back bedroom. "Jennifer sleeps a lot of the time now. If she's awake, see if you can get her to take something to eat and drink." As we neared the door to the bedroom, he lowered his voice. "If she asks to use the phone, please don't let her have it. We've had some trouble…" He didn't finish his sentence.

The darkened bedroom was furnished with an old-style hospital bed, complete with metal side rails and a crank at the foot of the bed. Next to the bed was a table with a pitcher of water, a glass with a straw, a box of tissues, and a pill bottle. The walls of the bedroom were bare.

"Jennifer needs the simplicity," Pastor Jacob whispered, pointing to the walls.

I didn't know how Jennifer took it, but I felt like I had just walked onto the movie set of a psycho-thriller filmed in a mid-century mental institution.

"Honey, Elizabeth is here to read to you."

Jennifer lay inert under white sheets. Her dark hair was thin and cut short. Little spears of it stood up, giving her the appearance of either a waif or a junkie. She was pale, and her lips were dry and cracked. Pastor Jacob bent over her and gently applied some Vaseline. She drew back from his touch.

The whites of her eyes were jaundiced. She stared at me for a moment before she reached a thin hand out from under the covers. "You're a friend of Ramona's," she whispered. I noticed right away she had a red rash on her hands and wondered if this was part of the illness.

Pastor Jacob leaned in close when she talked. "Now remember," he admonished. "Elizabeth is a volunteer. Don't cause any trouble."

I thought he was kidding until I saw the expression on his face. His mouth had a steely set to it, and she appeared to cringe at the sound of his voice. For a second, her eyes grew wide. Then she shut them and let her hand collapse to the sheets.

Pastor Jacob said, "Let me show you where things are." He quickly moved me out of the bedroom. "She'll sleep most of the time. You don't have to sit in the room with her. I know it's not pleasant."

"What's wrong with her?"

He shook his head. "We don't know." Abruptly, he turned away. Beads of sweat rolled down his forehead even though the parish house was only moderately warm. Was he nervous around me?

"Hilda, my mother, will be here in a couple of hours. If you need anything, my cell phone number is on the refrigerator. Please don't worry about the kitchen floor."

Abruptly, he walked out the door. I stood among the walls of folk art and felt a little chilled. My Hallmark Channel television romances were looking mighty good to me right now. I even missed the cat—sort of.

A small voice called out from the bedroom. "Is he gone?"

I hurried into the bedroom only to find Jennifer's eyes closed and the soft sound of snoring. Was I hearing things?

For the next half hour, I wiped up the Miracle Whip mess and roamed the parish house. The sun had moved, and the front window was now in the shade. I opened the drapes to let in some light and to get a better look at the artwork on the walls.

I studied the photos hanging over the couch. In one, a boy who looked to be around fourteen, lounged against a chipped stucco wall. He gazed straight into the camera with an expression I could not read. Another was of two teenage boys in white shirts and dark pants standing in front of a little wooden church.

"Missionaries?" I asked out loud. No one answered in the stale, still air of the house. Something about the portraits of the boys bothered me, but I couldn't place it.

I checked on Jennifer and noted she was still breathing. While I waited for her to wake up, I perused the bookcases in the study and resisted the urge to snoop upstairs. Most of the books were either college texts on philosophy and religion or various books on the Bible. None of it appeared to be leisure reading. I wondered what I would do if Jennifer woke up and wanted me to read to her.

Peeking out the back door by the kitchen, I noted the yard had the same neglected look as the front, except the grass was worn down in a path to the detached garage. I considered going out to sit on the back steps to get away from the stillness and bad feeling in the house but decided I'd better not. My job was to remain vigilant to Jennifer's needs.

In the back hallway was a door I assumed led to the basement. It had a deadbolt on it that opened only with a key. Why would anyone lock a basement door like that? Were they trying to keep the dirty laundry from escaping? I tried the door and found it was locked.

When I checked on Jennifer again, her eyes were open. I stood by her bedside table and asked if she'd like anything to drink.

"You're a friend of Ramona's. Aren't you?" She whispered.

"I tutored Ramona so she could get her GED."

"Ramona knew about it, didn't she? Is that why she died?"

"I don't know what you mean."

She turned away for a moment. When she turned back, she said, "This is a house of sin. We are being punished."

Since I had no idea what she was talking about, I decided the best thing I could do was try to distract her. I sat down on the straight-backed chair by the bed. "You can call me Liza if you like. Elizabeth is way too formal."

She nodded. "I like that name."

"Do you prefer Jennifer or Jennie?"

She shrugged. "Don't care."

Outside, a garbage truck rumbled down the alley, creaking and making beeping noises.

I asked her about Hannah.

A troubled look crossed her face, and she waggled a finger at me. "Hannah shouldn't be here. She's a good girl. I taught her in Haiti."

"Why shouldn't she be here?"

She pulled her hand back under the sheet and closed her eyes, "I loved being with the children and teaching them about the Lord Jesus Christ." She opened her eyes and stared at the ceiling. "But how could they learn when they didn't have enough food to eat?" She turned to me. "What would you do?"

I thought about all my low-income kids and said, "I'd feed them first."

She nodded and whispered, "It's not right—what's in the basement? Hannah shouldn't be there."

"What do you mean?"

An airplane rumbled overhead, rattling the windows. We were close enough to the airport that when the wind was from a certain direction, South Minneapolis was hit by the noise. Jennifer didn't answer my question.

"Would you like something to drink?"

She thought for a moment. "Will you promise to give me clean water?"

Pastor Jacob wasn't kidding. Jennifer wasn't tracking well at all. I poured some water from the pitcher by her bed. When I offered it, she batted it away. "No. No. I need clean water!"

She must have gotten mixed up and thought she was back in Haiti. "I'm sure it's clean."

Jennifer pointed at the glass with a look of desperation. "Get it straight from the sink. Please get it straight from the sink."

I took the glass to the kitchen, rinsed it out a couple of times, and filled it with water. By the time I got back, she was dozing again. This was going to be a long afternoon.

The minutes dragged by. I sat in the dark next to her bed and wondered what was wrong with her. Perhaps it was some weird tropical disease. I picked up the bottle with pills in it and was surprised to find out it had a hand-printed label that simply said, "Give four times a day." I opened the cap, and an odor of skunk wafted out. It mingled with the vague aroma of garlic I'd noted when I first came into the bedroom.

When Jennifer stirred again, I said, "I have water from the tap. It's clean. I had some myself."

She stared at me for a long time before she said, "Show me. Drink some."

I took a sip from the glass. "It tastes like it came straight out of the Mississippi."

She smiled a little and took the straw. "Thank you."

That was the last thing she said to me until the front door opened an hour later.

"Hannah?" A harried voice called. "I need some help here."

"Hilda," Jennifer whispered, her eyes still closed. She wrestled with something under the covers and finally brought out a wad of tissue. "Please take this quick and hide it."

While I was stuffing god knows what into my pocket, Hilda, the mother-in-law and church organist, strode into the room. She had the kind of briskness I've often seen with teachers who were ex-military.

"Well," she stood at the foot of the bed. "Who are you, and where is Jacob?"

I introduced myself and said I met Jennifer yesterday at Ramona's funeral, and she asked me to come and read to her.

After glancing at Jennifer, Hilda motioned for us to leave the bedroom. "Best to let her sleep."

"She drank a little water," I said, standing up. "But mostly, she slept."

We stood at the front door. Hilda seemed distracted and in a hurry to see me leave.

I pulled the keys to my car out of my bag and turned to her. "What's wrong with Jennifer? She seems quite sick."

Hilda's answer was the same as her son's. "We don't know."

"What do the doctors say?"

A car pulled into the driveway, and Hilda patted me on the shoulder. "Thank you for coming. We appreciate all the volunteers."

As I walked out the door, I heard a little squeak that could have been a cry or could have been a door that needed some oiling.

This place was creepy. Part of me wanted to settle in on the couch and watch the Hallmark channel. The Charlee part of me, however, said Jennifer needed help. When I got home, I pulled Jennifer's tissue out of my pocket. It contained an oblong blue pill.

Chapter Seven

The phone rang while I stared at my empty refrigerator, looking for the last beer. I could still smell the garlicky, skunky odor from the parish house as I closed the door.

"Liza?" His voice still had its nasal tone, but he sounded older and more assured.

"Jason. It's been a while." I sat down at the kitchen table and dug into a nearly empty box of crackers.

"My office said you needed to talk with me—about the ring?"

After coming back from the parish house of horror, I'd spent at least an hour tearing through my drawers, looking for the engagement ring. Goldie sat on the bed watching. I could have sworn she had an amused expression. I finally gave up and retreated to the kitchen for a beer.

"I'm sorry, Jason. I needed to get through your defensive line. The only other way I could talk with you was to make an appointment for some time around Thanksgiving. It might be too late by then."

"Is something wrong?"

I told him about Chester's ALS diagnosis and Mother's plea for me to talk with him.

"Well," he said with reluctance, "I'm a surgeon, not a neurologist. Perhaps I can have you talk with one of my colleagues in the clinic. I don't handle patients with ALS."

Wasn't a doctor a doctor? Had we become so specialized that he couldn't give me the basics of the disease? No wonder healthcare costs were so high. Imagine if you walked into a coffee shop and needed a latte specialist or a certified dark roast brewer just to get your caffeine fix. We'd be drinking thousand-dollar java.

"Listen," I said, remembering now how much Jason could irritate me. "Could we meet for coffee?"

The line was silent except for the cell phone echoing.

I noted his hesitation. "I'm sorry about the ring, and I'd like to return it. Your mother wanted it back."

"She died last year."

This conversation was not going well. I remembered that, in our college days, Jason was a noted tightwad. "Would it help if I offered to treat?"

I heard a little chuckle. "Okay."

Now I had to find the damn ring.

We met the next day at 6:30 a.m. at a French bakery near the hospital. I drove through the South Minneapolis neighborhood with my windows down. The air was fresh and smelled of morning dew. It held the promise of a beautiful summer day.

Unfortunately, I hadn't found the ring. I even checked the back of my closet, where I kept a bag of clothes I'd planned to donate to Goodwill. Goldie had meowed at me with some consternation. I think she was afraid I'd do something with the beloved slipper she'd adopted.

At the bakery, the croissants were fresh out of the oven, and the barista created a design in the milk foam of my cappuccino.

"Wow," I said, looking at it. "It's a work of art."

The barista shrugged and moved on to the next customer. The place was busy for such an ungodly hour in the morning.

Jason arrived fifteen minutes late. He was dressed in khaki pants and a neatly pressed white shirt. His clothes contrasted with the shock of curly hair that looked like a fifth grader had cut it. I wondered if his wife ironed his shirts and did the barbering to save a little money.

We sat at a table by the window. Jason had dark circles under his eyes.

"You look tired."

"Emergency surgery in the middle of the night. I didn't get much sleep." He regarded me with the light-brown eyes that I had once found so attractive.

I'd like to say those eyes didn't have an effect on me anymore, but it wasn't true. They were still sensual, and I felt my heart speeding up. Or perhaps it was the triple shot in my cappuccino.

"How have you been?" He sounded genuinely interested.

I wasn't sure I wanted to talk about my life over the last ten years. "Well, I guess we've all been living in interesting times."

What would he, the neurosurgeon brain specialist, say if I told him that Charlee, the other voice in my head, had suddenly shown up again? If I recalled correctly, he was one of the only people who knew about Charlee. I'd confessed during a night filled with cheap wine and Doritos that my long-dead twin sometimes whispered to me. I'd wondered the next day, as I nursed a pounding headache, if he'd dump me for being crazy. Near as I could remember, he never spoke of it again.

"And how are things with you?" I sipped my coffee. I decided he probably didn't want to hear about my summer of sloth, the cat that now shed on my couch or Ramona's death.

He shrugged. "My practice is going well."

I concentrated on eating my croissant while he fidgeted with his phone. The silence was too long. I finally broke it by telling him about my teaching career and my master's degree project on using music as a teaching tool for students who didn't speak English.

"You'd be amazed at how they respond to rap."

"Hopefully, you aren't using X-rated lyrics." Jason sat back, smiling.

God, he did look good when he smiled, but somehow it didn't seem genuine.

I told him about being outbid for the summer teaching position.

"Usually, they have at least two positions open. But budget cuts, etcetera. Let's just say I'm currently 'at liberty' until the fall when school starts again." I paused and added. "At least I have tenure, so I still have a job."

"So, for the summer, you're lost." Jason did still understand me.

I could have told him about Ramona and about the cat, but instead, I asked. "How's your family?"

"Fine." His lips tightened. He did this when he was stressed. I remembered the upper lip tightening when I told him I wasn't going to give the ring back.

"Hey, we were only together for a short time, but I know that tone of voice. You are not fine, are you?"

He shrugged. "I'm busy. Sometimes it's hell to be poking around—literally—in people's brains." He turned away from me and looked out the large storefront window.

I waited a few moments and then brought up my mother's concern. "Tell me what you know about ALS." I described my conversation with Mother and Chester's diagnosis.

He settled back in his chair. "It's one of those degenerative neurological diseases where we haven't been able to find either the source or the cure."

"Is it always—you know—fatal? I mean, how long could Chester live?"

Jason shook his head. "It's not good. But he has some choices."

"Oh?"

"People who die from it usually die because it eventually paralyzes the respiratory track. He can choose to go on a ventilator and live longer."

I thought about Stephan Hawking with all his equipment and his voice synthesizer. It didn't fit Chester.

We talked for a little longer, but Jason couldn't add much to what I'd already read online. Our conversation was winding down, as I thought more and more about Chester and mortality. I stared at the design in my coffee and decided it looked like a piglet.

The door to the coffee shop opened, and a woman wearing a clerical collar walked in. It reminded me of Pastor Jacob and Jennifer. I thought about how ill she seemed.

"What do you know about a disease that causes weight loss and paranoia?" I stirred away the piglet in my coffee.

Jason smiled. "You seem to be after a lot of free medical advice today."

"Hey, it's costing me a very expensive coffee."

Without naming names, I described what I was seeing with Jennifer.

"She seems so sure someone is trying to keep her quiet. Does this make sense?"

"Hmmm. It could be a number of things. What does the doctor say?"

I shrugged. "The family tells me they don't know what's wrong."

"One thing I've learned over the years is to not try to diagnose without seeing the patient. Too many people are diagnosing themselves, their relatives, and their neighbors using the internet. They come up with some of the stupidest ideas." He shook his head, "Who would have guessed that people would flock to a medicine made to deworm horses, thinking it would cure a virus?"

"Well, I guess it might not cure the virus, but it might take care of the worms if they have them." I chuckled.

Jason sighed. "Sometimes the misinformation out there makes my life interesting. Like the woman I saw a couple of weeks ago with a glioblastoma."

"A what?"

"A nasty brain tumor."

"Oh." I felt a little stupid.

"Her husband came in with something he'd printed out from the internet. It was from a wacko dentist who claimed the tumor was because of the mercury in all the old tooth fillings. If we just took the fillings out, he was sure the tumor would go away." He shook his head. "They refused the surgery, and I read her obituary in the paper three weeks later."

He finished his croissant, and a little crumb stayed on his chin. It was all I could do not to reach over and wipe it off.

I was picturing myself trying to talk Pastor Jacob into taking Jennifer back to the doctor when I accidentally bumped my cappuccino, and the piglet tried to escape. Suddenly my coffee cup tipped, and the milky brown liquid went flying right onto Jason's clean shirt.

"Damn it. I'm so sorry." I fumbled with a napkin and tried to wipe off his shirt. Lucille Ball couldn't have done it better because, in my haste, I dumped the rest of the coffee on the table.

For just an instant, Jason's face had the look of a toddler who was just ready to wail. The expression said to me, "Look what you've done. You've ruined my life."

At the same time as this drama, Jason's phone vibrated. As I was trying desperately to mop up the mess, he waved me away.

The barista noted the chaos and came over with a wet towel. Jason punched some numbers into his cell. The barista and I managed to clean things up while he talked.

His shirt was blotched with coffee stains that even the best wife would have trouble getting out.

"I've got to go." His tone was abrupt. I didn't blame him.

"Sorry," I felt clumsy and sheepish. "I guess I owe you both a ring and a shirt."

Jason stared at me for a minute, and I thought he was going to ask me to call his lawyer. Instead, a grin slowly emerged. "Liza, honey, you gave that ring back to me six months after we broke up."

"I did?"

As I looked at him and the stain on his shirt, I had a vague memory of sitting at a bar with him. But when?

"We met in Dinkytown. After several Margaritas, you gave me the ring, and I poured you into a cab."

It was coming back slowly. I'd met Jason and his new girlfriend for reasons I couldn't remember. Maybe it was to return the ring.

"Oh yes. I have a vague memory of it. Didn't you marry the girl you were with?"

Pain flashed across Jason's face. "We're divorced." He looked away, busying himself with his cell phone.

"I'm sorry," I stammered.

When he turned back to me, I saw genuine sadness. "It's hard on the kids."

He waved as he walked out. "I'll have my colleague give you a call about the ALS. I'm sure he can fill you in. Good luck."

I watched him leave and felt a sudden, overwhelming melancholy. I don't think it was about what might have been. It was more about what actually was—Elizabeth Catherine Johnson alone, temporarily unemployed, stuck with a voice in her head, and worst of all, dealing with Kitty Litter.

As I walked to my car, I muttered, "Maybe you could use some antidepressants."

At home, I found Goldie nestled in with my old slipper. At least someone

CHAPTER SEVEN

was at ease.

Chapter Eight

I sat on the couch with my laptop and did exactly what Jason told me not to do. I put together a list of Jennifer's symptoms, including weakness and paranoia. I even added a red rash. Nothing concrete came up. I thought about the blue pill and decided to try blue pills and garlic. "Blue pill" brought up numerous hits about erectile dysfunction, and garlic gave me a page full of great recipes. Nothing told me why Jennifer had handed me the pill. I needed to let it go. I was not a doctor; I didn't even play one on TV, and I'd only met Jennifer once.

I was about to shut down and go for another romance on Hallmark when I decided to make one more search. I typed in "Welcome Congregation Church, Minneapolis." An old feature article from the *Star Tribune* popped up almost immediately. The article talked about the storefront soup kitchen the church had organized in the Cedar-Riverside area where some of the new Haitian immigrants lived. The kitchen had operated for several months before the health department shut it down for not meeting commercial kitchen standards.

The article noted that the church hoped to raise enough money to move to a defunct restaurant that had a regulation commercial kitchen. A color photo showed Jennifer and Pastor Jacob standing behind a counter. Jennifer had on a white apron. I stared at the photo for a long time. Two years ago, it looked like she weighed over 150 pounds. Her hair was long and thick, and she had a healthy glow to her cheeks. I couldn't reconcile the person in the photo with the wraith in the parish house bed.

I found one more article mentioning the church. It was older and featured a teenage Haitian immigrant who said that since coming to Minneapolis, he had found a family with the Welcome Church. I tried to picture the church as providing a warm, loving family, and all I saw were the empty pews and the dusty windows. Considering the current state of the church and the parish house, I wondered if the family he found had moved on.

"Why?" I asked the cat. "Why did your mistress spend time with that church?"

Goldie raised her head at the sound of my voice, then settled back down for her cat nap. While she slept, I switched on the television. This time, I went back to *NCIS*. As the characters bantered to each other, my irritation grew. Within ten minutes of the start of the program, I found myself talking to the cat again.

"Look," I pointed to the television. "We both know that the murderer always shows up in the first act, and he is never the primary suspect. After all these years, Agent Gibbs, why haven't you figured it out?"

I half expected the cat to answer. What was wrong with me today? At least Charlee hadn't appeared to tell me what to do.

A friend of mine who studied screenplay writing told me that one-hour commercial television programs were actually 44 minutes long and had four acts. In Act I, the crime is committed, and we see the first of the suspects. In Act II, the plot thickens as the heroes go down the wrong road. At the end of Act II, just before the commercial, the hero says, "Wait, maybe we're looking at the wrong person." Act III has them pursue the right person, and Act IV is the confession and the tie-up of the loose ends.

Fortunately, the phone rang before I worked myself into a rant about formulaic television and scared the cat back into the closet. Pastor Jacob's cell phone was on my Caller ID.

"Elizabeth? This is Pastor Jacob. I'm so sorry to ask on such short notice, but my mother has an urgent appointment this afternoon, and I'm wondering if you could stay with Jennifer for an hour or so." He paused. "She really enjoyed your visit yesterday."

I could have said no, but in the back of my brain, Charlee's voice repeated, *Go.* Besides, the blue pill intrigued me. We agreed that I would come at two.

Mrs. Wilkens called as I slid into the hot seat in my car.

"I've got news from my sister about Ramona and that church."

"I'm on my way to read to Jennifer." I buckled my seatbelt. "We can talk this evening."

Mrs. Wilkens paused. "Grace thought there was something not quite right about the church and worried that Ramona didn't realize it. I wonder if it's dangerous for you to be involved?"

The place was creepy, but I doubted it was dangerous. What could a sick girl do to me? "I'll be fine." I hung up the phone.

A dark van sat parked in the church lot. When I knocked on the parish house door, a man with short, slicked-back dark hair opened it. He looked to be in his mid-twenties and wore a long-sleeved black shirt open at the neck. Little tufts of brownish chest hair peeked out.

He studied me. "Yes?" The accent was foreign.

I put my hand out. "Hi, I'm Liza."

Mr. Slick-hair did not take my hand. He continued to block the entrance to the parish house. I quickly grew annoyed.

"I don't think we've met yet. Your name is?" I smiled broadly as I tried to slip past him.

He grabbed my upper arm before I could step into the living room. "Miss," he said. "You shouldn't come in." His fingers bit down on my arm. He had an Eastern European accent. Russian? Romanian?

I tried to shake him off. "Excuse me," I said loudly. "I was invited." I nearly shouted the last sentence.

He did not let go. I wondered if he was going to shove me back out the door when I heard a door close. It sounded like it was off the kitchen—perhaps the mysterious basement door. Pastor Jacob walked to the front entrance. He looked at Mr. Slick-hair and said quickly, "Welcome, Elizabeth. Jennifer will be so glad you came."

Mr. Slick let go.

Pastor Jacob said without smiling, "Elizabeth, this is one of my church deacons, Nicholas."

Nicholas nodded at me before walking out the front door.

"I thought deacons were more friendly than that."

Pastor Jacob shrugged it off. "He's new to this culture and very protective of Jennifer. He was a great help in Haiti."

Doing what? I wondered. Robbing widows and orphans?

"How is Jennifer?" I rubbed my arm where the deacon had held me.

Pastor Jacob watched me, and I thought I saw a look of concern. Was he sad for Jennifer or sad that his henchman had been so rude?

"She's doing as well as can be expected."

"And Hannah? How's her hand?"

"She's fine." His tone was abrupt and dismissive.

I waited for him to say more, but he turned away from me.

The bedroom was again dark, with the shades pulled against the afternoon light. Today, the room had a smell to it that covered the garlic, something like a combination of baby powder and an herb. Had they been burning incense?

Jennifer's eyes were closed.

I leaned over the bed and said softly, "Hi Jennifer. It's Liza."

Her eyelids fluttered.

"Would you like me to read to you?"

In the gloom, I thought I detected a slight nod.

"I brought a classic with me, *Jane Eyre*. I thought since we both like children, you would want to hear her story."

Sitting down on the straight-backed chair, I turned the little bedside table lamp on and opened my crumbling paperback copy of *Jane Eyre*.

I began, "There was no possibility of taking a walk that day. We had been wandering, indeed, in the leafless shrubbery an hour in the morning, but since dinner (Mrs. Reed, when there was no company, dined early), the cold winter wind had brought with it clouds so somber, and a rain so penetrating, that further out-door exercise was now out of the question."

When I was a teenager, my mother thought I should read the classics. She brought home a box of them from the Goodwill store. They smelled like mildew, and as soon as she wasn't looking, I dumped them all in the neighbor's trash. It wasn't until my first college literature class that

I discovered why the classics were called classics. I spent one whole summer catching up with the Brontës, Jane Austin, and George Eliot. After that, I discovered Maya Angelou, James Baldwin, and Edwidge Danticat. Oh, the richness I'd missed out on in my anger with my mother.

I read to Jennifer until I noted the rhythmic rise and fall of her chest. *Jane Eyre* had put her to sleep.

When I stopped, though, her hand emerged from under the sheet. In it was a crumpled piece of paper.

"Please," she whispered. "Please hide this. They don't know I have it."

I took the paper and said, "Jennifer, this scares me. I don't know if I'm doing you harm or good right now."

She opened her eyes. "Please," her voice was a mere scratch. "I made a mistake in trying to say something. Now I'm part of it."

"Part of what?"

"The pills."

"Jennifer, what is this all about?"

Her lips moved, but no sound came out. Before I could press her more, I heard the sound of the front door opening.

I leaned as close to her as I could, "What are you saying?"

"I pray Jesus will forgive me and protect me." She turned her head away from me.

Hilda walked in the door just as I shoved the paper into the book.

"What are you doing here? Where's Jacob?" Her voice had a puzzled edge to it.

People certainly were suspicious around here. I stood up and motioned her out of the room. Once in the living room, I turned to Hilda and asked, "What is wrong with Jennifer? Are you trying to hide something?"

Hilda pressed her lips together in a tight line. If eyes could truly flash, which they can't, hers were doing it. "I don't think it's any of your business."

I thought about the paper pressed into the pages of the book. Jennifer was afraid of something, and I didn't know if it was her illness or a conspiracy. I took a chance and said softly, "You're right. It isn't my business. I'd be happy to call the reporter who did the story on Jennifer and the soup kitchen two years ago and ask her to do a follow-up. Reporters are good at digging, and I think the public and the congregation would be interested."

Color rose up Hilda's neck all the way through her cheeks. Her mouth worked. I thought she might either spit at me or tackle me. Instead, she stared for a minute, and suddenly, her eyes filled with tears.

"Jennifer has a problem," she pointed to her head. "Sometimes she makes herself sick—for attention."

"You mean this is psychiatric?" I suddenly felt cheap for threatening the family.

"She had a difficult childhood. Her mother was mentally ill, and her father was an alcoholic. Jacob met her after his motorcycle accident. She was an aide in the rehab hospital. He showed her the way to our Lord Jesus Christ. She married Jacob and helped him through Bible College."

Hilda sat down in the living room under the photo of the teenaged boys. She rubbed her face, "I warned Jacob, but he's always been a rescuer."

From inside the bedroom, Jennifer's thin voice called, "Jacob, are you there?"

"I have to go see to her. She won't stop calling until someone comes." She stood up.

Before she walked out of the room, Hilda turned to me, "The Reverend prefers that we don't say anything about it." Her voice trailed off.

The front door opened, and Reverend Jennings walked in. He carried his thin body as if every joint ached.

"Who is this?" He looked at me and then at Hilda. Forget any ministerial warmth. His eyes were cold despite his frailty. I had a hard time seeing him as a welcoming presence for new immigrants and wondered how he ended up as the senior pastor of this church.

I walked over to him and held out my hand. "I'm Elizabeth Johnson. I've been sitting with Jennifer."

Hilda appeared to shrink in his presence. The briskness went out of her voice as she said, "This is Reverend Jennings, my husband."

He took my hand with a bony grip. "Are you saved?" he asked.

I debated whether to say, "Saved from what?" but decided I was now a grown-up, not a sassy teenager. I dodged the question.

"I was at the funeral for Ramona. That's where I met Jennifer."

Reverend Jennings's eyes narrowed. Before he could say anything, though, Jennifer called out again. Hilda hurried out of the living room, and I turned to follow her. He grabbed my arm. "No. Let her take care of it."

I felt like he used the word "it" to describe Jennifer.

Pastor Jacob walked in before we could have more of this charming conversation. I held on to *Jane Eyre* tightly as I fled the parish house. This was more dysfunction than I knew how to handle. Yet, Jennifer trusted me. Mystery or no mystery, I would stick it out with her at least a little longer.

"See what you got me into!" I spoke aloud to the absent Charlee as I slid into the car.

Chapter Nine

I slept badly that night. This time, I dreamed I was in the parish house with Jennifer walking toward me, holding something in her skeletal hand. Her eyes were closed, and she kept repeating, "I can't stop. I can't stop." Except no sound came out.

At 8:00 a.m., my cell phone pulled me out of the thick, suffocating dream. Goldie was curled on the pillow next to me, her whiskers barely brushing my cheek. I looked at her before answering the phone and wondered if Ramona had let her sleep in bed like this.

I fumbled for the phone, blinking hard to wake up my foggy brain.

"Liza, are you up? How's the weather?" Mother sounded far too perky for the hour.

"Mother?" I struggled to pull myself out of the parish house dream. The light of the brilliant dawn streamed through my partially open blinds and laid a striped pattern on my tangled sheets.

"Vincent was here yesterday…" The perkiness drained out of her voice.

I kicked off the sheets and stretched, accidentally elbowing the cat. She let out a loud cat meow and scurried off the bed.

"Liza, are you okay? Was that a cat I heard?"

I wasn't ready to confess to my mother that I was sharing a bed with a cat. "Just half-asleep," I mumbled. I checked the clock again and noted that, while it was eight in the morning here, it was six in California.

"Vincent was here yesterday," she began again. "He upset Chester."

Mother wasn't one to gossip or say bad things about anyone, but I knew she thoroughly disliked Vincent, Chester's only child. I'd met him once, and when he started complaining about all the illegals taking jobs from real Americans, I'd walked away. Near as I could tell, Vincent didn't know how to work. He was a fat, middle-aged boy whose only talent was wheedling money from his father. From what I'd been told, he was continually broke and continually scheming. I put him in the category of entitled deplorables.

"Mother, what happened?"

"He wants Chester to move to Oregon with him."

"Why?"

"Because … because …" her voice broke.

"Mother, take a nice deep breath. Can you do that?"

I heard her slowly let the air out. "Death." Her voice broke again.

This time, I simply waited for her to collect herself. While I waited, a stack of *Star Tribunes* thudded against the front door of the apartment building. Our building must have been one of their biggest paper version customers since no one under fifty reads the paper in that form anymore.

Mother's voice was wobbly when she spoke. "They have that law that says you can get a prescription if you want to die."

"Ah." The fog cleared from my head. I knew about the law because Mrs. Wilkens worked with a group that was trying to get it passed in Minnesota. It was called "Death with Dignity" or "Physician Aid in Dying," and the law allowed doctors to prescribe a lethal sedative to someone who was terminally ill.

Oh boy. I wouldn't put it past Vincent to want to hasten his father's death and get his hands on the retirement account.

"Hold steady, Mother. Chester needs to stay with you. California has the same law. If Chester wanted to use it, he could without moving in with Vincent."

"Oh?"

"I don't think it's anything you need to worry about right now."

I heard a dog barking in the background as Mother breathed deeply once again. "I feel better now." The dog continued to bark. I assumed it was the mop creature she rescued several years ago from the pound. He liked to bark, and he particularly liked to shed all over me whenever I visited.

"Mother, Jason is putting me in touch with a colleague who can tell me more about ALS. We'll make sure Chester is safe with you."

Mother filled me in on Chester's condition. He was getting an ankle brace because of some foot drop, but otherwise, it was fine. "His appetite is good, and he walks every day."

Maybe it was time to put the Ramona mystery aside and fly to California. "I can come out if you'd like."

The silence on the other end said Mother wasn't quite ready for me. "We'll be fine. The house is full right now. I'll let you know when we'll have space."

On one of my visits, her log house was so filled with people in need of sanctuary that I ended up getting a room at the Holiday Inn Express in Grass Valley. At least I could get up in the morning and not sneeze out dog hair.

At nine, Mrs. Wilkens came charging into my living room. She handed me a coffee and a fresh bagel from the deli down the street. Today she wore saggy cargo shorts and a bright blue "Nevertheless She Persisted" T-shirt.

"Well, it's nice to finally see you after my visit to the parish house of dysfunction." I noted her bright orange tennis shoes and wondered if she glowed in the dark.

"A little cranky, are we? Have some cream cheese with the bagel." She opened the little packet of strawberry cream cheese and handed it to me. "I had a long conversation with my sister about Ramona. She said Ramona was evasive about all the time she spent volunteering for the church. Grace suspected something was going on, but she didn't know what."

"You mean going on with Ramona at the church?"

"Ramona told her she was getting help from Pastor Jacob." Mrs. Wilkens took a bite of her bagel, leaving a blotch of cream cheese on her cheek.

"What kind of help?"

Mrs. Wilkens hesitated, then picked at her bagel. "They are better fresh. I never buy the day-old ones."

"You're not telling me everything, are you?" I handed her a napkin and pointed to the cream cheese on her face. Mrs. Wilkens had an amazing face for an 84-year-old—high cheekbones and smooth, blemish-free skin. I wondered what I would look like at 84. I pictured myself shrunken down from my five-foot, eight-inch frame, blonde hair turned bleached white, wearing a ragged Taylor Swift concert T-shirt. It wouldn't be a pretty sight.

I was pulled out of my reverie when she cleared her throat. "Sometimes people aren't who you think they are."

I resisted the urge to say, "Duh!" Instead, I asked, "What do you mean?"

"Grace told me Ramona was being investigated by the assisted-living place where she worked. Drugs were missing. My sister knew something was up, because Ramona borrowed money about a month ago—she said to fix her car. But it turns out Ramona sold her car after Christmas and was taking the bus to work."

I finished my coffee while Mrs. Wilkens filled me in on Ramona's sad background. Ramona's parents had owned a bodega in Fargo. Most of their customers were migrant workers who came every year to harvest the sugar beets or immigrants who stayed. Her parents did well enough to buy a house and start a college fund for Ramona. When she was thirteen, a man with a shaved head and a swastika tattooed on his neck walked into the store and shot Ramona's father. He trashed the store and wrote nasty things on the walls. Ramona's father lived but was paralyzed from the chest down.

"Wow." I thought about the increase in hate crimes with the ugliness of the current politics. One of my students, a petite little girl of ten, came to school one day with a split lip. She wouldn't tell me who did it. She'd shrugged. "Some people don't like that I wear a hijab."

"Did they catch the guy?" I asked Mrs. Wilkens.

She shook her head with a sad expression. "Ramona told my sister that she didn't think the Fargo police looked very hard."

Ramona's parents lost the store, their house, and Ramona's college fund due to the assault.

"At fourteen, she was living in a small apartment in a dingy part of town, while her mother worked three jobs. Poor girl. She was stuck caring for her younger brother and her father. She didn't see a future."

As Mrs. Wilkens told her story, I ached for the Ramonas in this world. Many of my students faced the same hardships. For a moment, I felt a surge of anger that the school district had cut back my summer program.

Education was the key to a better life for my kids.

Mrs. Wilkens continued. "One day, she met a guy through a so-called friend. He was older, wore fancy clothes, and he told her she was beautiful. He told her she could be a model and make lots of money. All she had to do was come with him, and he'd set it all up. She was fourteen and miserable, so she went with him."

"He took her to Minneapolis, put her up in a motel, bought her designer jeans, and introduced her to cocaine. After a couple of days of partying, the motel kicked them out. She moved with him from place to place, because she didn't know what else to do."

Mrs. Wilkens sipped her coffee. "It's an old story. He was a pimp and an addict, and she was his dope money. Ramona stayed with him until she was sixteen and pregnant. He beat her up for being pregnant. She found a shelter that helped her get into a program for teenagers like her. After her daughter was born, though, she couldn't make it on low-paying jobs, so she went back to her pimp. At eighteen, she had another daughter. After that, it was a cycle of treatment, clean-up, and relapse. The poor little girls spent years in and out of foster care."

"Ramona had shared a little of this with me when I tutored her, but not the whole story. Those poor girls." I pictured their grim faces at the funeral.

Mrs. Wilkens grimaced. "They've had a tough life. But Ramona finally turned it around when she met Grace's stepson. He was a minister, you know."

As with the other day, I wished I had a flip chart so Mrs. Wilkens could sketch out the family tree. "I didn't see him at the funeral."

"Don't you remember?" she looked at me with those lovely blue eyes. "He died almost five years ago. He was a National Guard chaplain, and he got sent to Afghanistan."

"Oh." I did sort of remember because Mrs. Wilkens joined the peace group that picketed outside the Federal Building about that time.

"Poor Ramona. She slipped again after that—until she got into a good treatment program last year."

We sat in silence, finishing off the bagels. I thought about my own upbringing with my hippy/artist mother and how we moved from place to place until we landed in Josiah's lair. At least, after Josiah nearly killed me, she had the sense to stay away from cults. And I had the sense to stay away from drugs.

My coffee was cold by the time I told Mrs. Wilkens about Hannah and Pastor Jacob's reaction to the cut hand. I told her about Jennifer and the pill she'd shoved into my hand. I told her about Hilda and her comment that Jennifer's condition was in her head. And I told her about Nicholas, the Russian Mafioso deacon. I forgot to tell her about the piece of paper shoved into the pages of *Jane Eyre*.

Mrs. Wilkens was silent as she took this all in. Suddenly, she stared at me. "Damn," she exclaimed. "That's it!"

"What's it?"

"Human trafficking. That's what Ramona uncovered. That poor little Hannah with the beautiful voice. She's probably their slave."

I laughed out loud, trying to picture Pastor Jacob, with the limp handshake, Reverend Jennings, of "Are you saved?" and Hilda, the staff sergeant, involved in human trafficking.

Sometimes little old ladies can say the darnedest things. And sometimes, little old ladies can be quite astute. I wasn't sure which little old lady I had in front of me.

Chapter Ten

I felt drained after my breakfast with Mrs. Wilkens. Ramona's story had touched a nerve. I wanted the American dream for my fifth graders—or at least a chance at a decent education and a decent life. Now, for some of them, they faced a life of hardship and hiding. I thought about little Diego Nuñez. He was short with a mop of thick black hair and a dazzling smile. His undocumented parents brought him here when he was a baby.

One day last spring, he came to school in a dirty shirt and grass-stained jeans. Up until that day, Diego's clothes had always been immaculate. His face was tear-stained and haunted.

"Hey, amigo, what happened?" It was as if the lights had dimmed in his eyes.

"La Migra, they got my mama and papa. I don't know what to do."

He'd come home to a dark van parked in front of his house. He'd watched from behind a hedge as the officials marched his parents and older sister out and put them in the van. That night, he'd slept huddled in a shed in the back yard, afraid they'd come for him.

Diego's parents were hardworking and loving, and now they were in some goddam detention.

I took his hand and walked him down to the school social worker. She spent more and more of her time dealing with situations like this. As I gently nudged him into her office, I felt such a sense of loss and rage. Diego and his family contributed more to this country than the louts who paraded with their guns and their tiki torches.

"The world is not a perfect place, and right now, it's even less perfect,"

I told the cat. I thought about the Welcome Congregation, a church that was supposed to be there for people like Diego and his parents. Instead, it appeared to have lost its soul.

"Is that what has happened to us? Have we lost our souls?"

Goldie licked her paw with a dainty lap of her tongue and did not reply.

"Okay. Time for some action." I pulled out my cell phone and called Detective Pete Peterson from the Minneapolis Police Department. I'd worked with him a few years ago when one of my students told me her uncle was touching her in a funny way. I respected how he handled the delicacy of the case. It took immense courage for the child to speak up in the first place and great care on his part to investigate it fully. The uncle was now in prison.

He answered on the second ring. I pictured him at his desk with a suit jacket draped over the back of his chair, wearing a precisely pressed white shirt. He was probably in his late forties, balding, and always impeccably dressed.

"Peterson."

"Hello, Detective Peterson. It's Liza Johnson." We'd never reached the point of familiarity where I could call him Pete, and he could call me Liza.

For a moment, I wasn't sure what to say next. How do you approach a seasoned detective with an old lady's delusion that her niece was murdered? And what business was it of mine in the first place?

He paused. "Ms. Johnson. What a pleasant surprise." He covered the receiver to cough. Detective Peterson was an unrepentant smoker.

He chuckled before he started to cough again. I heard him take a sip of coffee as the cough subsided.

"Haven't quit smoking, have you?" I chided.

"Is that why you called? To check up on my health?"

"And Phil's." Over the years I'd known him, Detective Peterson had gone from being closeted to finally marrying the love of his life. I knew about it because Phil worked as a school liaison with the police department, and I'd often talked with him at parent-teacher functions.

"We're fine, thank you." I heard the puzzlement in his voice. "What can I do for you?"

Goldie jumped up on the couch and sat next to me, her tail brushing against my hip. It was the most affection she'd shown me since Mrs. Wilkens had plopped her down in the carrying case. Looking at the cat reminded me of my mission.

"I have a question for you."

"Shoot." In the background, I heard a woman's bray of laughter. At least someone was having fun.

"I have a friend …" I knew this sounded hokey as soon as the words came out, but I continued. "Her relative was found dead with a needle in her arm."

"An addict?"

"Well, supposedly in recovery."

Detective Peterson grunted as if to say, "Oh, sure."

"What my friend wants to know is how you would determine if it was suicide, accidental, or something else?" I let the words "something else" hang.

He paused long enough that I wondered if my phone had cut out. I pulled it away from my ear to check. It was still connected.

"Ms. Johnson?" He finally came back on. "Is everything all right with you?"

The concern in his voice almost brought me to tears. He must have thought I was contemplating doing something stupid. "I'm fine. Really. It's my neighbor's relative."

"Oh?"

"I couldn't be better. Really. Just to prove it, I now have a cat." I turned to Goldie. "Can you meow for the nice man?"

She hissed instead and jumped off the couch. So much for golden moments with Goldie.

"Good to know." He coughed and cleared his throat. "About the overdose/suicide thing with addicts, it's basic detective work."

"You mean like finding a suicide note?" I hadn't asked Mrs. Wilkens if they'd found a note.

"That's a big one, of course. But we look at other things, too. This relative, where did he die?"

I realized I knew very little about the actual circumstances other than that Ramona had been found in her apartment. "At home."

"Did they find any stash? If it's accidental, there's usually a stash. Suicidal addicts will often use up everything they've got. You know, no sense wasting it."

I tried to remember if we'd heard anything about drugs found in the house. "I don't think they found anything."

"Makes a pretty good case for suicide—especially if there's other stuff going on."

I thought about the accusations of drug use at Ramona's work. Could that have triggered it?

Detective Peterson said, "Excuse me," and put his hand over the telephone mouthpiece. I heard a muffled directive to someone in the room. "Get me a BLT on whole wheat." After a few moments, he came back online. "Okay, where were we?"

"Suicide versus accidental versus something else?" I couldn't say the word "murder." It sounded too dramatic.

He told me there was often evidence that it was accidental. "We tend to find more drugs. Like they aren't planning to off themselves. Or it happens in a setting that doesn't look like suicide." He paused. "Like the stories you see on the news of a mom and dad overdosed in the car while the kids are strapped to car seats in the back."

I grimaced, recalling those news photos. Those dead parents could have been the moms or dads of my fifth graders.

Detective Peterson continued. "Suicides don't like to leave a mess. They'll do things like shoot up in the bathtub because they know they might soil themselves if they seize."

From the hallway, I heard Goldie scratching in her cat box. Life was so much less complicated for a cat.

"What if it was something else? You know, like homicide?" For some reason, I felt better using the word "homicide" than "murder."

I heard the squeak of the chair as Detective Peterson shifted his weight. I pictured him rolling his eyes to one of his desk mates. "Why do you ask?"

"Because my neighbor thinks this was murder."

He chuckled. "I'm sure if it had any hint of foul play, the police at the scene would have investigated."

"What would a 'hint' be?"

"Blood, chaos, bruises on the body, neighbors reporting a ruckus—that sort of thing."

I shivered, trying not to picture the scene with Ramona and the needle in her arm.

"All right. All right. Too much information." How could I say any of this to Mrs. Wilkens?

We made a little more small talk before I said, "Well, thanks, I guess."

I sat with the phone on my lap, wondering how to tell Mrs. Wilkens that I thought Ramona had probably killed herself.

Chapter Eleven

"I need a break," I told the cat. She yawned and walked away.

Instead of thinking about Ramona and drugs, I decided to bicycle over to see my friend Ed. Until he retired two years ago, Ed had been our school custodian. I learned by accident that Ed had a hard time reading and took it as a challenge to help him. In the process, I discovered that he was a bit of a savant. He could tell me anything I ever wanted to know about baseball, particularly about the Minnesota Twins. Had he been a child in school now, he probably would have been diagnosed as high-functioning on the autism spectrum.

When he retired, I helped him with all the paperwork, including applications for Medicare, Veteran's benefits, and Social Security. I was astounded by the complexity of the system.

"Like figuring which players to pull up from the minors," he'd remarked when he saw all the paperwork.

Since his retirement, I visited him a couple times a month. We would have coffee and Oreos, and Ed would read to me. We were currently working through W.P. Kinsella's *The Iowa Baseball Confederacy*.

Ed lived near South High School in a working-class neighborhood. His house was a small Craftsman painted white with brown trim and a blue roof. Today, he greeted me the way he always did, with a rough grunt. We sat in the backyard on cheap lawn chairs with a plate of Oreo cookies and glasses of lukewarm lemonade.

"Bet you didn't know that, in 1962, the Twins were the first major league team to hit two grand slams in one inning." He paused. "Yup, it was Killebrew and Allison."

"Well. Well." I never knew how to respond to his bits of trivia, but it felt good to hear something that wasn't about drugs and murder and churches.

We sat in the quiet, watching as two squirrels chased each other up the trunk of an old oak tree. I wondered if this was a pursuit related to love, food, or fun.

Finally, Ed turned to me. "Been busy, haven't you?"

How did he know? I told him about the parish house and reading to Jennifer. "She seems so sick. I can't imagine that it's all in her head."

Ed's foot tapped the lawn in a fast up-and-down rhythm. He frowned. "Not good. Not good at all."

Even though his social skills were poor, Ed had an uncanny ability to read people and situations. Back when he was the janitor, he always had the mop and the sawdust mixture ready almost simultaneously with the upchucking kid.

After I finished telling him how the Reverend had asked me if I was saved, he said, "They are not people of God. People of God help others. The Bible says to 'do unto others.' That girl is in big trouble."

I had to agree that I didn't see Pastor Jacob, Hilda, or the Reverend doing much for the betterment of mankind. I also thought whether it was in her head or not, Jennifer was very ill.

"The little girl, Hannah, she's being used."

It surprised me Ed could pick that up from the little I'd said about her. I nodded as a noisy airplane flew overhead, close enough to the ground to rattle our plates.

Ed read to me a chapter from the book. His voice was a monotone, and he stumbled over some of the words, but he kept at it, grunting from time to time. We only did ten pages for each visit. That was the routine. When he put the book down, he looked straight ahead and said, "You got that voice in your head, don't you?"

I gasped, "How did you know?"

He shrugged, and I guessed he didn't have the words to tell me. "I just do."

I'd once told him about Charlee and how Dr. Slack had been very clear that she was part of my imagination. To this day, I don't know why I'd sat in his cramped, little janitor's closet inhaling the chemical scents of toilet cleaner and floor polish, talking about the voice that was part of my childhood.

To Ed's credit, he had listened without comment. When I was done describing Charlee and how she was my long-dead twin, he'd nodded and said, "If she ever comes again, you listen to her."

A white, fluffy cloud floated overhead, dampening the brightness of the sun for a few moments. A fly landed on the empty plate of cookies. Ed reached over and flicked it away as he waited for me to respond.

I inhaled deeply and slowly let it out. "She thinks I should help Mrs. Wilkens, keep the cat, and stay volunteering for Jennifer."

"You listen to her. You keep going to that parish house. You know it's the right thing to do."

I was getting a little tired of the phrase "the right thing to do," but, of course, Ed was right.

By the time I was ready to leave, I was back in the funk I'd tried to shed by visiting him. I promised to return in a couple of weeks.

"Not during a Twins game." He clasped his hands and rocked in his chair.

I always checked the game schedule before visiting Ed. "No, not during a game."

"New guy pitching today. Just traded for him. Bad ERA, though." Ed stood up and walked me to the gate of his yard. "Goodbye."

I smiled and waved, but he didn't notice. The game would be on the radio in twenty minutes.

Mounting my bicycle, I headed for the Greenway Bike Trail. One thing about Minneapolis, even though we can have miserable, bone-chilling, endless winters, we do have some of the best bike paths in the country. The day was mild and sunny. People everywhere were smiling. I had a lovely ride back until a jackass on a racing bike tried to take me out while passing on the Greenway trail. He didn't even call out the polite, "On your left." He whizzed by, clipping my shoulder just as I was moving over to pass a young mother pushing a stroller. My last sight of him was his butt pumping furiously. Then I careened onto the gravel shoulder. I ended up with a leg full of pebbles and a bent fork.

"Bicyclists are supposed to be the good guys, you son of a bitch," I muttered as I picked little pieces of gravel out of my knee.

Mrs. Wilkens found me in my living room surrounded by Band-Aids, Bacitracin, and a very badly made gin and tonic.

"Well," she said. "It looks like we skinned our knees and elbows."

"No kidding." I told her about Ed and about the nice mother/baby combination who stashed my Trek in the back of her minivan and brought me home. I didn't tell her about my conversation with Detective Peterson. "I always thought of cyclers as part of the people working on saving the environment, not jerks who hog the bicycle lanes."

Mrs. Wilkens shook her head. "We're living in a time of jerks." Before I could say anything more, she picked up my gin and tonic, sniffed it, and said, "What did you make this with? Lighter fluid?"

She walked into the kitchen, her orange tennis shoes still aglow in the late afternoon light, and mixed a decent gin and tonic. When she handed it to me, she said, "I still don't think Ramona would kill herself."

When she sat on the couch, Goldie appeared from nowhere and jumped onto her lap. The cat purred and regarded me with a look that said, see? I can be affectionate.

I really wanted the whole Ramona thing to go away. "Maybe it was an accident. I've been reading about the spike in accidental overdoses—dope laced with bad chemicals and stuff like that." I paused, weighing my next words. "Did they find a stash? You know, like more drugs?"

Mrs. Wilkens' eyes flashed with indignation. "Her apartment was drug-free."

"Hmmm." I thought about what Detective Peterson said about using everything up before committing suicide.

Mrs. Wilkens continued. "I asked Grace to see if she could get a copy of the police report and the autopsy. The piece I don't understand is that Ramona was addicted to powder and pills, not needles. She once told Grace she'd never in her life ever shot up. Needles scared her."

"Addicts lie sometimes."

Mrs. Wilkens folded her arms with a tense set to her jaw. "She didn't commit suicide, and it wasn't an accident. I know it. And if we don't do something about it, whoever did this to her will go free."

Abruptly, Mrs. Wilkens stood up, splashing a little of her drink. Goldie barely had time to jump off her lap. "We're going to get to the bottom of this."

I said nothing as she stomped out of the room. Forgive me, Charlee, I thought, but this is a losing battle.

Goldie meowed at me and trotted to the bedroom. I was left alone to finish my gin and tonic and contemplate mankind's nasty streak.

Chapter Twelve

Just as I settled in bed with the sheet pulled lightly over my damaged knees, Goldie suddenly leapt off the bed and into the closet. I felt but didn't hear Charlee's voice.

"Charlee?"

I wished she was real so we could have a regular chat. I pictured her sitting on the edge of the bed, an exact duplicate of me—tall, slender, and blonde with Mother's greenish-blue eyes. I'd love to settle into the covers and have a normal conversation with her. Maybe we'd talk about the future—travels, love interests, work. Maybe we would play word games like we did when I was little.

"Charlee?" I asked again. In the closet, Goldie settled into my slipper as if politely leaving me with my guest.

Yes.

"Am I imagining you? Are you really unresolved issues with Mother—or something?"

Hardly. You should have grown out of the mother issues by now.

Nothing like being chastised by the voice of someone who didn't exist.

No, I am not a figment of your imagination. I am part of you. Remember when you asked Mother why I was gone, and she said, "Oh, Liza, she will always be in your heart."

"Yes, but she never mentioned you'd be in my head. Can't you let me believe you don't exist?"

You need to help Mrs. Wilkens and Jennifer.

"You've said that before." I pressed my lips together in irritation.

And find yourself a decent man.

"What?"

Relax. I'm kidding. Maybe.

"Geez." I sighed. "I've tried, but all the men I meet are like cartoon characters. You know, two-dimensional."

Maybe you need Match.com.

"Really? You're telling me to try internet dating?"

Well, you haven't had much luck with regular dating.

"You mean you've been keeping track?"

Hah!

"Remember, I was once engaged, and I did once have a live-in boyfriend."

You scare them off.

"I don't want to talk to you about this right now. You aren't real, so quit bothering me."

The room was quiet except for an occasional cat squeak from the closet. The golden warmth inside my head was fading.

"Wait. What about Jennifer and Ramona? What should I do?"

Stay with it.

Once again, she was gone. Thanks to a sleeping pill from Mrs. Wilkens, I fell into a deep sleep.

The phone rang at 8:30 the next morning.

Goldie was back on the pillow next to me as I reached for the phone. She lifted her head up, regarded me for a moment, then settled back onto the expensive down pillow as if she owned it.

As I said a sleepy "Hello," I vowed to demand that Mrs. Wilkens find another home for her. This cat-sitting was supposed to be temporary. The last thing I wanted to do was wake up every morning to a nose full of cat hair.

"Is this Liza Johnson?"

"Uh-huh." I blinked in the early morning sunshine that eased through the window of my bedroom.

"I'm John Trapper. Dr. Epstein asked me to call. I'm from his clinic."

John Trapper? Wasn't he a character in some medical sitcom from the seventies? Or was it Trapper John?

"Hi," I rubbed my eyes, hoping the mists from the sleeping pill Mrs. Wilkens had given me would clear.

"He said you had some questions about ALS."

I yawned and tried to stretch. My skinned and bruised knee from the bicycle accident howled for a moment. I groaned.

"Are you all right?"

"Sorry," I mumbled. "I had a little run-in with a bicycle yesterday. I'm stiff."

"Oh."

For the next minute, I stumbled through a conversation, trying to remember what I was supposed to ask. Finally, I said, "Would you like to meet me for coffee? I'll buy."

The voice on the other end of the line chuckled. "That's what Dr. Epstein said you'd offer. Sure."

"One request, though. Please, not at six in the morning."

Instead, I met him at the Caribou Coffee a mile from my house at noon. He said he had a long lunch break because of a couple of cancellations. The place was packed. I found a small table in the corner and waited for someone who looked like a Hollywood movie star to walk in. Didn't Donald Sutherland play Trapper John in the movie? Or was it Alan Alda? And weren't they now old men with grandchildren?

The person who approached my table was definitely not a movie star. He was a bearish-looking fifty-year-old with a neatly trimmed dark beard. He was in pretty good shape for a middle-aged guy and had the ramrod-straight walk of someone in the military.

"Liza?"

"Dr. Trapper?"

He smiled. "Yes and no. I have a doctorate in nursing science. I'm not a medical doctor. I'm a nurse practitioner."

I tried to hide my disappointment. I asked for a specialist, and Jason sent me a nurse. Crap.

71

He read my face. "I'm a very good nurse practitioner."

I blushed, ashamed of my reaction. "Um, sorry. Could I buy you an expensive coffee?" I gave him a ten and hoped that it would cover everything he wanted.

When he came back with his coffee, we chatted about the weather and the Twins baseball team. As we remarked on the unusual success of the team this year, I noted that John Trapper had interesting eyes and a nice, crooked smile.

Finally, he said, "I'm guessing you want to know why Dr. Epstein hooked you up with a nurse instead of a doctor?"

I cleared my throat, knowing I had insulted him. "Jason is a tightwad. I assumed he figured your time was cheaper." It came out before I could stop myself.

John tipped his head back and laughed. "He's my boss, you know."

"I hope he pays you well because he's always been careful with money. I've never known him to pick up a tab when he didn't have to."

A cell phone rang at the table next to us. The ringtone was a little Irish jig. I turned to look, half expecting a leprechaun. Instead, a large, brassy woman with platinum hair answered, "It's about time."

I turned back to John and apologized. "I'm sure you are good at what you do, or Jason, for all his skinflint ways, wouldn't have sent you."

John nodded, "The truth is that nurses know more about this disease, because we know how to look at the patient holistically. Doctors are trained to be experts in disease pathology. We're trained to be experts in health."

I smiled, even though I wasn't sure what he meant by experts in health. "Okay, I'll buy that."

The woman behind me finished her call with a "Screw you, don't you ever call me again." One more example of why cell phones should be banned everywhere but in the privacy of one's own home. Cell phones were problematic for all teachers these days. I'd had trouble with my fifth graders and cell phones. They were sneaky enough and skilled enough to send text messages by feel through the pockets of their little jeans. Considering how many of them came from families that barely eked by, I was constantly amazed at how they could afford the phones.

I filled John in on the little I knew about Chester and his condition. "Mother says it started a couple of months ago when he began to have some weakness in one leg. The doctor was stumped and sent him to a physical therapist. She said the physical therapist suggested he see a neurologist."

He nodded as if he knew the symptoms.

"It's gotten worse now. He's walking with a cane, and he just got an ankle brace."

"Ah yes, foot drop."

"Does this sound like the right diagnosis?"

John shrugged. "Unfortunately, it probably is. Chester is the right age for onset, between 40-60. If he's a smoker or a former smoker and if he's been in the military, he fits the profile. More importantly, sometimes ALS is genetic. Do you know if he's had any family members with it?"

I had to admit I knew nothing about Chester's family other than his worthless son. "I can check."

The Irish lilt rang again. Brassy Lady answered with, "Screw you." Instead of hanging up, though, she continued with her stream of swear words, growing louder with every expletive. People were getting annoyed.

"Excuse me," I said to John. I stood up and walked over to Brassy Lady. Before she knew what was happening, I'd swiped her cell phone from her hand. It was a maneuver I'd perfected in my classroom.

"You want this back? You follow me."

The woman gaped at me, grabbing at the phone. "Gimme that, you bitch."

I marched out of the coffee shop as she stumbled after me, yelling not nice things. Once outside, I handed it back to her. I said in the voice that caused my unruly fifth graders to sit up straight. "Finish your conversation here."

She glared at me open-mouthed, and I could see a litany of expressions on her face that started with surprise and worked their way up to rage.

"Go to hell!" She finally barked, dropping the cell phone as she wound up her arm to land a punch. Before she could get herself into gear, however, John grabbed her arm and held on tight.

In a low, controlled voice, he said, "Would you like me to call the police?"

I stooped down and picked up her cell phone. I looked at John and said, "911?"

Suddenly, the rage disappeared. Brassy Lady mumbled, "Never mind," and reached for her phone.

"No more swearing, please." I handed her the phone, and she walked to the corner, punching numbers into it. When we walked back into the coffee shop, several people applauded.

"I hate loud cell phone conversations," I said mildly to an older woman who reached out and patted my hand as we walked by. "I used to confiscate phones from my students."

"Then I guess that lady is lucky she still has her phone." She smiled, her eyes large and blue like Mrs. Wilkens's.

Once we sat down again, I commented, "You must have been in the military."

John nodded. "Perceptive of you. I was a Marine medic."

After a long pause, I resumed our conversation about ALS. "What will happen to Chester?"

John told me about slowly losing control of muscles and the downward slide I'd already read about on the internet. Prognosis was somewhere around four years for the best-case scenario.

"Isn't there something he can take?"

"Riluzole can sometimes slow it down. Otherwise, we treat the symptoms as they come up. Hopefully, he's got a good physical therapist and a good occupational therapist." He took a sip of his coffee. "And good insurance."

I wasn't sure about any of the above, and it occurred to me that I needed to get out to Northern California to scope out the situation.

"One more thing that sometimes helps."

"What?"

"Marijuana."

"Oh.

John looked at his watch. "Looks like I have to go."

Before he stood up to leave, I remembered Jennifer and her illness.

"Tell me if this sounds like anything." I described what I had seen with

74

Jennifer.

"Any twitching or muscle weakness? Can you understand her when she talks?"

I shrugged. "Honestly, to me, she looks like a concentration camp survivor. I don't know what other symptoms she has except that she thinks someone is poisoning her water. Her mother-in-law tells me it's all in her head, but to me, she looks really sick."

I pictured Jennifer in the bed and remembered something else. "She has a funny-looking rash on her hands and arms." I tried to describe it but finally gave up.

"Hmmm. Let me do some research, and I'll get back to you."

By the time we walked out of Caribou, Brassy Lady was gone. I was relieved. My knee and hip still hurt from the bike fall, and I didn't want to get into any more fights.

On the way home, I reflected on John Trapper and our conversation. He'd described the likely scenario of Chester's illness. It followed the course I'd witnessed with my teaching colleague. I wondered why good people endured terrible illnesses while people like Chester's son Vincent waltzed through life, never having said a kind word to anyone. I didn't have the answer to the age-old question about suffering, and by the time I parked in my spot behind the apartment building, I felt a cloud hanging over my head.

"This is not my idea of summer fun," I muttered as I let myself into the apartment. It was time to get back to my television serials. They always got the bad guy in the end.

Chapter Thirteen

Before I could hit the remote control on the television, my phone rang. Once again, it was Pastor Jacob, wondering if I would come for an hour or two on short notice. The sane part of me said it was time to bow out. There was no conspiracy. Jennifer had mental problems, and Ramona was an addict who died of an overdose.

I agreed, not because I was a good person, but because an old lady, a voice in my head, and an autistic retired janitor said I should. I would stay with Jennifer from three in the afternoon until five. Pastor Jacob said his mother would be back by five at the latest. I did another quick search on my laptop for any more information on Reverend Jennings or his son but found nothing more.

After that, I typed in John Trapper's name. I found one on Facebook who lived in Massachusetts and was into old cars. Nothing about a John Trapper, nurse practitioner in Minneapolis. While I was searching, Goldie jumped up on the coffee table and meowed.

"What do *you* want? If it's someone to love you, you've come to the wrong coffee table."

She continued to meow until it occurred to me that I'd forgotten to feed her. As I dished out the liver dinner, I thought about the easy life of a house cat. Someone to feed you, provide a soft, expensive pillow, and clean your kitty toilet. Not a bad way to live. Then I remembered that the poor cat had spent two days beside her dead mistress in a hot apartment.

"Okay," I said as Goldie chewed her food. "I'm sorry—for now."

The afternoon was again sunny and mild. A few wispy clouds floated overhead. The next-door neighbor had just mowed his lawn, and the parking lot of my building smelled like fresh grass. It's days like this that I remember why I was never attracted to Mother's Northern California log house. Summers were hot and dusty, winters were wet, and the in-between times were often filled with smoke from forest fires.

As I stepped into my old Toyota Corolla, *Jane Eyre* accidentally fell out of my hand and onto the ground. A piece of paper slipped out, and a little breeze gently pushed it under the car. I'd forgotten that Jennifer had given me the slip of paper the last time I was there.

"Damn." It was far enough under that I had to get down on my still sore knees to retrieve it. When I stood up, my white pants were covered with parking lot dirt. It was almost three o'clock, and I didn't have time to change. I stuck the paper in my back pocket and drove like a New York cabbie to get to the parish house on time.

When I arrived, the ever-friendly deacon was on the front step as if he was guarding the house. As usual, he was wearing a dark suit coat that looked out of place on this warm summer day. I wondered if he'd been watching a few too many mobster movies. I had to remind myself I was only a volunteer, and whatever was going on with the church and its deacons was none of my business.

"So nice to see you again, Nicholas."

Nicholas looked at me with disdain and frowned as I walked by.

Pastor Jacob came out of Jennifer's room. His hair was wet as if he had freshly showered, but he had deep circles under his eyes.

"You look tired," I said.

He ran his hand through his hair. "We had a rough night."

"Oh, is Jennifer okay?"

"What?" His brow wrinkled in confusion. "Oh, yes, she's fine."

"But you had a rough night."

He waved his hand as if he were waving away a fly. "No, no. It was one of the parishioners. Her daughter ran away last night."

"Teenager?"

He nodded.

In my experience, kids didn't run away unless something was really wrong at home. I remembered the little curly-haired girl with the large dark eyes who was in my class for only a few weeks. One day after school, she came up to me and said, "I don't want to go back home." I did a little gentle prodding to find out that she was afraid of her mother's boyfriend. All she said to me was, "He does stuff that I don't like."

I called the school social worker, who called child protection. Two days later, she was back in my class. When I asked her how things were going, she said, "Okay," but she wouldn't look at me. The child protection worker later told me she was too afraid to say anything, so they had to leave her in the home. A week later, the principal told me she'd run away.

I was much younger and more naïve when that happened. I was willing to go out, find her, and take her in myself, but I never saw her again. To this day, when I'm driving by some of the drug and prostitution corners, I look for her.

Pastor Jacob interrupted my thoughts. "My mother will be here by five. Jennifer is sleeping right now. Can you make sure she gets her pill at four? It's in a bottle by the bed."

He was out the door before I could say anything else.

I woke Jennifer at four for her medicine. "Would you like to hear more *Jane Eyre?*"

She blinked and didn't argue when I handed her the pill.

"Do you know what you are taking?" I asked.

"Don't care anymore. Doesn't matter. They've won."

I helped her to sit up and watched as she took the pill in her hand and threw it in her mouth. With a quick gulp of water, she coughed a little, swallowed another sip, and it was gone.

"Jennifer, what do you mean, 'they've won.'"

She pulled the sheets up further and whispered. "I can't save the children."

"What children are you talking about?"

"The boys. I know about them, and I can't save them." She shook her head and was quiet for a few moments before she spoke again. "When I was growing up, my dad got mean when he drank. I was scared of him, and when Mom had to go to the hospital, I told my teacher I didn't want to go home. She helped me find a place to stay, and that's when I decided I wanted to teach, too. I wanted to help the children like my teacher did."

I nodded, "Teaching is my passion."

"I took Jesus into my life so I could teach about His goodness." She shuddered, breathing rapidly.

I wanted to know more—especially about the boys. "Can you tell me about the boys? The ones you want to help?"

Jennifer's eyes opened wide while she gasped for breath. "Can't. Not now." Her fingers grasped at the bedspread.

I didn't want her agitation to escalate. It was time to talk about something else. Patting her arm, I spoke in a soft voice, "Why don't we read more of Jane Eyre and see what she does."

I opened *Jane Eyre* and read part of a chapter until I saw the regular rise and fall of her chest as she slept. With her eyes closed, she looked like a child herself.

The parish house was quiet except for the high-pitched buzz of the refrigerator. The windows were shut, and the air in the bedroom smelled stale and of sickness. I stood up to open the window a crack when I thought I heard a noise. It sounded like a heavy object being dropped.

All was quiet again as I searched for the sound. The house was impeccably clean, including a newly waxed kitchen floor. I thought about Hannah with her crystal voice. I wondered how her hand was. I listened again but heard nothing.

I should have gone back into the bedroom to sit with Jennifer. I should have read her the next chapter of *Jane Eyre*. I should have kept my nose out of the affairs of the Welcome Church parish house. But, the oddness of it all niggled at me, like that kind of itch you can get on the bottom of your foot. The one that even when you scratch, it won't go away.

When I looked in on Jennifer, she snored lightly. I headed to the bathroom. Again, the bathroom was spotless and smelled of a piney disinfectant. Above the sink was an old-fashioned medicine cabinet, the kind with a mirror as the door. When I opened it, the hinges creaked, and I stopped to listen. No more sounds in the house. All three shelves were filled with prescription bottles—mostly for Reverend Jennings. I pulled two of them out and realized that I didn't know exactly why I was there or what I was trying to find out. I didn't recognize the names of the drugs. None of the bottles had Jennifer's name on them. The pill that I had given her had come from the bottle with the handwritten label. What were they giving her?

The medicine cabinet door squeaked as I shut it.

The front door closed, and Hilda's voice called, "What's going on?"

I quickly turned on the faucet and was washing my hands when she swept into the bathroom.

"What are you doing?" she demanded.

I held up my wet hands and smiled. "Do you have a towel I could use? I had to do a little cleaning up." I hoped she wouldn't ask anything else.

"Oh," she said. "I thought I heard the medicine cabinet open."

I looked at my feet with a rueful shrug. "Um, I was looking for some Tylenol. I have a headache, and I didn't bring any with me."

She ushered me out of the bathroom and into the kitchen. "Here," she said, "we keep it here."

I took the bottle and dutifully took out two tablets.

"Next time," she added, "use the guest bathroom."

By the tone of her voice, I wondered if there would be a next time.

Chapter Fourteen

When I returned home, I slipped off my scuffed white pants and threw them in the pile of dirty laundry. Once into a comfortable pair of shorts, I checked the refrigerator for anything edible. The best I could do was a package of limp organic carrots, a carton of expired eggs, a bottle of soy sauce, an assortment of condiments, and a nearly empty bottle of tonic.

"Shame on you," I said to myself. "You have a better supply of food for a cat that you don't like than for yourself."

Mrs. Wilkens met me at the door as I stepped out to do some grown-up grocery shopping.

"Do you want to join me?" I asked reluctantly. Mrs. Wilkens always lectured me on my grocery choices. I'm never organic enough, sustainable and local enough, or high fructose sugar-free enough.

"No, I'm on my way to help Grace and the girls with some of the estate things. Ramona might have had her problems, but she did buy a life insurance policy."

It fit with my experience with Ramona. She truly did care about her girls.

"Anyway," she continued. "I think we should go to church on Sunday."

I sighed. "You aren't going to give up on this church-involvement thing are you?"

She smiled and shook her head. "Not until I'm convinced that Ramona voluntarily overdosed."

That night I dreamed I was back in Josiah's Household huddled in a dark closet. I knew that something evil approached as I tried to press myself back further into the closet. The doorknob rattled, and I gasped.

I woke up to Goldie's meowing from the closet. I was panting and covered in sweat.

Bad dream?

"It's like it was happening again."

I feel your fear.

"Please don't tell me to get over it. I know it happened twenty years ago, but, like you, the dreams don't always go away."

I know.

I got up, splashed my face with cold water, and took some ibuprofen. By the time I crawled back into bed, Goldie was sleeping peacefully on the pillow beside me. Charlee had disappeared once again. Part of me hoped it was a permanent departure, and part of me hoped she'd be back soon.

Sunday morning brought dark, roiling clouds and a mild thunderstorm. Mrs. Wilkens and I skittered through the puddles from the Welcome Congregation parking lot into the church. As with the funeral, the church was less than half-full. The same usher who had given us the program at Ramona's funeral stood like a sentinel at the door. I took a program from him and felt something creepy in the back of my neck when his fingers touched mine as he handed me the paper. Without thinking, I jerked my hand away and moved quickly inside.

Mrs. Wilkens pointed to one family with two blond teenage boys and a girl about the age of ten who had dark, almost black skin. "What if they're using that little girl to do all the housework?"

I whispered back, "Let's ask them when the service is over."

Mrs. Wilkens' eyes narrowed. "That sounds like a good idea. Maybe we can get to the bottom of this."

I sighed and shook my head. "I was kidding." What was wrong with old people anyway? Didn't they recognize sarcasm when they heard it?

We stood and sang the processional as the acolytes, two young boys with light brown skin and dark, closely cropped hair, led Pastor Jacob and Reverend Jennings to the altar. Hilda's voice soared like an aria as she played the organ. The rest of us struggled with the unfamiliar hymn. Why were we singing this Germanic dirge in a congregation of mixed cultures? I wondered where Hannah was. We needed her clear, youthful voice.

Sweat trickled down my forehead by the time we reached the sermon portion of the service. Lightning flashed through the round stained-glass window behind the altar as Reverend Jennings took the podium. He blessed us, peered at us as if looking for a sinner, and began.

Reverend Jennings clearly didn't get his sermons from "Church Sermons for Dummies" like his son. His voice was practiced. He could lower it to a whisper, then slowly raise it until it filled the church. The power in his ability to speak was surprising, considering how frail he looked.

Unfortunately, it was filling the church with vile words. Both Mrs. Wilkens and I stiffened as he ranted against those who would "defile God" by demanding the marriage of two men. And he raged against those who "chose" the life of homosexuality and depravity.

"You," he intoned, "must go forth and cleanse this state and this nation." He pointed an accusing hand at the congregation. I swear his eyes bore into me as he waggled his finger.

Since the Supreme Court had already ruled on the marriage equity law and allowed gay marriage, he was a little late in asking for the "cleansing." What was he suggesting?

The church was absolutely silent until the usher, with a high voice, said, "Amen to that."

Pastor Jacob sat in his chair behind his father, robed in white and looking like he was in a trance. I wanted to yell at him, "Wake up to what your father is saying."

"That's it," I said. "Let's go."

Mrs. Wilkens put her hand firmly on my knee. "Sit," she hissed.

I seethed through the rest of the service. Once the reverend and company had processed out, I stood up, ready to charge out and demand to know what Reverend Jennings meant by "cleansing the nation." Again, Mrs. Wilkens stopped me. "Wait," she said.

She led me out a side door away from the receiving line at the back of the church.

Once outside, I turned to her. "Why did you stop me?"

She assumed a stance with folded arms that reminded me of my tenth-grade math teacher when he caught people cheating. "Because you need to go back and watch over that poor girl in the parish house. Something is so rotten here. You can't get kicked out."

I cursed all assertive little old ladies under my breath as we headed to my car. It fairly steamed when I opened the door, which perfectly matched my mood. As we drove away, I noted that the congregation had quickly dispersed, and the usher and the Reverend Jennings were engaged in a serious discussion. Pastor Jacob stood like a stone, away from them and away from the parishioners as they headed for their cars.

Back in my apartment, I cranked up the air conditioner too high and glowered at Mrs. Wilkens as she sipped iced tea at my table. Goldie sat curled on her lap, purring like she'd saved it up after all these days with mean Liza.

"I want to be done with that church. I feel like I should take a shower and get the stench off me. What was Ramona doing associating with them?"

Mrs. Wilkens stirred her iced tea with her pointer finger and said nothing. She was silent for a long time. The only noise in the apartment was the rattle of the air conditioner and the sound of my sandals scuffling on the floor. Finally, she pushed herself up. "I need to go home now. Go take a shower. We'll talk later."

"They are evil, Mrs. Wilkens. They're no better than the ignorant mullahs who throw acid in the faces of little girls for going to school."

The shower helped. While shampooing my hair, I remembered the slip of paper that I'd stuck in my now dirty white capris. Maybe I could figure out what poor Jennifer was trying to tell me.

I rescued the pants from the dirty clothes hamper, which was beginning to grow a life of its own. This summer, with its steady stream of hot, sticky days, had caused the pile to mushroom. The apartment laundry still took quarters, and since I usually bought everything with either plastic or my phone, I never seemed to have enough of them. Someday, I promised myself,

I would splurge and buy an apartment-sized washer and dryer.

The folded piece of paper was wedged in the pocket of my pants. It was a plain white small tablet-sized piece of paper. She'd written two words. The first was "Vivorna." The second was harder to read. All I could make out for sure was the letter "F."

I googled the word "Vivorna," and what I found left me more puzzled than ever. Without hesitating, I pulled out the card that John Trapper had given me and called him. His voicemail told me he was unable to take my call, but he'd get back to me as soon as possible.

Why had Jennifer given me the name of a drug used to treat AIDS?

Chapter Fifteen

Mrs. Wilkens was right. I needed to get back to the parish house. While I dug under the cushions on the couch, looking for quarters for the washing machine, I raised lots of questions with no answers. Who was Deacon Nicholas? Or the sleazebag usher? What did any of this have to do with Ramona? What was wrong with Jennifer, and why was she trying to save the boys? For that matter, who were the boys?

Despite Charlee, Ed, and Mrs. Wilkens, I thought seriously about going online and buying an airplane ticket to California. Mother needed me, too. I could have left Mrs. Wilkens a voicemail asking her to take the cat and pick up my mail. I could have escaped, except that Reverend Jennings thoroughly upset me with his sermon. I was tired of living in an era where Reverend Jennings could proclaim that he was a Christian while preaching such vile words. I felt my blood pressure rise as I recounted what he had said. I wanted to catch him in something that would destroy his credibility. I wanted to shake his son until his teeth rattled, and I wanted to know what was wrong with Jennifer. I had to get back to the parish house.

I called the parish house. When Hilda answered, she sounded just like the cranky receptionist at my school. Marcy was fifty years old, slightly hard of hearing, and she thoroughly disliked children—which probably explains why they flocked to her.

"This is Liza Johnson." When Hilda didn't respond, I went into teenager mode and ended all my sentences with a question. "Jennifer's volunteer? I was there yesterday?"

"Yes."

"Um, I can't seem to find a bookmark. It's silly, I know, but it was given to me by one of my students just before he…" I paused for emphasis, glad she couldn't see how much I was staring at my feet. "Did you happen to find it?"

"I'm sorry, I haven't seen it." She was too quick in her answer. I think I was overplaying the teenager part. I switched to "mature adult."

"Could I stop over for a moment and look? I think I know where it might be."

I heard noise in the background, including what sounded like a box being dropped.

"Is everything all right?" I asked.

Hilda cut me off, "Right now isn't a good time. I'll look into it." The phone clicked off. She hadn't asked what it looked like or how to reach me.

It was time to switch to Plan B. Unfortunately, I didn't have a plan B, short of calling the police. I imagined a call to Detective Peterson: "Hello, this is Liza Johnson. I think they're killing the minister's wife at the Welcome Congregation parish house and doing other unusual things. I know because my addled upstairs neighbor and a voice in my head told me so."

And his response would be, "Would you like to talk to a counselor?"

I shook the conversation out of my head and hoped my phone might ring with some significant information to help solve the case. It stayed mute. The only sound was the irritating whine of a leaf blower down the street. It was time to do my laundry.

Mrs. Wilkens once almost instigated a rent strike over the condition of the building's laundry room. It was a musty, windowless room down the hallway from my apartment. Sometimes the machines worked, and sometimes they filled with water and quit. When she and the couple next door to her advocated to the new landlord that he replace the washers and dryers, he'd balked, claiming they should appreciate that he hadn't raised the rent. They could damn well go to the laundromat on Lake Street.

"We're a building full of old people. That's ridiculous."

When she tried to organize a rent strike, however, the landlord said he'd evict everyone before he'd bow to the pressure. I didn't know the legalities of eviction, but I knew I didn't want to move.

Instead of a strike, I talked with Ed, who was a whiz at machinery repair. He fixed the machines for a small fee, Mrs. Wilkens settled down for the moment, and no one got evicted. I decided that someday when I won the lottery, I'd buy the building and replace the elderly machines—but not the elderly tenants.

Today, I was able to scrape together enough change to take care of my hamper full of stinky clothes. They were still warm from the dryer when I dumped them on the bed to fold. Goldie immediately found my favorite T-shirt and curled up on top of it.

"You hairy beast."

She appeared to be immune to insults.

The phone rang while I sorted through the mismatched socks.

"Hello, this is John Trapper returning your call." He sounded so formal, like he was answering a work page, that it unnerved me.

"It's Liza Johnson. We had coffee the other day."

"Ah yes, the cell phone enforcer. What can I do for you?"

At that moment, Charlee returned. Goldie looked at me and settled deeper into my favorite t-shirt, oblivious to the annoying voice in my head.

Go back to the parish house. Take him with you.

"What?" I spoke out loud.

"Are you there?" John's voice had a note of concern.

"Sorry. I was distracted by the cat."

Go now. You know you shouldn't wait.

I hesitated, and the voice became more urgent. *Go!*

Clearly, this was not the time to argue with Charlee. I took a deep breath, "This is going to sound strange, but how would you like to go on a field trip with me?"

He didn't know me, and it occurred to me that he might think I was nuts. I would certainly have that impression if I knew this person I was talking to was hearing voices.

Instead of an instant "no," he said, "Tell me more."

I explained the information I'd found in the Parish house and how I'd called to say I'd lost my favorite bookmark. Did he want to accompany me to take a quick peek at Jennifer?

The line was silent. Liza, I said to myself, this is certainly one of your dumber ideas.

No, it's not.

"Okay." His voice had a tentative quality to it.

"How about if we meet at Caribou Coffee in an hour to map out a plan?"

"Okay." Again, he sounded skeptical. Then he added, "A lost bookmark? Is that the best you could do?"

After John hung up, I waited for Charlee to talk to me.

Good work.

"I wish you would sit down beside me and explain what is going on in that church. I feel like I'm in an episode of *NCIS*, and the writers have screwed up the plot."

Watching too much television?

"No kidding. Can't you tell me the ending? Do we find out if Ramona died by accident, suicide, or murder?"

She didn't answer. Charlee was gone once again. Goldie glared at me when I shooed her off my t-shirt. It had little clumps of cat fur on it, thanks to her.

Unconcerned, she sat on my bed, licking her underbelly. "See? See what you have done?" I threw the shirt into the laundry hamper and grabbed a peasant blouse from the closet. "By the way, this is not how I planned to spend my summer."

I tugged the blouse over my head as Goldie padded over to the pile of folded laundry and settled on top of my second favorite T-shirt.

"I hate cats," I muttered as I gathered my car keys and phone.

Chapter Sixteen

"A full-blown case of AIDS definitely has neurological implications, but I'm no expert." John Trapper sipped an iced tea. The coffee shop was eerily empty when I joined him. The only other customer in Caribou sat at a high table, squinting at the screen of his laptop.

I ordered an Americano, and the barista immediately asked if I wanted it iced. One thing I have never understood is why anyone would put ice in their coffee. Despite the 90-degree heat and 70% humidity outside, I asked for it extra hot. She flashed me a puzzled shrug and later handed me a coffee that needed two sleeves before I could carry it back to the table.

"So, you are sure this drug is used to treat AIDS?"

"Oh yes. This one is a variation of the combination of three medications. It's new on the market and used for people who have tested positive for HIV. There are others called PrEP drugs that are used for prevention, but this one is definitely for someone who has HIV in their system."

"Wow." I raised my eyebrows. "I'm impressed with what you know." I surreptitiously pulled the cover off my coffee to let it cool down.

John smiled. "Sorry, I just finished an advanced pharmacology class. I like the study of drugs."

"I can tell."

"Anyway, in layman's terms, these drugs interrupt the virus from duplicating, which may slow the spread of HIV in the body."

"Could they be used for something else?" I found it hard to think that Jennifer might have AIDS, but she was sick enough that it could be possible. And she'd spent time in Haiti.

I brought out the pill that Jennifer had given me the first time I visited and put it carefully in front of John. "Could this be the pill?"

John studied it, turning it over, noting its shape, and pulled out his iPhone. In seconds, he had pulled up a photo of Vivorna. He held the phone for me. "It's the right color and right markings."

I showed him the pencil scratching that Jennifer had made after writing the word Vivorna. "Does this make any sense to you?"

He smoothed out the piece of paper, then took a penlight out of his pocket. Using the light, he studied the faint letters and finally shook his head. "Looks like an 'f', but that's all I can see."

I told him about Mrs. Wilkens and her niece and how I ended up as a volunteer reader. I didn't tell him about my hiatus from teaching due to budget cuts. I also didn't mention that I was doing this at the urging of a voice belonging to my dead sister.

Our plan was simple. We'd drive to the parish house; I'd ask to look in Jennifer's room and bring John with me. While I pretended to search for a bookmark, he'd take a quick look at Jennifer. What could possibly go wrong?

We took my car. The streets were quiet, with little traffic. When I pulled up to the curb to park, John shook his head. "It looks kind of—forlorn."

"No kidding."

Hilda met us at the door before I could ring the bell. She opened it with a look of expectation. Apparently, we weren't who she was expecting. I thought I saw a flash of apprehension in her eyes, but it could have been my imagination. She stood in the doorway like a barrier.

"I am sorry to intrude, but John and I were in the neighborhood, and I thought I'd pop in to see if I could find my bookmark."

Pop in? When had I ever used that phrase?

I think that Hilda wanted to "pop" me. She furrowed her brow, and a blush flooded up her neck. "As I said on the phone, this is not a good time." She made motions to close the door. I thought about wedging my foot in before she could slam it shut. Fortunately, John saved the day.

"My goodness. You're Miss Grieg, aren't you?" He stuck out his hand to shake hers.

Hilda looked totally bewildered. "Excuse me?"

I gaped at him as he flashed a genuine smile. "I'm Johnny. I used to be in the back of the choir." He paused before explaining. "Miss Grieg was our elementary school music teacher at Pratt."

Hilda's mouth dropped open.

"Don't you remember? You once told me that I shouldn't sing so loudly—maybe mouthing the words would be better."

He edged past Hilda, still smiling. "You were a wonderful teacher. We were sad when you left."

Wonderful teacher? Hilda? I felt as bewildered as Hilda.

I followed him into the living room, completely amazed. Did my subconscious know about this coincidence? Is that why Charlee insisted I take John? I shook my head. No, not likely.

Usually, at this point in a conversation in the olden days, we would stop and have a nice chat about, "Remember when…" Instead, Hilda folded her arms and said nothing.

John quickly countered her silence. "Did you ever sing on Broadway? You told us that was your dream."

Hilda continued to look at John as if he were an apparition. She blinked so hard it actually made my eyes hurt. Finally, she said in a flat voice, "No. I married the Reverend. I only sing to praise the Lord."

Scare the Lord is more like it.

John looked at me. "I still remember her beautiful voice. She would have made a wonderful Maria in *Sound of Music*."

I clamped my teeth together to keep from giggling. Hilda as Julie Andrews? No way.

"We'll just scoot into Jennifer's room for a minute. I'm sure I know where I left the bookmark. We won't disturb her at all." I didn't wait for a reply as I made a quick exit into the bedroom, tugging John along. I needed to get in and out before I started using more words like "scoot" and "pop."

Instead of the usual gloom, the Venetian blinds were open, and outside light filled the room. The walls seemed even starker in the daylight. Hannah held a basin of water. At first, she looked frightened, then when she saw it was me, she smiled. Jennifer lay uncovered on her back with her eyes tightly shut. She looked gray and sunken beneath the pink cotton gown.

"How is your hand?" I whispered to Hannah.

"Good," she said.

I introduced John. "He's a nurse," I whispered.

She nodded.

John leaned close to Jennifer. "Hi, Jennifer. I'm John. How are you feeling today?"

Her eyes fluttered open, then widened.

"It's okay," I said. "He's a friend of mine."

I wasn't sure she recognized me until her face relaxed, and she whispered to John, "Hello. I'm Jennifer."

John lightly touched her arm. "Liza tells me you like to listen to her read."

She smiled as she looked at him. What is it about some men that cause women, even women who are ill, to respond like that?

"Do you mind if I help Hannah get you straightened up a little in bed?"

Jennifer continued to gaze at him as he nodded to Hannah. Between the two of them, they picked up the ends of the draw sheet under Jennifer and hoisted her up higher in bed. Jennifer grabbed his wrist when they moved her and grimaced.

"Did that hurt?" His voice was gentle.

"Makes me dizzy," she answered.

"Jennifer, can you tell me what medicine you are taking?" John asked.

I picked up the note of concern in his voice.

She shook her head, "Don't know anymore."

"When was the last time you saw the doctor?" John gently held her wrist as he quickly scanned her body.

"No doctor. Can't have a doctor. No insurance."

My jaw dropped. Could she be saying that she was this sick and no one had consulted a doctor?

"I'm scared." She whispered.

"I can see that." John's voice was so calm you'd think he'd just said, "Nice

93

day." He turned to me. "Go tell Miss Grieg to call 911, please." He looked at Jennifer again. "I think we should get you to the hospital."

Her eyes grew wide. I could see how jaundiced they were. "They won't like this," she whispered.

I started for the door to find Hilda but stopped. I didn't trust her to call. Instead, I pulled out my cell phone and dialed 911. When the dispatcher answered, I gave the phone to John. Quickly, he stepped out of the room. I stayed with Jennifer and Hannah. Hannah looked more frightened than Jennifer.

"John is a great nurse," I assured Jennifer. "He's one of the best."

Jennifer grabbed my hand and squeezed tight. "Will I be safe?"

I stroked her forehead the way Mother used to touch mine when I was sick. "They will take good care of you."

In the hallway, I heard the words, "Dehydrated and pulse weak and thready." Then I heard Hilda's sharp voice.

"What are you doing?"

Calmly but firmly, John told her that Jennifer was extremely ill and needed to be in the hospital. Hilda replied, "Nonsense, she does this sometimes. We pray her through it. She always gets better."

John didn't argue with her. He simply instructed her to have all of Jennifer's medications ready when the paramedics arrived.

I peeked out into the hallway to see Hilda's face grow the color of a red balloon, ready to pop. "The Reverend is going to be very angry about this. The church can't afford the cost to treat her imaginary illnesses."

John came back into the room, also looking like he was about to explode.

In the living room, I heard the high voice of the sleazy usher. He, too, sounded angry. "Why did you let them in?" Within moments, Hilda hurried in, her face still flushed.

"I tell you, Jennifer's problem is in her head."

John replied in a low, terse voice. "She's critically dehydrated. Please get her medications together and any notes you might have from her doctor." He emphasized "please and doctor."

"She's not taking any pills!" Hilda's voice rose. She had a panicked expression.

I stepped in. "Pastor Jacob had me give her something last time I was here." I pointed to the bottle on the nightstand.

"Those aren't pills! They're supplements." Her voice rose to a higher pitch.

In the distance, I heard the sound of sirens. In the parish house, I heard the sound of a door slamming. In the bedroom, Jennifer dozed while John sat on the edge of the bed and held her hand.

When the paramedics arrived, I did my best to stay out of the way. They asked numerous questions of Hilda. "How long has she been this way? What medications is she taking?" They worked for several minutes to get an IV line started.

With John's help, they were finally able to find a vein. I closed my eyes as they put the needle in. I was a coward when it came to needles. I could handle kids throwing up, getting fat lips, and scraping their knees, but needles were a different thing.

John stayed with Jennifer, holding her hand as they wheeled her out. Once she was in the ambulance, he spoke quietly to one of the paramedics.

Hilda stood with me, a shocked expression on her face.

Once they closed the door to the ambulance, John came back and glared at Hilda. "I can't believe you let her get so sick."

She looked down at her feet and said nothing. Her hands trembled by her side.

"They're taking her to Hennepin County General. I think you'd better get the family together and go to the emergency room as quickly as you can."

Hilda turned on her heel and walked back into the parish house. Before slamming the door, she glared at me. "Don't you come back here!"

I guess I wouldn't be "popping in" anymore.

Chapter Seventeen

We stood by my car in the heat and humidity. My hands were shaking. "Wow, I don't know what to say." I felt stupid. Why hadn't I done something on my last two visits? Why had I assumed that the Jennings were taking care of Jennifer? Thank God for Charlee's insistence that I go today.

John said nothing to me as he tapped a number on his phone. "Can you put me through to the emergency room, please?"

A mosquito landed on my arm. I slapped it while another buzzed around my ear. The door to the parish house remained shut. Sweat trickled down the side of my face as I waited for John to finish his call.

"Hi, Dr. Ellis. This is John Trapper from the neuro clinic. I wanted to give you a heads-up that the ambulance is bringing in a young woman from south Minneapolis. I don't know what is wrong with her, but she's severely dehydrated, and I suspect she's been poisoned with some kind of heavy metal."

Poisoned? I froze for a moment before swiping at the mosquito buzzing my head. Jennifer had told me she was afraid of the water. Now, I felt even worse for not doing anything.

John talked for a little longer before putting the phone away. He sighed and said, "I could use something cold to drink."

"Amen."

We drove to Rosie's Tavern on Lake Street. When I walked in, Joey, the bartender, nodded at me, pulled a Summit beer glass out of the freezer, and held it up.

"Friend of yours?" John asked as we settled into a battered wooden booth.

"He's a good listener." Joey was a lot cheaper than trying to get my insurance company to cover a therapist. Besides, therapists didn't normally provide beer.

The bar had been in the neighborhood through several generations of mostly blue-collar workers until the gentrification of this part of South Minneapolis. Now, at least half the customers were lawyers, doctors, and accountants. The food and drink stayed the same—artery-jamming burgers and fries—comfort food for people on their feet all day long. In deference to her new customers, Minnie, the cook, had added a veggie burger to the menu. I suspected that she made it with hamburger and a few garbanzo beans, but I never asked.

Joey brought the beer over and took John's order of a club soda with a twist.

"Not a drinker?"

"Ten years sober."

I didn't know what to say to that. I liked my beer, my gin and tonic, and an occasional hangover. I couldn't imagine giving it up. But I also couldn't imagine living through the horrors of addiction.

We tried small talk until John's soda and a basket of fries arrived.

He took a bite of one and sighed with pleasure. "These could stop your heart."

"I know." I dredged a fry in ketchup and confessed. "I feel like a fool, not catching on to how seriously sick Jennifer was."

John waved my comment away. "The damn fools are the family. What the hell have they been thinking?" He took another fry. "Did you notice the smell of garlic in the room?"

"Not today. But I did the first time I was there. Why?"

John pulled out his phone and poked at it. "Here it is." He handed the phone over to me. On the screen was a description of arsenic poisoning. It listed the smell of garlic as one of the symptoms.

"Scroll down."

I scrolled through a series of photos of skin problems associated with arsenic poisoning. One of them was familiar. "The fingernails. Those look like hers! How did you know to look?"

"Mees lines. That's what the stripe in the nail bed is called." John finished his club soda and the last French fry. "I saw it in Bangladesh when I was on a medical mission. One of the biggest mass poisonings by arsenic."

"Who was poisoning people?"

I assumed it was some big American chemical company exploiting the poor workers in a third-world country.

John shook his head. "It wasn't a who; it was a what. It turns out that one of the water wells was dug deep into an area with naturally concentrated arsenic. People were drinking toxic levels of arsenic."

"What happened to the people who were poisoned?"

"Some died. Some we were able to save."

I signaled the bartender for another beer. "Wow."

We sat in silence while I absorbed what he was saying. The darkened bar, with soft country twang music in the background and the beer, felt good. The silence was nice for the few moments it lasted.

"I can't believe she wasn't under a doctor's care." John shook his head.

"Hilda told me that Jennifer has a history of unusual illnesses. They come and go, and no one can figure them out." I reached into the pocket of my cargo shorts and pulled out a medicine bottle. A little sheepishly, I handed it to John. "Since it didn't look like Hilda was going to give any medicines to the paramedics, I took this off the bedside table. I was going to give it to them, but I forgot." I'd stuck it in my pocket when they were trying to get the IV started.

He examined the bottle. "It's got handwritten directions on it."

"And it smells like skunk."

He opened the bottle and made a face. "Looks like some of the homeopathic junk that my patients bring in. They're so desperate for a cure that they'll try anything."

"Do you suppose it has arsenic in it?"

"Can I keep this? I'll drop it off at the hospital when I do my rounds tomorrow. I'm guessing that Jennifer will still be there."

I hoped Jennifer would still be alive. I wondered where Pastor Jacob fit into all of this.

"You know, I saw Pastor Jacob, her husband, a couple of times with her. He seemed genuinely affectionate."

John didn't say anything. He studied his French fry as if deep in thought. When he finally looked at me, his expression was troubled. "I don't see how Jennifer's husband could be so oblivious to how critically ill she was."

I had no answer for him. We sat in silence for a while.

I scratched a mosquito bite on my arm. "What about the Vivorna? Could this all be part of having AIDS?"

"I've never seen AIDS manifest itself in this way, but as I said before, I'm no expert." He looked at me. "In case you are worried, AIDS is not very catchy."

I frowned at him. "A good friend of mine died from it. I helped take care of him. It doesn't scare me."

Even in this day and age, some people were afraid they would catch AIDS simply by being around someone who was HIV positive. Last year, Troy, a new fourth-grade teacher, made the mistake of telling someone that his partner was HIV positive. After that, some of the teachers would leave the break room if he was there. I caught a kindergarten teacher using antiseptic wipes on the chair he'd used. I hated that kind of ignorance. I especially hated that kind of ignorance in teachers. If they couldn't get it right, who could?

The door of the bar opened, and a noisy group of men and women tumbled in. They wore red jerseys and baseball caps that said, "Rosie's." This was the bar softball team. I once played for them.

John noticed the look on my face as I watched them pull tables together. "You were a jock at one time." He didn't ask; he simply noted.

"You are observant."

"Yup, that's what good nurses are." He settled back in his chair. "Tell me about your sports career."

Maybe it was the need to take a break from this afternoon's drama, but I found myself telling John about my high school days playing basketball and my intramural exploits in college. I finished with my swansong on Rosie's softball team.

"I crashed into the second baseman on a bad slide and dislocated my shoulder."

"Bad luck."

I smiled at the memory. "Not exactly. The second baseman became my boyfriend." I thought about how Terrence had expertly popped my shoulder back into place as I lay writhing on the field. Then he had taken me to the hospital. When I emerged from the little curtained exam room with my shoulder all trussed up, he was still there.

John interrupted my thoughts. "Not to be nosy, but are you still with this second baseman?"

I looked away. I didn't want him to see my eyes tearing up. I really liked Terrence. "We broke up."

I didn't want to go into the painful details of Terrence's spiral into depression and his suicide attempt. Yet another example of my pathetic love life.

"Oh." John frowned. "I'm sorry."

An uncomfortable silence followed until I lightened it. "I now have a shoulder that the orthopedic surgeon assured me will have to be replaced before I turn sixty. I don't play sports anymore."

He nodded. "My mother was a hockey nut. She came from Canada and thought that all boys should be happy to slap pucks into other boys."

I looked at his burly build and pictured him as a hockey player. "You look the part."

He shook his head. "I couldn't skate. I was terrified of the ice."

"Oops. I guess that could get in the way." I laughed. "On the other hand, my mother was appalled that I was in competitive sports. After our basketball team won the Regionals in high school, she came up to me and said, 'But Liza, look at all those girls crying over there because they lost.'"

To this day, I remember that her hair was down to her waist and that she wore dangling earrings, Birkenstocks, and a long cotton skirt. I was still so angry with her over Josiah's Household that I'd stomped off and left her bewildered on the auditorium floor.

The softball team laughed in unison as someone recounted the play of the day. I tuned them out and asked John, "What should we do about Jennifer?"

He pointed to the door. "Let's talk outside."

I paid the tab and left a hefty tip for Joey, the bartender. I knew that he was in graduate school and had lots of student loans. He told me one quiet Sunday night when I was sick of reruns and needed a break that he owed over $60,000. "My major is philosophy. How am I ever going to pay that back?"

I sympathized. It took me ten years of teaching to put most of my loans to rest. I blamed it on the mentality that if you weren't rich, you weren't worth it. Mrs. Wilkens blamed it all on Ronald Reagan. I couldn't argue with her because I didn't remember Ronald Reagan. She said he started all the anti-tax hysteria. "And it's gotten worse. Don't let me get started." Of course, she did get started and ranted on until I was ready to "cancel" her.

Outside, the sun moved toward the horizon, but the air remained muggy. We walked onto the Lake Street Bridge and looked down on the Mississippi.

"I love this river. The mighty Mississippi." He leaned a little over the rail to watch the water lazing its way downstream. "I've always had a dream of canoeing it to New Orleans." He smiled, "Have you ever been there?"

I grimaced. "Once in my junior year in college. Spring break coincided with Mardi Gras. A bunch of us got a couple of cheap hotel rooms and joined the party. I remember catching beads, but I'm not sure what happened after my third Hurricane. My friends assured me I had a good time."

I didn't tell him how I ended up in an alley that smelled of sewer gas, throwing up and wishing I could die on the spot. I have not been back to New Orleans since.

John's phone rang.

"Excuse me," he walked away from me, talking into the phone in low tones. Even with his back to me and the noise of the cars crossing the bridge, I heard the tension in his voice. When he was done, he turned to me with a flushed face.

"I'm sorry, I need to go."

"Emergency?"

"Ex-wife. Everything is an emergency for her. Let me call you tomorrow."

I dropped him off at his car and headed home. When I pulled into the parking lot of my building, it was bathed in a greenish-yellow light. The air had turned still, and the slight arthritis in my shoulder told me a low-pressure front was moving in. I looked up and noted that the clouds were coming in from the east, which was never a good sign. We were in for another evening storm.

I found Mrs. Wilkens pacing in front of my apartment door. She held a notebook in one hand and her phone in the other. "Oh, finally, you are here. I was about to call."

An overheated apartment greeted us. Goldie was nowhere in sight. She was probably on my bed, happily shedding on more of my clean clothes.

"Ramona might have left some clues." She could hardly contain the excitement in her voice. "I found this in her apartment." She lifted the notebook.

I didn't think I could stand any more drama. In the distance, thunder rumbled.

Chapter Eighteen

I poured Mrs. Wilkens a glass of iced tea and filled her in on my trip to the parish house.

"I should have done something earlier."

Mrs. Wilkens looked at me with a wry smile. "Ah, yes. You have a bad case of the 'shoulds.' My sister-in-law, long dead now, spent her life feeling guilty about everything. Behind her back, I confess I called her Miss Shoulda. What she 'shoulda done' was go to the doctor earlier when she noticed lumps under her arms."

She stirred a teaspoon of sugar into her tea. "Did you think Jennifer was that sick?"

I shrugged. "I'm not a medical person. I'm an elementary school teacher. All I knew was that she looked awful, but Hilda and Pastor Jacob seemed well aware of her condition."

"Well, then. There you have it. You did the right thing by bringing John in, and now what's done is done."

Ah, yes, thanks to Charlee. I still didn't feel much better.

I pointed to the notebook. "What's in it?"

Mrs. Wilkens wrinkled her brow, tapping her fingers on the cover. "I'm not sure. I only read a couple of pages. Ramona's spelling and grammar are...were terrible." Her voice dropped off as she took a drink of the tea.

I waited for her to talk again. One thing I've learned over the years with fifth graders if you wait with an expectant expression long enough, they will tell you everything.

Finally, she took a deep breath and let it out with a long sigh, "I went to her apartment today with Grace and the girls. They have to get everything out by tomorrow, or the landlord will charge them for another month." She paused, stirring her tea once more. "Other than the life insurance policy, Ramona didn't leave any money."

"This must be hard for her girls."

Mrs. Wilkens slowly shook her head. "They're angry, and they're young. All they want is to get it done with. Chrissy, the oldest, said to throw everything away."

Outside my kitchen window, lightning from the distant storm brightened the sky. A low rumble followed.

Mrs. Wilkens continued. "Ramona didn't have much—a few sticks of furniture from Goodwill, a couple of knickknacks, you know, little ceramic angels, and lots of photos of the girls. We found a couple of these notebooks under her bed. She must have been writing in them at night. They're journals she kept after her last go-round in rehab. Chrissy was going to dump them in a garbage bag when I stopped her. I told her that someday she might want them."

Mrs. Wilkens placed the notebook on the kitchen table. "This is the most recent one. I think we should read it for clues."

I suppressed a sigh. Of all the mysteries from this week, Ramona's was the easiest to solve. Despite what Mrs. Wilkens thought, I was convinced Ramona overdosed, either accidentally or on purpose, and that it had nothing to do with the church. I guessed she had a side of her Mrs. Wilkens and her sister simply didn't know about.

"Did Ramona's apartment look like she'd had some kind of a confrontation? You know, things scattered around, chairs overturned?" I didn't add blood.

"Her place was so clean, a mouse would have starved in it." Mrs. Wilkens said with pride.

Outside, the air had grown deathly still. In the distance, a siren blew. Goldie, who had joined us, suddenly ran back into the bedroom with a loud "meow." I wondered what spooked her.

With the sound of the siren, I should have turned on the television to get the weather warning or at least checked my phone, but I was tired and hungry, and Mrs. Wilkens needed my attention. I decided to wait before I quizzed her more on the state of the apartment.

"I'm going to fix some supper. Would you like to join me?"

"Uh-huh." Mrs. Wilkens leaned over the notebook. I took that as a yes.

Fortunately, I had the ingredients for a vegetarian chili that I could have ready in 30 minutes. What better dish for a hot, sultry evening in my hot, sultry kitchen than chili? While I sautéed onions and cut up carrots, Mrs. Wilkens studied the pages. Every once in a while, she nodded, "Uh huh. Interesting …"

By the time I set the bowl of chili in front of her, she'd finished reading. Outside, the rumbling of thunder grew. "Just as I thought. Something fishy was going on."

She handed me the notebook. "Take a look at page five."

It was a cheap, school-sized, spiral-bound book made with recycled paper. I opened it. The entries were printed in a cramped, childlike style. I recognized her writing from my tutoring lessons.

Mrs. Wilkens reached over and flipped the pages for me until we reached page five. The entry was dated January of this year.

Cold, cold, cold. Had to give myself a pep talk to go to meeting. D.G. called to say the meeting place changed 'cause of furnace problems. Met at Welcome church. Cold there, too. Boy called Rennie in group wanted to leave but counselor made him stay. Rennie says church is bad place. Wouldn't say why. Hope he comes back so I can find out.

I looked up at Mrs. Wilkens. "Did he come back?"

"Look at the next entry."

Went to Welcome church. Wanted to know why it was bad. Pastor Jacob was very nice. Hardly anyone in church. Heard they used to do services in Spanish, but new ministers don't. Rennie back at meeting today. Says minister is a hippocrit. Not sure what that means.

Outside, the leaves began to stir. "So far, I'm not seeing much that damns the church." I said.

"Read the next entry."

Pastor J came to meeting today. Has sweet eyes. Rennie said he wouldn't talk if Pastor J stayed. D G asked PJ to leave. PJ very apologetic. Rennie cried after PJ left but wouldn't say why. Says he doesn't want to come back to meetings here. Bad vibes. I like Pastor J. Plan to see him next week to talk about joining. Don't know why R. is so upset.

"I still don't see what you are getting at."

Mrs. Wilkens reached across the table and grabbed the journal. "It's here somewhere." She paged through it, her lips moving as she scanned the entries. "Here." She slid the notebook back to me.

The entry was dated April 8th. It was hard to read because Ramona had apparently spilled coffee on the pages. I squinted hard to make out the writing, wondering how Mrs. Wilkens, with her eighty-four-year-old eyes, could read it so easily.

Rennie back. Looks terrible. Sick or something. Says he's gay and no one cares about him. Says Jennings gave him something that he could never get rid of. Saw Pastor J after meeting. Asked about Rennie even tho I shouldn't. He was really sad and said he cant tell me. I took his hand. Felt so good. Says I'm the only one who understands.

The idea of comforting wimpy Pastor Jacob made my skin crawl. I pictured his limp handshake and his emotionless funeral sermon.

The journal had a few more entries, mainly about work at the assisted living facility. The last entry was written in such a scrawl that it was hard to read.

Won't do it! Won't do it! Not going back to the old days even if he needs a supply. He says he needs me.

"Wow," I said, "I wonder who *he* is?"

The trees began to rustle as the wind picked up. A gust swept through my kitchen window, sending the napkins on the table skittering to the floor. Immediately, the rain came down hard against the side of the building and into the kitchen. I rushed around, closing all the windows to the roar of the wind and the slap of the thunder outside.

Goldie was in the closet, nuzzling my old slipper. She looked at me with scared eyes.

"Hey, it's a little rainstorm. Nothing to worry about. You poor thing."

A white-hot bolt of lightning lit up the sky. Immediately, the building shook with a loud "bang!" and we were bathed in darkness. The apartment smelled like burned electrical wires.

"Damn," I said as I stumbled around in the dark, trying to find a flashlight. "With all these storms this year, you'd think I would be smart enough to Velcro one to my thigh."

I thought about the cadre of idiots who refused to admit the weather patterns were changing. Somehow, "global warming" was an example of "fake news." Fake or not, we'd had more nasty storms in the last two years than in my entire lifetime. This looked like another one.

I groped my way out to the kitchen and found a couple of candles. Mrs. Wilkens and I sat in the flickering light, eating our chili. Wind and rain slammed the apartment building.

At one point, I heard a loud crack outside and wondered if a tree had fallen.

"Must be some damage somewhere."

Little did I know.

Mrs. Wilkens was so quiet, I finally leaned toward her and said, "You aren't telling me everything, are you?"

She shook her head and sighed. "When Ramona wasn't using, she was a lovely, bright creative person. She had a lot of good years, especially after she met Grace's stepson Bobby. He was an assistant pastor at the church where the AA and Narcotics Anonymous meetings were held. They fell in love, she got her children back, and everything went well until Bobby was called up to the reserves. Remember, he was killed in Afghanistan."

Even in the candlelight, I could see Mrs. Wilkens's face darken. "Damn war with a disastrous ending. And where did it get us?"

I chose not to comment because it might have caused Mrs. Wilkens to go into lecture mode about the current politics. I wasn't in the mood for that.

I agreed with Mrs. Wilkens about the war. Too many lost lives, limbs, and dreams for something that never made any rational sense. And too many of those who lost their limbs and their lives and their dreams were poor and of color.

Mrs. Wilkens continued. "Ramona fell into a black hole again. Chrissy and Lena were in and out of foster homes. Ramona would clean up for a while and then fall back. We thought she'd finally pulled herself up after her rehab stint last year."

She fell into silence. When she looked at me again, she said, "There was some talk a couple of weeks ago about missing pills at the assisted living facility. Naturally, the finger pointed at Ramona. I think she was close to losing her job."

It seemed like another reason Ramona might have committed suicide, but I didn't point this out to Mrs. Wilkens.

"We need to go back to her apartment. There's got to be another notebook."

Outside, sirens wailed as the storm receded. The lights flickered and clicked back on, and Goldie emerged from the closet. At least the drama of the wind and thunder was over—or so I thought.

We were interrupted by a loud knock on the door. When I answered it, Mr. Diaz, our caretaker, stood next to a fireman wearing all his gear. "Ms. Liza, you better come here."

Chapter Nineteen

Mr. Diaz led me out the backdoor of the apartment building. The rain had stopped, and the air smelled fresh and cool. Overhead, wisps of clouds floated over the quarter moon. The peaceful scene was ruined, however, by the bright flashing red lights from the fire truck. They shone on what used to be my beloved Toyota Corolla. A huge tree limb sat on top of it, crushing the roof into the front seat. I stared. I'd bought the Corolla with my first teaching paycheck. It had seen me through a lot of turmoil, including the breakup with Terrence. Through all the ups and downs, the bad boyfriends, and the good ones, the Corolla had been my Rock of Gibraltar.

"Oh hell."

Mrs. Wilkens patted my hand. "Oh my."

That night, I sat on the couch in semi-darkness with a gin and tonic that was more gin than tonic. Goldie curled up beside me, as if she understood my distress.

"Oh, why don't I have someone besides an old lady and a figment of my imagination to help me mourn the loss of my car?" I stared at the lime floating in the drink.

I thought about John Trapper and how good he was with Jennifer. He had a combination of tenderness and command that Jason Epstein would never have. If I'd mixed myself one more gin and tonic, I probably would have called him for some sympathy. Better sense prevailed.

"This is really not a good day." Goldie lifted her head but provided no solace.

As the night quieted and the storm became a distant rumble, I finished my drink and dragged myself to bed. My body felt like I'd run a marathon without practicing. Goldie settled comfortably on the pillow beside me and immediately started to purr.

"Could you keep it down?" But in truth, the sound she made had a note of comfort to it.

I fell almost immediately to sleep and dreamed of Jennifer lifting a cup of tea to her mouth as I was trying to tell her it was poison. Her eyes said, "It's too late." Then she morphed into Chester, who also lifted the cup to his mouth. I must have flailed in bed as I tried to shout, "No! No!" because Goldie meowed in irritation and jumped off the bed, waking me up.

The rest of the night I tossed around never quite finding the right position. My brain was going at the speed of light with images of Jennifer, of the shimmer that was Charlee, John Trapper, and the dead Ramona. On top of that, Josiah lurked deep in the background. Like being stuck with Charlee, I felt doomed to have him haunt me. Nothing worked to shut down my brain until about five in the morning when I finally dropped into a deep sleep.

I woke with a start to a knock on my bedroom door. Mrs. Wilkens stood with two coffees and a concerned expression. She pointed to the tangle of bedclothes.

"It looks like you had a riot in here."

Once again, I'd forgotten to lock my apartment door.

From the bedroom window, I saw the scattering of branches and leaves on the lawn from last night's storm. Outside, the neighborhood was abuzz with the sounds of chainsaws and the beeping of trucks as the city worked to clean up the storm debris. Inside, my head was also abuzz. My temples throbbed from a headache that had either been brought on by last night's gin or my miserable night's sleep.

"Get yourself showered. We need to find that other notebook before they haul the trash out."

I stared at her, blinking away my sleep haze. "Um, I have things to take care of here?" In my exasperation, I'd taken on my teenaged persona.

"Oh, never mind your car. The insurance people will take care of it. You've called them, haven't you?"

"Um. No?"

Mrs. Wilkens folded her arms and said sternly. "We haven't got time for you to revert to adolescence right now. Get in the shower." She added. "Now!"

I sulked for a minute or two, feeling sorry for myself and the loss of my beloved car, before I downed more than the over-the-counter recommended dose of ibuprofen and stood in the shower. The water washed away the haze, and the ibuprofen dulled the headache.

While Mrs. Wilkens paced in the kitchen, I called the insurance company and arranged for someone to come out and do a damage estimate. I was pretty sure that whatever they wanted to pay me for the Corolla wasn't enough to replace it.

"We'll take my car." Mrs. Wilkens was already halfway out the door. "Don't forget your phone."

Before we left for Ramona's apartment, I took one last look at the car. In my musings last night, I'd imagined that once they got the branch off, the roof would pop back like new. Workmen had removed the tree branch, but the top of the car was still caved in. So much for wishful thinking.

"I guess I should see if I have anything valuable in the car before we go. In case they tow it..."

Mrs. Wilkens nodded impatiently.

The front passenger door still opened enough for me to squeeze in. I rifled through the glove compartment and pulled out a Minnesota road map, an array of expired insurance cards, and a small survival kit with matches, a candle, hard candy, and gum that was probably ten years old.

Squeezing myself out, I walked around the car. Branches and woodchips covered the gravel. An aroma of fresh, clean wood permeated the parking lot. None of the other cars, including Mrs. Wilkens' antique Geo Prism, had been touched. Why my Corolla? I glanced into the smashed back window on the driver's side. Something was on the floor, wedged under the driver's seat.

"What is that?" I was talking to myself while Mrs. Wilkens stood nearby with an impatient expression.

I tried the door, but it was crunched into the frame.

"Are you coming?" she called.

I moved around to the back passenger door and tried it. Like the front door, I could get it open enough to squeeze in. The object looked like a book. For a moment, I wondered if I'd left *Jane Eyre* in the car. Reaching through the rubble of broken glass, I grabbed the book.

It was a leather-bound, embossed Bible. The leather still smelled fresh. I had no recollection of ever putting a Bible in the car.

"What have you got?"

I handed the Bible to Mrs. Wilkens. She opened it with a puzzled expression. "Oh my."

One-third of the way through the book, the pages had been hollowed out. A scrap of paper was tucked into the hollowed-out portion. She took it out and held it up to the light. I looked over her shoulder. In a barely readable scrawl was the word "Fake."

Chapter Twenty

We stared at the book and the little slip of paper.

"This is like a Bible I saw in the parish house," I whispered.

Mrs. Wilkens pressed her lips together. "I told you something was wrong with that church."

Before I could say anything more, she handed the book back to me. "Keep this for evidence. But we have to hurry to Ramona's apartment before someone gets there to pick up the rest of the stuff."

Mrs. Wilkens' tone had a drama queen pitch to it. I found as I gazed at the wreckage of my car, that I was tired of drama. I wanted to go back to my apartment, crawl into bed, and wake up later with my car intact, Ramona alive and Charlee vanquished. Oh yes, and the cat, happily living somewhere else.

Mrs. Wilkens grabbed my arm and tugged me in the direction of her car. The ibuprofen was wearing thin, and a headache roiled behind my eyes.

"Come on!" She pulled harder. "You're worse than a dawdling schoolchild."

I stumbled along, unable to come up with an appropriate retort. Then, I made the mistake of not insisting that I drive. The trip to Ramona's involved one near collision and two runs through red lights. As we sped along, I resisted the temptation to open the glove compartment and see how many traffic tickets were hidden inside.

Mrs. Wilkens screeched into the one available parking space at the side of Ramona's apartment building. I closed my eyes as she threw the car into park and thanked God or whatever Supreme Being existed for getting us here safely. As we stepped into the sunlight, an image of the body bag being taken out the front door hit me. For a moment, my knees weakened. Fortunately, Mrs. Wilkens was so focused on getting inside that she didn't notice.

"Grace told me this is section-eight housing, and many of the tenants are low-income immigrants. Ramona had to wait almost two years to get an apartment here." We hurried into the building's entrance. The hallway was filled with the smells of curry and spices intermingled with mildew and garbage. To get to Ramona's third-floor apartment, we walked up a set of stairs covered in a worn carpet that had probably been put down before my mother was born.

Mrs. Wilkens opened the door with the key Grace had given to her. The apartment was completely empty.

"Grace told me the girls were coming today to pick up the last few boxes. They must have gotten here very early."

She tapped out a number on her phone while I surveyed the room, remembering how shabby the apartment was. The carpeting in the living area was worn and in places, threadbare. In the kitchenette, off the living room, several cupboard doors were missing. The nicks and cigarette burns on the countertop indicated hard usage. The white porcelain sink was chipped and had a large rust stain where the faucet dripped.

Remembering what Detective Peterson had told me about crime scenes, I glanced around for any evidence of violence. Ramona had been found in the living room. Would there be bloodstains on the carpet? Or the walls? I saw nothing but a dilapidated room and a carpet needing a new home in the garbage dump.

Mrs. Wilkens stood near the front window, talking into her phone. "I'm on hold." She glanced over at me. "Can you look around for the notebooks?"

What was she on hold for?

My assignment was to look for a missing notebook. Since everything appeared to be gone, I guessed it would be a short investigation.

Lead on.

I felt the vibration in my head as I walked into the bedroom. The room was big enough to hold a double bed and a dresser. A small closet had built-in shelves and a rod to hang clothes. Several wire hangers dangled from the rod. The shelves were lined with old newspaper and completely empty. My nose filled with dust and mildew as I peered in. I sneezed several times. It brought back memories of dusty closets like this in the many apartments we lived in when I was a child. I didn't want to think about those days and the false bravado Mother put on every time we had to move. She'd say with a smile that didn't match her eyes, "We're going on another adventure." At least after our stay with Josiah's Household, we finally settled into a reasonably decent duplex.

"There's nothing here," I shrugged as I turned to leave the room.

Keep looking.

"You are like a dog with a bone."

Little touchy today?

I wanted to snap back at her about Jennifer and about my car, but it seemed pointless since she was nothing but a voice in my head.

Back at the closet, I stared at the shelves. Something was slightly different. One of the shelves had an extra layer of newspaper. I pulled off the top one and brought it into the light.

I'd seen the article before. It was a full page from an old *Star Tribune*. Maybe dogs and bones weren't such a bad thing.

"Mrs. Wilkens, come and look at this."

She came in with her phone pressed to her ear. "You mean the girls didn't come this morning? But the place is completely cleaned out." She looked at me in exasperation. "I'll call you back."

I showed her the article on The Welcome Congregation Church that pictured Jennifer in an apron serving food to the homeless. Pastor Jacob stood beside her, and next to him was a smiling Reverend Ellis—not the stern Reverend Jennings. Pastor Jacob's face had been circled.

We moved closer to the window, and I reread the article. What I hadn't noticed before in my search of the Welcome Congregation was that this was not the same minister. The article listed Reverend Martin Ellis as the senior minister of the Welcome Congregation. It made no mention of Reverend Jennings and named Pastor Jacob simply as Jacob Jennings and his wife,

Jennifer.

"We need to find that notebook," Mrs. Wilkens said, handing the paper back to me. "We should keep this for evidence."

I was about to say, "Evidence of what?" when her phone rang with a chiming ringtone. While she talked, I reread the article. It mentioned the church services in English and Spanish and also said that Reverend Ellis conducted a special service every week for new immigrants. The article noted how much the congregation had grown with the influx of African Christians.

I needed to find out more about the church and how the Jennings fit in. I was doing a search on my phone to see if I could find Reverend Martin Ellis when a call came in. The ID said, "Neuro Specialty."

"Liza? It's John Trapper."

He was at Hennepin County Medical Center making rounds on the neuro clinic patients and wanted to fill me in on Jennifer.

"I dreamed about her last night," I confessed. "She was about to drink poisoned tea."

He laughed. "Well, you weren't too far off. I couldn't look at her chart, of course, because she's not our clinic patient, but I did talk with my doctor friend in the ER."

John told me they'd admitted her to the ICU unit, suffering from dehydration and probable kidney failure. "I asked him about the arsenic. He said they did the lab work and were waiting for the results, but he did talk with poison control, and they confirmed that the symptoms he was seeing could be consistent with arsenic or some other heavy metal."

"So," I said, "She was poisoned."

"It's a good guess."

"Do you think I can visit her?"

"I'm not sure."

He was interrupted by an overhead page that called out, "Code silver, emergency one."

John stopped talking until the page was over.

"What's a code silver?" I asked. I knew from watching too much television that a code blue meant someone's heart stopped.

John sounded a little rattled when he replied. "Sorry. I'm just a hallway down from the ER. Silver means someone has a gun. I'd better go."

"Oh my god. Please take care."

His phone abruptly clicked off. I stared at it, praying that he would be all right.

Mrs. Wilkens emerged from the bedroom with an angry expression. "Someone took all the stuff in here. Grace checked with the girls, and they said friends were coming this afternoon to pick things up. I'm going to see the caretaker and give her a piece of my mind."

As I hurried after her, I told her about the "Code Silver" page.

"Too many guns," she muttered as she marched down the stairs to the caretaker's apartment. Judging by Mrs. Wilkens's tone, I was glad she wasn't packing. I felt sorry for the poor caretaker.

For a brief moment, Charlee came back.

I like John.

And then she was gone.

Chapter Twenty-One

The caretaker's apartment was in the basement. I sympathized with anyone who had to try to manage an old, decrepit building filled with people living on the margins. I had spent a summer between my junior and senior year in college, caretaking a small apartment building in Southeast Minneapolis. Most of the residents were University of Minnesota students, and I figured they wouldn't be a problem. Oh sure. I could count the nights I didn't have someone at my door at all hours—forgotten keys, plugged toilets, noisy neighbors, loud parties—you name it. I vowed after that to never bother a caretaker unless it was a matter of life or death.

Mrs. Wilkens banged on the door. "I want to know what happened to all the things in apartment 306," she demanded.

The caretaker's door was painted a shiny red, which contrasted with the gray, crumbling walls of the basement staircase. Behind the door, someone fumbled with the chain. When it opened, the woman we'd met when Ramona had been found looked out.

"Yes?" She wore a deep purple headscarf. I wondered if she was Somali.

Mrs. Wilkens calmed down when she saw the woman. In the background, a well-modulated voice on the television pitched exercise equipment. It was a sad commentary on the state of my summer that I knew the ad by heart. If I ordered in the next twenty minutes, I would get a free gizmo, good for creating six-pack abs.

Mrs. Wilkens articulated her words carefully. "Who took the things in apartment 306?"

The woman blinked. "They come with truck and took last night."

"Who?"

She shrugged. "Man with dark hair and man with light hair. He have key and say family asked."

"Did he say where he was taking things?"

"He give key to me after he put things in truck. He not saying much."

I thought about the newspaper article that Mrs. Wilkens had stuffed in her handbag. I asked her to pull it out.

"Did either of the men look like this?" I pointed to Pastor Jacob.

The caretaker shook her head, hesitated, and then said. "I see him sometimes, but not last night."

Mrs. Wilkens gave her the key her sister had given her. "Thank you."

Before the woman closed the door, she said, "They put trash by big box." She pointed toward the back of the building.

In the distance, I heard the beep, beep of the city garbage truck making its rounds. "Let's take a quick look before they haul it away. Maybe they threw out the notebooks—whoever they were."

Mrs. Wilkens nodded and headed for the dumpster. I had to run to keep up with her.

We hurried through the alley as the squealing roar of the garbage truck drew closer. The dumpster was overflowing and smelled ripe with rotted garbage. I stopped before we got too close to the blue container. "Maybe we are being a little silly about this."

On television, the crime scene people put on jumpsuits and heavy gloves before they go through the trash. I had on a pair of cargo shorts, a T-shirt and sandals. Mrs. Wilkens had plaid shorts, a "Get in Gear" running T-shirt from 1987, and her neon orange tennis shoes.

"Nonsense. Let's see what we can find."

Gingerly I followed her. The alley was strewn with crushed cans, broken beer bottles and all manner of plastic trash. Dirty puddles of water from last night's storm created an obstacle course to the dumpster. Down the street, the garbage truck beeped and rattled as it lifted cans and dumpsters.

Mrs. Wilkens charged ahead with the focus of a major league pitcher going for a no-hitter. Several black plastic lawn-sized bags sat outside the dumpster.

"I recognize these," she exclaimed, pulling open the first bag. "Lena dumped the notebooks in a bag like this."

She ripped open the bag only to jump back as rotting vegetables and a meat tray filled with maggots leaked out.

"Let's go." I had no time for maggots.

Mrs. Wilkens ignored me and tried the second bag. Behind us, the garbage truck was backing into the alley with the rhythmic beep, beep, beep. The driver stuck his head out the window of the truck and yelled, "Hey ladies, get out of there!"

Mrs. Wilkens grabbed the trash bag and dragged it behind her as she skirted the garbage truck. I caught up with her and took the bag from her. "Here," I said in total exasperation. "Are you hauling more rotten stuff around?"

"Put it in the trunk of my car." She replied. "It's got some of Ramona's things."

I half-carried, half-dragged the bag to her car. The bag felt like it might be filled with clothes.

Before we got into the car, I politely and firmly asked Mrs. Wilkens for her car keys. "I'll drive."

When we arrived back at our apartment building, the Corolla was gone, and only scattered windshield glass indicated that it had ever been parked under the old oak tree. I looked at the empty space and felt a sense of loss. How could I replace the old workhorse?

Mrs. Wilkens popped the trunk and waited impatiently for me to pull the garbage bag out. "We'll go through it in your place."

"Excuse me? What if it's full of maggots and flies?"

"Nonsense. I recognize the bag. Chrissy put her mother's clothes in it."

It occurred to me as I hefted the bag out of the trunk that I had never been in Mrs. Wilkens's apartment. In the five years I'd known her, she had never invited me up. Perhaps she was keeping a group of conservative politicians hostage until they agreed to support universal health insurance. If so, she was probably forcing them to watch MSNBC.

"Why don't we take it to your place?" This would be my opportunity to finally see how she lived.

"Yours is closer." Her tone said the decision was made. Out of respect for my elders, I didn't argue. However, I did resolve that if one ugly critter crawled out of the bag, I was picking the whole thing up and throwing it in the dumpster.

It turned out that Mrs. Wilkens was right; the bag was filled with Ramona's clothes. She had several blue striped smock tops from work along with white polyester pants. Ramona was not a large woman. Most of her clothes were a size six, and most of them had labels indicating that they came from either Target or Walmart.

Goldie joined us, staring intently as I examined one of the smocks. She meowed loudly and rubbed up against the cloth. Poor kitty. I'm sure it smelled like her mistress.

Mrs. Wilkens carefully folded the clothing I pulled out of the bag and stacked it neatly on the coffee table.

"I don't see any notebooks in here."

"Maybe the girls took them." Mrs. Wilkens held up one of the smocks. "Life is so fragile. Last week, she wore this to take care of people. This week, it'll go to Goodwill."

Yes, I thought. One day Terrence, the kindest softball player I'd ever met, and I were laughing about a movie. The next, he was heading in his car toward a concrete abutment without his seatbelt.

I took out another smock. Something rattled in one of the pockets. "Didn't you say Ramona was under suspicion because of missing drugs at the assisted living?"

"Of course, if anything got misplaced, they'd look at Ramona first because of her history." Mrs. Wilkens frowned with indignation.

I pulled a prescription bottle out of the pocket and handed it to her. The bottle was half-filled with oxycodone, and the label on the bottle was someone other than Ramona.

"Oh shoot." Mrs. Wilkens looked crestfallen. "Maybe she accidentally kept it—you know, put it in her pocket and forgot to put it back."

"Maybe." I didn't add that I doubted very much that this was an act of forgetfulness.

We stopped looking in the bag after that. I offered to take it up for her, but Mrs. Wilkens insisted on carrying it back to her apartment without help.

I kept the bottle of pills.

After she left, I sat on the couch and stared at the bottle. Was this the key?

Goldie sat next to me, and for a few moments, I felt like we bonded over loss—sort of. Goldie lost her mistress, and I lost my car—hardly a fair comparison.

"You know," I finally said to the cat. "You'll have to get over it."

So here I sat alone in my little apartment. My main companions consisted of a cat who didn't like me and a crazy old lady. Plus a voice that showed up randomly to tell me what to do.

"I must be insane." I stood up and stretched. It was time to take another field trip. I needed to see Jennifer and make sure she was all right.

Goldie followed me to the kitchen, looked at her dish, and meowed. Ah, yes, I thought. Maslow's hierarchy—basic needs first. I fed the cat.

Chapter Twenty-Two

I left a message for John and took a bus downtown to Hennepin County Medical Center. I hoped he might be able to meet me at the hospital and help me through the medical maze. If Jennifer was lucid, maybe she could tell me more about Ramona and her cryptic remark, "Jacob would know." If she wasn't, maybe I could read to her. I stuck my copy of *Jane Eyre* in my bag.

In the hospital gift shop, I bought a small teddy bear. Stuffed animals always worked with my students when they needed more comfort than I could give.

As I took the elevator up to the ICU, I felt an unpleasant tightening in my stomach, like I was going someplace I shouldn't. The sensation continued as I stepped into the ICU waiting room. It was filled with worried people. An African-American family huddled in one corner, silently holding hands and staring while a chaplain talked in a low voice to them. A middle-aged woman paced the floor in front of a teenage boy playing games on his cell phone. I heard her say to him, "Grampa will be glad to see you." He barely looked up as he mumbled, "Do I have to go in?"

I was relieved to see that the Jennings family was nowhere in sight.

All the ICU rooms were behind a swinging door that required a badge to open. I checked with the clerk at the desk and asked if I could see Jennifer. The clerk had short, steely silver hair and an expression that said, "Don't mess with me." She studied the visitor's pass I'd gotten at security before coming to the waiting area.

"Are you family?" Her voice was surprisingly gentle, but she surveyed me with suspicion.

Somehow, using the phrase, "I'm her volunteer," didn't seem like it would work with this woman. I crossed my toes inside my Nikes and said, "I'm her stepsister." I must have had enough of a concerned relative look about me for her to pick up the phone and call back to the nurse's station.

"You can go back, but only for a few minutes." She buzzed the door.

As it swept open, I faced a centralized nurse's station surrounded by patient rooms. They all appeared to be occupied. To my left, as I walked in, a man talked loudly to the patient in the bed.

"The doctor says you are going to be fine." He shouted. I peeked through the door to see an elderly man leaning close to a wizened old woman who had so many lines and tubes going into her that I wasn't quite sure she was human.

Something deep inside urged me to leave. I pushed myself forward to Jennifer's room. As I entered, I counted five bags of IV solution hanging from poles. It was hard to find Jennifer among the medical trappings. A tube was taped to her mouth, and a machine quietly whooshed in air. The room was humid and smelled of a poorly disguised disinfectant. Jennifer's eyes were closed. Nothing in the room indicated that the family had come—no cards, no flowers, no balloons.

I stared at her. Her face was puffy, as if someone had tried to blow her up like a balloon. A nurse whisked in wearing an ID badge on a lanyard that said, "Ellen RN."

A flush crept up my neck to my cheeks as a tingling sensation grew. This room was so crammed with equipment that it barely fit a chair to sit on. Yet, something about it was so familiar. I took a deep breath to calm myself and pulled out the little teddy bear from the gift shop bag.

"Can she have this?"

The nurse looked at the bear and said, "It's cute. I'm sure she'll like it."

"Her face looks so puffy. Is she all right?"

While the nurse checked all the digital gauges and all the lines, she said, "Her kidneys aren't working well, and that causes the fluid to build up. Sometimes people get that way when we put a lot of fluids in them."

"Oh." On television, they always look pretty normal except for a bandage or two.

I'd read somewhere that you should talk to people even if it didn't look like they were conscious. I leaned over to talk with her, but my throat was so dry the words came out almost in a squeak, "Hello, Jennifer. I brought *Jane Eyre* in case you'd like me to read."

The nurse looked at me. "Are you all right?"

A bead of sweat rolled down my temple. What was wrong with me?

"Has her husband been in to see her?" I forced the words out. The room felt like it was closing in.

"Not on my shift. They said the family signed papers for her treatment but didn't come up to see her."

My eyes filled with tears, and I blinked hard. "But, he's a minister. I thought he'd be here."

She shook her head. "You're the only visitor I've seen today." When she finished straightening out the sheets on the bed, she beckoned me out the door. Once we were out of earshot, I felt a little less dizzy.

"Maybe you could talk to her family. She isn't doing well. We're wondering if she might have an advance directive."

"Advance directive?" I knew what the nurse was talking about, but I thought those were for old people like Mrs. Wilkens.

Ellen appeared to be a little uncomfortable now. "You know, what Jennifer would want if she wasn't going to make it..." she left the word hanging.

The floor wobbled beneath me, and I grabbed the nurse's station to steady myself.

Again, Ellen asked. "Are you all right? Sometimes, this can be really hard on the family."

I said nothing.

An alarm went off in the room next to Jennifer's. Ellen quickly excused herself. I turned to see several other people run into the room. The last one pulled the door closed behind her.

I steeled myself and walked back into Jennifer's room. When I sat down and opened *Jane Eyre* to read to her, I felt a bit steadier.

A doctor walked in while I was reading. She wore a white lab coat and looked to be younger than me. I didn't introduce myself other than to say, "She hasn't stirred since I came."

The doctor stood in front of the bedside computer and tapped through the electronic medical record.

"We're going to try dialysis as well as blood transfusions." She quoted me some lab values that meant nothing to me. "However, it looks like our best bet will be Dimercaprol, but of course, there are risks."

Ellen, the nurse, entered the room and said softly, "Dr. Hooper, perhaps we could step out to talk about this."

The doctor's cheeks reddened. "Oh, sure."

In the hallway, Dr. Hooper apologized. "I get so caught up in the technical part that I forget ..."

I had one question for her and hoped that she would answer it. "They said it was arsenic. Is that true?"

Dr. Hooper nodded. "We don't see it often. Someone alerted the emergency room doctor to look for it."

"Do you have any idea how this could have happened?"

Ellen studied me. "We were hoping someone in the family could tell us."

I shook my head. "I don't know, except that she was taking pills that didn't look like they came from a regular pharmacy."

The sounds and smells of the unit rose up, assaulting me as I spoke. Again, the floor wobbled beneath my feet. I realized I needed to get out. "I'm sorry, but I have to go. I'm sure Pastor Jacob, her husband, will be here soon. You should talk with him."

I fled before they could ask me about the pills. I needed to talk with John and find out if the pills I'd given him were full of arsenic. And I needed fresh air.

On the way out, I again looked for signs of the Jennings. The old man I'd heard talking to the woman in the bed by the door sat in a chair in the waiting room with an anguished expression. "I think we should let her go." His eyes were reddened, and he sniffled when he spoke. Two middle-aged women sat next to him. I heard one of them say, "But Dad, you can't give up.

CHAPTER TWENTY-TWO

If they think surgery will help."

I walked as quickly as possible to the corridor. I had to get out of this place. At the elevator, several people stood waiting. Two of them were wiping their eyes and holding each other. I looked around for an exit. If the elevator didn't come soon, I planned to flee down the staircase.

As the elevator dinged, something flashed in my brain. It was a snippet of a man in a bed, his eyes open and staring at nothing on the ceiling. I waited for people to step off, fighting off the image of the man. To my chagrin, the last person off was the unfriendly young deacon named Nicholas. I looked down, pretending to dig in my purse, and hoped he hadn't seen me. None of the others from the parish house were on the elevator.

I merged onto the elevator with the grieving family. As they sniffled and cried softly, it struck me that Jennifer might actually die. The overpowering smell in the ICU came back to me. Was it the smell of death? What was I doing getting involved in this? My face felt tight, and the back of my throat ached as I pictured Jennifer with all the tubes and lines—Jennifer alone to fight this battle.

"Hold the door, please." Nicholas stepped on and assumed the elevator position of looking straight ahead at the door with his hands folded in front of him. I stayed in the back, cursing the fact that I was tall and the people in front of me were short. As we descended, I pretended to be totally occupied with my phone. Maybe he hadn't seen me.

On the main floor, he stepped off. I positioned myself in the middle of the herd, again hoping he hadn't seen me. Once off, I looked around and didn't see him.

"Dodged that bullet," I mumbled, heading for the revolving door. The outdoors had never looked so good. Before I could reach it, a hand grabbed my arm from the back.

"We need to talk," his accented voice whispered in my ear. I smelled the hair oil on him and the sourness that goes with wearing a polyester suit coat in the Minnesota summer. I knew I was in trouble.

Chapter Twenty-Three

"Let me go!" I hissed.

I looked around for a security guard or a friendly face in the lobby, but the security desk was vacant. The hand on my arm tightened. "We go for coffee."

"What?" I turned to him to see if he was kidding. Who assaults someone by taking them for coffee? For a moment, I thought maybe it was an Eastern European code word, probably meaning "kill her now."

He steered me toward the coffee kiosk in the lobby. Without taking his hand off my arm, he ordered an Americano and then turned to me. "What you want?" His voice had a demanding tone to it.

I looked for the most expensive coffee on the menu and ordered a Carmel Frappuccino. If I was going to be kidnapped, at least I would have plenty of sugar and caffeine in my system.

He pushed me toward a little table in the corner. "Go sit."

I could have run at this point while he was picking up the drinks, but I thought, why waste a good coffee? Besides, I was curious.

We sat glaring at each other while we sipped our coffees. Mine was entirely too sweet, and I could tell by his expression and the number of packets of sugar he dumped in his coffee that his was too bitter.

Finally, he said. "Did she tell you about drugs?"

"Are you talking about Jennifer?"

"Of course." He looked at me with an expression of pure annoyance.

I wasn't about to tell him anything. "She's on a respirator and unconscious. She can't talk."

He shook his head in exasperation. "No, not today. Before when you come to the house."

I studied him, perplexed. "Why are you asking me? Why don't you talk with Pastor Jacob or Hilda or somebody?" I took another sip of the too-sweet coffee. "I don't know anything about 'drugs.'"

"No talk about drugs?" He repeated.

I hoped he couldn't see that my toes were crossed again. "She hardly talked to me. She was way too sick." I leaned a little closer to him. He was younger than I had first thought. As he fumbled with the sugar and slopped his coffee, I realized that he wasn't much older than Jennifer.

"Nicholas," I said. "What are you talking about?"

Instead of answering the question, he said, "What is wrong with her? She is very sick, yes?"

This was not the conversation I expected to have with the Russian mafia. "I think she is gravely ill. Do you know what that means?"

"She could die?" The gruffness and demanding had gone out of his voice. "They don't tell me nothing."

A young mother with a toddler sat down at the table next to us. She talked lovingly to the little girl, "When we get home, I'll read you a book. Okay?"

"More cookie, Mama. More cookie."

It flashed to me what Jennifer had said about growing up. Mother gone and father a mean drunk. Hilda had also said Jennifer hadn't been cared for by her mother. What were Hilda's words? She had a rough upbringing.

"Why do you care?" I asked.

"Jennifer, she be nice to me. Not like the others, 'do this, do that.'" I heard the anger in his voice.

"What others?"

He scowled, but he didn't answer. Instead, he again asked. "What is wrong with her?"

I saw no reason not to tell him. "She's been poisoned with arsenic."

He wrinkled his brow. "What is this arsenic?"

What had John told me? It was found naturally in a deep well in India. Otherwise, my knowledge of arsenic began and ended with the play *Arsenic*

129

and Old Lace. We'd done it in high school, and I'd played one of the sweet, homicidal little old ladies. We'd put the poison in the tea if I recalled right.

"I don't know much about it, but it can cause convulsions and the kidneys to stop working. They're trying to get the arsenic out of her system now."

Nicholas scratched his head. "Somebody give it to her?"

I shrugged. "Maybe it was an accident." Like hell, I thought.

Nicholas wrinkled his brow like he was trying to sort all of this out. I reached over and touched his wrist.

"You know something, don't you? What is it about drugs? Does this have anything to do with Ramona?" I was trying to put it all together, and nothing fit.

He stared at me, his eyes hard. "Who this Ramona?"

"She was a friend of Pastor Jacob and volunteered to read to Jennifer." I paused. "She's dead now. It was a drug overdose." I watched his face, hoping he'd give me a clue that he understood what I was talking about.

Instead, he wrinkled his brow with a bewildered look and mumbled, "I don't know no Ramona."

While we sat in uneasy silence for a few moments, a couple of Minneapolis policemen walked through the main door. Nicholas had his back to them. If I was afraid, this would be the time to make a run for it. However, as I studied his expression, I saw worry, not anger or danger.

"You must really care about her."

He didn't answer.

One of the policemen walked over to the coffee bar, all the equipment attached to his uniform rattling as he moved. Nicholas glanced up at the officer, and suddenly, his expression changed from worry to fear.

Abruptly, he stood up. "I must go now. Don't come by the church no more." He left his unfinished coffee and hurried in the opposite direction of the coffee bar.

"Wait." I wanted to ask him more questions, but he didn't look back, and he didn't stop.

I stirred my syrupy, sweet concoction and watched him rush out the door. I noticed that he walked with a slight limp, as if one leg was shorter than the other. What was his story? Undocumented? Wanted? What secret did he carry with him, and how was he connected to Ramona and the Jennings? All the questions gave me a brain ache.

At the table next to me, the little toddler dropped her drink on the floor. She wailed as her mother sopped up the mess. It was time for me to go.

Perhaps I would have been okay as I walked out the door. The dizziness and shakiness I'd felt in Jennifer's room had disappeared when Nicholas caught up with me. Perhaps I would have made it home to deal with my car, feed the cat, and tell Mrs. Wilkens about Jennifer. Except that just before I walked out of the hospital, the overhead operator announced a code blue. The words, so familiar, turned me cold.

"Code blue."

I couldn't catch my breath.

"Code blue."

I felt as if someone had me around my chest and was squeezing as tight as possible.

"Code blue."

I broke out in an icy sweat. Panting and stumbling, I lurched to the door and outside with the words still ringing in my head. When I closed my eyes against the bright sunshine, I saw that man again in a hospital bed, staring with dead eyes. Josiah. *Code blue.*

Chapter Twenty-Four

I made it across the street to a bench in a little sitting area. My peripheral vision clouded as darkness threatened to overcome and smother me.

Call John. Call him now!

Charlee's voice encased me, holding off the darkness that was after me. I hardly remember punching in his number. I gasped, trying to get oxygen to my brain. What was happening to me?

"This is John Trapper."

I prayed it wasn't his voicemail. "I...I...can you help me?"

"Liza, is that you?"

Talk to him.

I'm not sure what I said, but I must have told him where I was sitting. "Can't breathe. Please come."

"Hang on. I'm just across the street." His voice was calm, and it helped keep the blackness away. "I'll be there in a few minutes."

You need to remember. You need to talk to him, or this will never go away.

"I can't, Charlee." I gulped at the air. Sweat poured down my face.

A woman with several bags settled down on the bench, looked over at me, and abruptly stood up. "Not getting Ebola from you."

I don't know how much time passed. Several busses whooshed by while I sat with my head down, repeating the alphabet. If I kept repeating it, everything would be okay.

He's here. Talk to him.

"Liza?" John sat next to me and put his arms around me. When was the last time someone provided comfort to me? "Take slow, deep breaths. That's it."

The shaking subsided, and with his calming voice, I was able to finally catch my breath. The lady with the bags hovered close by and waggled her finger at John. "She's got that Ebola. You be careful."

Slowly, the world turned back to its normal self. Down the street, a car honked. A few feet away, smoke from a cigarette wafted in my direction. Even the lady with the bags decided it was safe to sit on the bench, although she kept as far away from John and me as possible.

"I'm sorry. I don't know what happened. They called a code blue, and I panicked."

John kept me in his embrace and nodded.

Talk to him.

"You stay out of this," I muttered.

John pulled away with a puzzled expression.

"Oops, not you."

He wrinkled his brow. I wondered if he was thinking that he'd just gotten himself entangled with a madwoman.

This is about Josiah. Talk to him.

"Can we go someplace and talk?" I wanted to reassure him that I wasn't crazy. But here I was—post-panic attack with a voice inside my head issuing orders. Maybe I was nuts.

"That might be a good idea." He called his clinic to tell them he'd be out for an hour, while we walked down the street to a little coffee shop. My legs felt wobbly and it was nice that he kept me steady with his arm firmly around my waist.

Once we settled at a back table, he brought us both iced teas. Sliding into the seat across from me, he said. "Okay. What was that all about?"

I took a deep shuddering breath and told him about Josiah and the Household. "When I was fourteen, my mother got involved with this group. She was kind of a hippie if you know what I mean. The group was really a cult, but she didn't know it. She thought it was a commune of like-minded people who lived together in a big South Minneapolis house. She moved us there the summer before I started eighth grade."

John nodded, his eyes filled with concern.

I continued. "Josiah was the leader. He reminded me of the sleazy caretaker in one of our apartment buildings. He had blue eyes that could look soft and warm and then turn mean in a heartbeat. I didn't like him from the minute I saw him. He liked to touch us and hug us, but it felt wrong to me." I paused to gather my thoughts. How much should I tell him?

"And?" John prodded.

I cupped my hands around the iced tea and felt the coolness on my palms. "Okay, here's the Cliff's Notes version. One evening, everyone went out to a neighborhood festival, except he told my mother I had to stay back because I was throwing off 'too many negative vibes.' That's how he talked. Josiah, the three moms, and the five kids left, and I had some quiet time to myself."

"But he came back?"

"He came back. Except I didn't know it. I was up in the room I shared with my mother, listening to music on this fancy new device called an iPod."

While I'd danced, feeling a raw sense of freedom, Charlee spoke to me—almost like I had eyes in the back of my head. She warned me. She said, *He's coming back! Get out!*

John reached over and touched my wrist. "I'm sensing this is very painful."

"No kidding. The guy was a predator. He brought single moms into the commune so he could get at their kids—boys, girls—he wasn't fussy. Of course, I didn't know that. I only knew that he gave me the creeps."

"I tried to run down the staircase and out the door. Except he caught me on top of the stairs. He had his oily hands around me." I closed my eyes and shuddered, remembering how his hands snaked under my t-shirt. "He...he was whispering foul things about what he was about to do to me. He told me he knew I wanted it."

I'll never forget that hot breath of his on my neck. To this day, I can't stand to have a guy kiss my neck.

Opening my eyes, I stared at the table. "Well, long story short, I was trying to push him off when suddenly, both of us ended up falling down the stairs. I landed on top of him. I was so stunned I just sat on the steps and stared at him. Something was wrong. He was bleeding from his mouth and making funny groaning noises."

I gripped the iced tea cup so hard the plastic lid popped off. Fortunately, it didn't spill all over the table. John took my hand. It felt warm and steady as things came back to me in fragments. "I honestly don't know how long before someone found us. It's a blur—ambulance, Mother holding me and crying, the emergency room." I paused and took a deep breath. "But the worst memory I have is of being in the emergency room and seeing them bring him in on a gurney. He was staring up at the ceiling, and suddenly, he turned his head and sneered at me like a snake ready to bite. Then I heard 'code blue,' and someone hustled me away."

"Was the code for Josiah?"

"I don't really know, but I ended up so frozen with fear I couldn't talk. They called it traumatic aphasia. I remember someone in the hospital whispering the words 'catatonic.' After a couple of days in the hospital, they transferred me to the adolescent psych ward. I don't remember how long I was there before Mother told me she was moving out of the Household. Later, I heard that two other girls told their mother's that he had raped them."

What I didn't tell John was that Charlee had stayed with me for the entire ordeal and that I'd confessed to Dr. Slack, my therapist, about her. Dr. Slack assured me that it was a normal reaction to the trauma and Charlee would eventually go away.

I did go away for a long time. But, see, you need me now.

"I wish you'd leave. My life was so much easier without you."

John pulled his hand away and looked startled. "What?"

"I'm sorry, I wasn't talking about you." I tried to backtrack. "It's what I wanted to say to Josiah, I guess."

"What happened to him?"

"He died. Or at least that's what Mother said. I never asked."

For the first time in years, I felt the dribble of tears down my cheeks. Sniffling, I grabbed a napkin and tried to blink them away. "Usually, I'm the sanest person I know."

You think?

John leaned forward with a sympathetic smile. "Remember, I was in the military. I know how bad things can come back to haunt you when you least expect it."

I took a drink of the iced tea that was no longer icy. What I needed right now was to change the topic. Smiling and blinking back the tears in a way I hoped didn't appear maniacal, I said, "On a lighter note, the storm last night? It dropped a tree on my car. I need to get back to deal with it."

For a moment, John peered at me like I might be an extra-terrestrial. His face broke into a big smile. "You sure know how to lighten the mood."

We parted after I assured him that I was now fine. Actually, I was fine. I felt a weight had been lifted from me and hoped the feeling would last. I also felt like I might actually see John again sometime when I wasn't having a nervous breakdown. On top of that, the voice that was Charlee had disappeared. Silently, though, I thanked her.

Chapter Twenty-Five

The bus grunted its way down Lake Street. I had hoped for some quiet reflection about my mini-nervous breakdown on my way home from the hospital, but instead, I ended up sitting behind an unwashed teenaged couple who were talking about where they could crash tonight. It was hard not to eavesdrop.

The girl, with tangled bleached hair, said to the boy, "I hear that they don't bother you if you go to that place under the Franklin Avenue Bridge."

The boy replied with a shrug. "Naw, it's all fenced off now. Jordy says they patrol down there, and besides, I don't want to sleep outside again. Look at all the mosquito bites." He showed her his arm. His arm was a mottled bluish-black from all the tattoos. From my vantage point, I couldn't see any of the bites.

"Shit, that's nothing."

"Didja hear that Danny-O got picked up yesterday? Dumb jerk tried to walk out of Target with a bunch of stuff he lifted."

"He's so screwed…"

These two could have been my summer school kids at one time. Or they could have been Ramona at fourteen. I knew for some of them the Franklin Avenue Bridge was a safer place than home or with an abusive pimp. When I was fourteen, I'm guessing the bridge would have been a safer haven than Josiah's Household.

I leaned forward. "Hey, in case you're interested, there's a place to stay on Lake Street. They don't ask questions."

The boy looked at me with eyes that were much older than his face. "What do you care?"

Shrugging, I said, "Just a suggestion. It's on Lake and Nicollet. White house with a red rocking horse on the porch. No signs."

I sat back, pulled my phone out of my bag, and ignored them. A former teaching colleague ran the place. She'd managed to get some of the kids back in school and connected with the right services. With the others, she asked no questions.

They got off at the next stop and crossed the street to the bus headed toward Nicollet. Maybe they could have a decent night with no mosquitoes.

Mrs. Wilkens knocked on my door shortly after I got home. She carried a fresh bottle of tonic and several limes.

"I'm assuming you have gin?"

I regarded the tonic and the limes for a moment. Between the panic attack, the sugary Frappuccino, and the lukewarm iced tea, my stomach felt a little queasy. Still, a gin and tonic sounded pretty good, all things considered.

"Sure, why not?"

I let Mrs. Wilkens mix the drinks.

We sat in the living room going over the day. Ramona's notebook, the bottle of oxycodone, and the hollowed-out Bible were lined up on the coffee table. Mrs. Wilkens prattled on about the notebook and the mysterious men who cleaned out the apartment while I sat, barely listening to her. Should I tell her about the panic attack? About how dizzy and sick I felt visiting Jennifer?

I raised my hand and stopped her. "I wonder if we should turn it all over to the police to sort out. What's happened to Jennifer scares me."

"What do you mean?"

I told her about Jennifer in the ICU hooked up to life-support. "She's on a respirator, and her face is all swollen up because her kidneys aren't working." The tonic fizzed inside my mouth as I sipped my drink. "They wanted to know about that living will stuff. I think she could die."

"Oh my." Mrs. Wilkens frowned.

Then I told her about Nicholas and our strange encounter. "He nearly ran out the door when a couple of policemen walked in. The whole thing stinks." I looked directly into Mrs. Wilkens's eyes, "These are real people, and I feel like I have been playing a grade school game. This isn't an Encyclopedia Brown mystery. It's serious business."

I expected Mrs. Wilkens to pat my hand and say things like "It's okay, dearie" and "Let's stay the course." Instead, she put her gin and tonic down, closed her eyes, and leaned back against the couch. She was quiet for such a long time that I thought she'd gone to sleep. I reached over to shake her when her eyes popped open.

"You're right. We've been tinkering. It's time to sort this out."

"Maybe it's time to butt out."

Mrs. Wilkens shook her head. "Someone put that Bible in your car. Someone is asking for help."

I half-expected Charlee to bug me with her "help them" mantra, but she left me undisturbed.

I sighed. "Okay, what next?"

For the next hour, we sorted through everything we knew and everything we speculated. I had flip chart paper left over from a school project in my closet. I brought it out, and we made two pages—fact and speculation. On the fact side, we had:

- Ramona was associated with the church in some capacity (volunteer for Jennifer)
- Ramona had some type of relationship with Pastor Jacob (counseling?)
- Ramona had someone else's oxycodone in her smock pocket
- Jennifer had been sick for at least a month (according to Hilda)
- Jennifer was suffering from arsenic poisoning and was afraid of the drinking water
- Someone took things from Ramona's apartment without the family's permission (as far as we know)
- Someone put a Bible with the inside hollowed out in my car
- Nicholas was worried that I knew something about drugs
- The church had declined since the article in the *Star Tribune* about their

soup kitchen
- Reverend Jennings preached ugliness from the pulpit

On the speculation side, we had:

- Ramona's death was not a suicide (need police and autopsy report)
- Jennifer's poisoning was not accidental
- The church was involved in something shady (check out Nicholas)
- The Jennings were creepy

By the time we got to the last bullet point, we were feeling both exhausted and a little giddy.

I read over everything and said, "I'm going to check out the church. The *Star Tribune* article named the previous pastor. Maybe he can shed some light on the Jennings." I looked to see what Mrs. Wilkens thought.

She sat with her head tilted back and her mouth open, snoring gently. It was time to put the old lady to bed.

When I woke her and offered to accompany her upstairs, she was quite firm that she was fine and could manage without my help. I had hoped that this might be my opportunity to see the inside of her apartment. Maybe I could rescue the hostages she kept upstairs. I pictured a group of scruffy men wearing red baseball caps forced to watch The Rachel Maddow Show and started to giggle.

Fortunately, Mrs. Wilkens was too tired to pay me any attention.

That night, maybe because I'd poured my heart out to John or because I was totally exhausted, I had a good, dreamless sleep. Even Goldie sleeping on the pillow next to me didn't bother me. When I got up the next morning and looked at the flip charts taped to my living room wall, it all seemed silly. The first thing I needed to do was get a new car.

Chapter Twenty-Six

The car rental place picked me up and efficiently set me up with an SUV. They were sorry, but all their sub-compacts were rented. I'd always disliked SUVs because they were gas hogs, too big and powerful for most people, and not nearly as safe as regular cars. However, this one was a hybrid, and when I sat in it, I felt like a royal rising above the common proletariat. I could picture myself atop a desert mesa, looking over a jaw-dropping vista.

It had a backup camera, a video console, and a radio that would play iTunes from my phone. We were now in the era where car mechanics weren't grease monkeys; they were IT whizzes.

At the Toyota dealership, I tested several of their models, including the Prius line. Somehow, none of them felt right, even if they could tell me when I was backing into a tree or a car was in my blind spot. Finally, I said to the saleswoman, who was being very patient with me, "Where do I find a thirteen-year-old Corolla with bald tires." She laughed and sent me to a used car lot down the road.

Okay, it was only seven years old, and the tires were in pretty good shape, but the color was the same as my old car. I made a deal with them that if they delivered the car to the car rental agency when I dropped off the SUV, I would pay cash. There went all the money I'd saved for my dream trip to Europe. Who wanted to go to Europe when they could stay home and binge-watch crime dramas, anyway?

I was sorting through all the paperwork on my new old Corolla and ruing the cash decision when Mrs. Wilkens came marching in.

She was livid. "They say the life insurance policy is void if Ramona committed suicide." She stood in front of me with her arms folded as if it was all my fault.

"Isn't that common with life insurance policies?"

"Well, the girls are upset. I told them we would meet them this afternoon to figure out what to do."

Why did Mrs. Wilkens decide that *we* needed to figure any of this out? "I don't think I can be much help. I don't know anything about life insurance." I pointed to the paperwork in front of me. "Besides, I have to fill out these forms, or my insurance won't issue a paltry check for my ruined car. I don't have time for life insurance." Of course, I had plenty of time—all day, in fact.

Mrs. Wilkens glared at me with an expression that said, don't mess with me. I felt the blush rising up my neck. Busted. Even Goldie flashed an accusatory hiss before she jumped off the couch and headed for the bedroom.

"I'll meet you at your car in two hours." She walked out the door before I could reply.

The old gal certainly was good at getting her way.

We met Ramona's daughters at a little neighborhood café nestled in a residential area of South Minneapolis. The building had once housed a hardware store. Next to it was the office of a Holistic Health practitioner, and next to that was a self-service laundromat.

The girls were waiting at an outside table when we pulled up. An umbrella shaded us from the afternoon sun. The air was fresh and clean, but I felt sour. I didn't want to be here meddling in something that was none of my business. On top of that, as we drove the new Corolla to the café, Mrs. Wilkens pointed out that the interior smelled of cigarette smoke. I hadn't noticed it in my haste to buy the car.

We sat down with Ramona's daughters. Mrs. Wilkens introduced me and told them how I had tutored their mother so she could pass the GED.

I smiled. "She was a good student."

Chrissy, the older one, held out her hand. "I remember you from the funeral. Aunt Grace said you've been very helpful."

Lena, the younger one, nodded, but said nothing. Both of Ramona's daughters had dark hair and large brown eyes. Lena was taller and had a slender build. I could see her modeling for fashion ads. Mrs. Wilkens had told me that Lena was very quiet.

"Too many years in different foster homes. She has a hard time expressing herself." Mrs. Wilkens also warned me that the girls didn't hold much trust with strangers. Another reason I should have stayed home.

I decided to play this low-key and let Mrs. Wilkens do the talking. I didn't know what I'd say to them anyway. I guessed they would have a long and probably losing battle with the insurance company. I worked with a teacher whose son did the twenty-one shots game for his 21st birthday. He'd downed the liquor while his friends cheered him on. When he passed out, they'd hauled him to a friend's house to sleep it off. He never woke up. My colleague had an insurance policy with the confusing language about self-inflicted death. The company claimed by doing the shots, he'd deliberately poisoned himself. She spent four years in the legal system trying to get them to pay and never saw a dime.

Mrs. Wilkens was all business with the girls. "We have to establish that your mother was not suicidal. Can you tell us anything about her state of mind these last few weeks?"

Lena stared at her iced tea.

Chrissy hesitated before she spoke. "We hadn't seen much of her lately."

Lena nodded, but said nothing.

"She used to try to get together with us on the Sundays when she wasn't working. But lately, she stopped calling much." Chrissy's voice dropped to a near whisper. "We were afraid she'd started using again."

The silence grew until the waiter brought our drinks. As I stirred sugar into my coffee, I felt a deep sympathy for Ramona's daughters. Clearly, they were affected by their mother's death. The school social worker once told me that the most complicated grieving she saw came from kids who had lost a toxic parent.

"It's like they always dreamed Mom would get better and start loving them. Now the dream is gone," she'd explained. I wondered what the two girls thought beneath their quiet and composed exteriors.

Chrissy finally spoke again. "I really don't care about the life insurance policy. Both Lena and I have scholarships and jobs. We'll be fine."

Mrs. Wilkens' eyes narrowed as she leaned toward Chrissy. "That's not the point. Your mother did not commit suicide, and the damned insurance company needs to pay." The vehemence in her voice took us all aback.

I cleared my throat. "Uh, maybe you need to wait for the coroner's report before taking on the insurance company. You have plenty of time to file a claim."

Lena nodded with enthusiasm as Chrissy agreed. "I think we need to wait."

We talked for a little longer, avoiding any mention of their mother. I found out Chrissy was in her first year of law school at St. Thomas and that Lena planned to follow her when she finished her undergraduate degree at the University of Minnesota.

Mrs. Wilkens told them I taught fifth grade. Lena, who had not said a word the whole time, looked at me with a smile that dazzled. "I had a grade school teacher who kept telling me that I was smart enough to do anything I wanted."

"Sounds like you took her seriously."

"I did."

As we drove back to the apartment building, Mrs. Wilkens muttered, "I won't let that insurance company get away with this."

I looked at how her cheeks had flushed, and it occurred to me that she was refighting an old battle.

"You've had problems like this before, haven't you?"

Over a cup of orange pekoe tea in my apartment, Mrs. Wilkens told me about her son.

"Peter was going to go to college after high school, but that summer, his girlfriend suddenly broke up with him, and after moping around for a couple of weeks, he told us he had decided to enlist in the army. He and a friend signed up together. Maybe he thought he'd see the world and forget his sweetheart." She took a deep breath. "It was a bad choice for him. I don't know what happened. It's not like we were at war. But when he was discharged and came back, it was as if someone had taken away his voice. He hardly talked."

She set her mug down on the coffee table. "In those days, PTSD didn't exist, but I'm sure that's what he had."

"Did he get help—like from the VA?"

She shuddered. "They claimed he was discharged healthy and didn't have any service-related injuries. But something happened that broke him. He got into drugs and alcohol and was never the same. He bounced around from menial job to menial job to surfing on couches. Not the same Peter who was so alive with wonder as a child." She closed her eyes for a moment.

I hesitated and finally said the word. "Did he commit suicide?"

Mrs. Wilkens didn't answer for a long time. The silence in my apartment became oppressive, but I needed to let her sift through her thoughts. Finally, she said, "I don't know. He was living with friends in a rundown place by the railroad tracks near Hiawatha Avenue. One morning, he didn't wake up. They found alcohol in his system and track marks on his arms."

"Did the coroner call it suicide?"

Again, she sat quietly while Goldie purred next to her. She spoke in a soft voice, "We didn't know it, but he was HIV positive. Between the drugs, alcohol, and HIV, his body gave up. The official cause of death was liver failure."

"I'm so sorry." My words sounded clichéd, and I wished I could have come up with a better reply.

She looked at me, and a fury grew in her eyes. "Someone hurt him when he was in the army."

A tear rolled down her cheek. I reached over and handed her a tissue. She dabbed her eyes with a little hiccup.

"Did the insurance company refuse to pay?" I wondered if they could make a case back then that HIV was a choice.

She shook her head. "No, that wasn't the problem. We bought the policy before he went into the army. Mr. Wilkens got snookered by a persistent salesman who convinced him that all of us needed to be insured. I thought taking out life insurance on our son was morbid. But Mr. Wilkens signed up."

I finished my tea and took our cups to the kitchen for more hot water. While I was in the kitchen, I thought I heard her softly crying, but when I came back, she was sitting up ramrod straight with a tissue in her hand.

"What happened?"

"We paid on that damned policy for years. Then, the year he died, we missed one payment. When we tried to collect, the company informed us that the policy had been canceled. No notification, no nothing."

"Did you appeal?"

Mrs. Wilkens folded her arms with a harrumph. "Of course, all the way to the state insurance commissioner."

"And you didn't see a dime, I'm guessing."

To my surprise, Mrs. Wilkens said, "Oh yes. We finally collected. Three years later, after Peter was gone."

Now, I was confused. "But you seem so angry about it."

"Of course, I'm angry. I'm still angry. The three-year fight took the life out of Mr. Wilkens and destroyed our marriage."

I watched the steam rising from the tea cup while I built up the courage to ask the question that was hanging in the air. I took a deep breath and said, "If the fight was so painful for you, why do you want to put Chrissy and Lena through it?"

"Because," Mrs. Wilkens snapped back. "Because they deserve the money, and Ramona wanted them to have it." She folded her arms and stared at my front window.

When she looked back at me, the defiance had drained from her face. She patted my thigh. "This was a good conversation. Now we have work to do. I think you should find out more about the church."

She stood up and walked out the doorway. Goldie watched her with what appeared to be a wistful look as she closed the door behind her. I stared at the backside of her shorts and muttered to the cat, "Why am I taking orders from an old lady who clearly has a screw lose?"

The cat jumped off the couch and sauntered away with a barely audible meow.

I should have booked a flight to California right then and there. But I kept thinking about Jennifer.

Chapter Twenty-Seven

After Mrs. Wilkens left, I stared at the flip charts until they blurred in front of my eyes. In my television mystery world, this would be the time when I'd have an "aha" moment. Nothing called out to me, however. Maybe it was time to roll them up, put them in the closet, and settle in for more television watching.

As I was reaching for the remote, Goldie jumped up on the coffee table and sat on the faded article about Jennifer and the soup kitchen from the *Star Tribune*. I picked the cat up and set her down on the floor.

"Couch, yes. Table no."

Goldie lifted her tale high and sashayed away. What arrogance, I thought, before I glanced down at the article.

I didn't exactly have an "aha" moment, but I did feel the need to talk with the former pastor of the Welcome Congregation. Maybe he knew about the hollowed-out Bibles and the Russians. I pulled out my phone and searched for an address or phone number for Reverend Martin Ellis. He did not have a Facebook page, and other than references to the *Star Tribune* article, the only hit was a dot com that offered to search for Martin Ellis. The first thing they wanted was my credit card number.

"Someone who doesn't want money must know where he is."

I called the Metropolitan Council of Churches.

"I'm a former parishioner, and I'm trying to reach Reverend Martin Ellis of the Welcome Congregation. Do you have contact information on him?"

The man who answered the phone said, "Have you tried the church? They might know."

The last thing I wanted to do was call the parish house, so I lied. "They didn't have the information."

"Curious that they wouldn't know." I detected a note of skepticism.

I jumped in with yet another lie. At this rate, my toes were going to end up permanently crossed. "The secretary was out, and the person answering the phone didn't speak much English. I'm only in town today, so I was really hoping to get hold of him…" I let my voice trail off.

"The Welcome Congregation isn't part of our organization, but I can put you in contact with Doctor Jamison from the seminary. He might know."

Doctor Jamison knew someone who might know. I left several messages with different people, feeling like a total fraud. No one called me back. In sheer frustration, I picked up the phone and called the *Star Tribune* reporter who had done the article. Her name was Mary Powell, and she answered on the first ring.

"Wow," I said, a little flustered. "I'm so used to leaving messages that I didn't know people actually answered their phones anymore."

Mary Powell was silent for a moment and then said, "Can I help you?"

I explained that I was trying to reach Reverend Martin Ellis and saw the article she'd written about the soup kitchen. "Would you know how I could find him?"

"I don't normally give out that kind of information. Can you tell me why you need to talk with him?"

I was out of fibs at this point. I simply said, "I've been to the church, and something is wrong. Your article made it sound so vibrant and inclusive, yet the pews are half-filled, and the current minister is a…" I stopped before I said a hardnosed bigot.

"Hmmm," Mary Powell answered. "I've heard some rumors that the church isn't what it used to be."

"I want to see if Reverend Ellis has a perspective on it." I paused and added, "I think a church like the Welcome Congregation serves an important need in the community. I hate to see it decline."

I heard some tapping on the other end of this line. "I hesitate to do this, but Reverend Ellis did give me his phone number and said to call anytime.

I'm sure he'd be interested in what you have to say."

She came back on the line with a phone number with an unfamiliar area code. "He told me he was retiring to the Pacific Northwest where he had family."

Ah, he moved to the West Coast. Very convenient for the Jennings. No one to check in on how the church was doing.

"While I have you on the line, do you remember much about that article? I've met Jennifer and her husband, and it doesn't look like they opened up the new soup kitchen."

Mary Powell typed as she talked. "I started exploring the church on a tip that they were bringing in children for adoption. I didn't get anywhere with that and ended up with a puff piece about the soup kitchen. Jennifer was enthusiastic about the project, but I didn't sense her husband really bought into it. He was quite distant. Jennifer told me he had some health problems related to a motorcycle accident."

He looked pretty healthy to me. But what did I know?

"What about the adoption angle? Couldn't that have been a feel-good story?"

The keyboard tapping stopped. "The tip said the children being brought in for adoption were actually being used as domestics."

"Oh." I thought about Hannah. Could that be the case?

"I interviewed a number of the families and saw no evidence that they were anything but loving."

"Why didn't you run that story?"

"My editor said it had been done before. The soup kitchen was the second choice."

Again, I pictured Hannah and her frightened way of answering my questions. "Was there any possibility of truth to it?"

In the background, I heard a cell phone ring tone. "Sorry," Mary Powell said. "I have another call. Reverend Ellis struck me as being honest and ethical. I doubt there was anything to it. Yet," she paused. "I don't know."

I thanked her for her help and hung up. Goldie sauntered back in and parked herself in front of me with a loud "meow."

"What? I've fed you, changed your litter box, and burped you. What else do you need?" I knew what she needed—a loving home with someone who actually liked cats.

I shook my head at her. "It ain't me, babe..."

I needed to find Reverend Ellis before I started singing the rest of the song to the cat.

Chapter Twenty-Eight

When I punched in the number the reporter had given me, a man with a rasp in his voice answered the phone after the third ring. "Good afternoon. This is Martin. How may I help you?"

I felt like I was talking to the concierge of an expensive hotel. Even with the lousy cell phone quality, his voice sounded cheerful. I identified myself as someone who was interested in the history of the Welcome Congregation.

"Mary Powell from the *Star Tribune* gave me your phone number. I hope you don't mind if we talk."

Reverend Ellis coughed and cleared his throat. "That church was my pride and joy. I'm happy to talk about it."

I imagined myself as a student planning to write a paper on the history of the church. Again, my toes crossed as I questioned the minister.

"How did you become involved with it?" I wondered if the church was a pet project or if he'd been thrown into it by his diocese.

"I came from a big suburban congregation and was tired of all the politics and all the focus on raising money to build an even bigger church. I thought we should use our funds to ease the lives of the poor. They thought we should use the money to add an education wing to the church." He chuckled. "I was a bit of a rabble-rouser in Edina. I don't think the congregation missed me much when I went off on my own."

"Was the Welcome Church there when you started?"

"Oh no. I mustered a few seminary students to help me and set up a storefront near Cedar Avenue. A lot of the new immigrants were living in the Cedar-Riverside high rises. We took off from there. When we outgrew our space, I found the current church building and parish house for sale."

I pictured him smiling over the phone. "It had been a Lutheran Church before all the young families moved to the suburbs. We revived it and made it nondenominational."

I thought about Reverend Jennings's rant against homosexuality. "I attended services last Sunday. Reverend Jennings was quite…" Again, I was at a loss for words.

Martin Ellis helped me. "Fundamental?"

"Uh, yes."

He sighed. "I've heard that, too, from some of my old parishioners. I've heard the church isn't doing well."

I described to him the nearly empty service and the neglected state of the church and the grounds.

"I'm sorry to hear that. Reverend Jennings was not my choice to take over."

Reverend Jennings was not my choice to be claiming Christian principles, but I didn't say this to the minister on the phone.

"How did he get the job?"

Again, I heard a sigh. "Churches are like any other institution—more political than you'd expect. A couple of the church board members pushed for him because of his work in Haiti."

"Oh?"

"They thought he would understand the congregation's needs because he'd worked in an impoverished country." I sensed that Martin Ellis was holding back. He paused and then said, "What is it that makes you so interested in the church?"

At this point, I could have told him I was researching churches that welcomed a diverse congregation for a project. What harm could it do? Yet, Mother's voice entered my head. "Liza, the more you make up, the more entangled you get with your lies."

Between Mother and the honesty I felt in Reverend Ellis's voice, I decided to tell the truth—sort of.

"I've been volunteering to read to Jennifer Jennings, Reverend Jennings' daughter-in-law. She's quite sick. In fact, she's in the hospital in intensive care right now."

"Oh my."

"Anyway, someone gave me a Bible with the inside cut out—as if it was being used to smuggle something. I think it came from the parish house."

Reverend Ellis was silent for a moment and then said, "Can you describe the Bible, please?"

I picked it up off the coffee table and described the leather binding and the tissue-like pages. I also read to him the inscription on the inside page of the Bible. "Revised Standard Version Translated from the Original Tongues. A.D. 2002. Furnished courtesy of The Word International Foundation."

"And you say the pages were hollowed out?"

"Not only hollowed out, but someone left a note in the hollowed portion that simply said 'fake.'"

The rasp in Martin Ellis's voice intensified as he spoke. "Part of the reason I retired was because several of the church board members—members with a little money and a lot of clout—wanted to create a non-profit to distribute Bibles around the world. I wanted to use any money that came in to make sure our parishioners were fed and housed."

"Were they the ones who chose Reverend Jennings?"

Reverend Ellis began to cough—a dry, deep, dangerous cough. He gasped and coughed more until I wondered if I should hang up and call 911. Finally, the coughing subsided, and he talked in a voice that was hoarse and weak. "I might be a man of God, but I've smoked since I was fourteen. God is calling me home sooner than I had hoped."

I murmured something about how sorry I was and waited for him to talk again. I didn't think of ministers as smokers, but of course, they were human beings also—with good and bad habits.

"You should talk to Ivan Rusov. He was the church board president at the time I left."

"Is he Eastern European, by any chance?"

Reverend Ellis started to cough again. "Sorry," he choked. "Need to take a nebulizer. God be with you."

I set my phone down and leaned back. My window was open to let in the late afternoon fresh air. The storm had cleared away the smog and the heaviness and left us with highs in the seventies and no humidity. Unfortunately, our caretaker had taken the opportunity of the dry weather to attack the dandelions in the yard with a chemical that no doubt would take thirty minutes off the life of anyone who breathed it in.

I got up, closed the window, and turned on the damn air conditioner.

On the flip chart paper next to the bullet point about the Bible, I wrote, "Call Ivan Rusov." I didn't know who Ivan Rusov might be, but based on my experience with Nicholas and the high-pitched usher, I wasn't looking forward to talking with him. Instead, I washed the dishes, vacuumed the living room, and avoided anything to do with the flip chart.

Goldie watched me scrub the kitchen floor from the hallway. Her expression said you are one crazy lady.

"I know. I know," I said, as I dumped the sudsy water down the sink.

After exhausting myself with the sudden spurt of cleaning, I sat down on the couch with the stack of mail on my end table that I'd set aside to read later. Some of it went all the way back to April. One was a flyer for a group fighting the local legislators who wanted to defund Planned Parenthood. The group called itself "Women Who Say No to Congressmen Who Say Yes." Planned Parenthood was one of the only safe oases for many of my former students to get health care. I couldn't imagine the loss to them if those clinics had to close.

I suspected the Reverend Jennings would approve the closure. The more I stared at the flyer, the angrier I became. It was time to fire up the Corolla and visit the parish house again. The Jennings had some explaining to do about Jennifer, hollowed-out Bibles, and true Christian principles.

"Hear me roar," I declared to the cat as I gathered my bag.

Chapter Twenty-Nine

I tried to reach Mrs. Wilkens to tell her about my discussion with Martin Ellis, but her phone went directly to voice mail. It was Wednesday, which I knew was a day that she and a ragtag group of elders, who called themselves Grammas and Grampas Against Assault Weapons or G-GAAW, picketed at the state capitol in the name of gun safety. Despite their efforts, the United States continued to be the home of gun carnage. I once asked her why she kept at it.

"We need to make sure they know someone is watching. Thoughts and prayers are not enough!" She'd pressed her lips into a tight line. I admired her tenacity in the face of heavy money pouring into the political arena to make sure Americans could continue the slaughter of innocents.

When I stepped into my car, I noted that it not only smelled of cigarette smoke but also a pine deodorizer. I should have done a little more research on the car before buying it. Perhaps someone or something died in it, and the used car place was covering up the smell that would never go away. Death can creep into a car and stay. I shivered. Too much thought about death.

The church and the parish house looked the same. No one had come since the storm to rake the leaves or pick up the fallen branches and twigs. No one had mowed, and the lawn, with a fresh burst of water from the storm, had grown more raggedy and neglected than ever. Both buildings, the house, and the church, looked derelict on this block of neatly trimmed yards. I wondered what the neighbors thought.

I stepped out into the bright sunshine and mild temperatures. A few fluffy clouds dotted the skies, including one that looked eerily like my temporary cat. Down the street, a lawnmower buzzed. Next to the parish house, an older woman wearing long sleeves and a floppy straw hat dug into her flower bed with a hoe.

As I approached the front door of the parish house, I tried to formulate my reason for coming. Would it be Jennifer? The Bible? Ramona? Maybe I would ask about Ivan Rusov.

Remembering the warning from Nicholas, I almost turned back. What had he said? "Don't come by no more."

I gritted my teeth and knocked on the door, listening for movement inside. Everything was quiet. I knocked again and waited. A car drove by with its windows down, blasting the bass beat of a hip-hop song. I loved the rhythms of hip-hop and used them with my students to create poetry. It was amazing how engaged they could become. The lyrics they came up with were also amazing. Some were joyful, and others spoke of the realities of being ten and living in a world where free school lunches were the only meals they had.

"Hello," I called, but no one answered.

The woman who was hoeing stared at me until I waved and walked over to her yard. She was working the soil around several neatly trimmed rose bushes. Fragrance from the roses filled the air.

I pointed to the deep red flowers and said, "Those are beautiful. How do you keep the bugs away?"

She straightened up and regarded me. Her hands were gnarled and misshapen, but her face still had youth to it. She spoke with a German accent.

"Ach, these are so much verk. Sometimes I vish they vould die." Her eyes twinkled.

"If you give me ten minutes with them, I'm sure I could kill them off. I've done in every houseplant anyone dared entrust to me." I laughed.

"Give them a little plant food, maybe?"

I shrugged, doubting there was a remedy for my dismal plant record. "Do you know the parish people?"

The woman shook her head. "I don't tink nobody's home."

"No one answered when I knocked. The yard looks so neglected. Is the church still active?"

"They haf services on Sunday. Someone is almost always at the church, though, because I see many delivery trucks come and go."

"That's curious. I wonder what they deliver."

The woman didn't answer.

As we stood in her yard, a brown delivery truck pulled up to the parish house. The delivery man hefted a box from the back of the van, checked his handheld digital clipboard, and carried the box around back.

"Do they always deliver to the back of the house?"

"Ya, sometimes two or tree times a day."

"That's curious." I thanked her and wished her well with her roses. After the van left, I tried the parish house door once again. No one answered, and the door was locked.

I noted a well-worn path around the side of the house. I followed it to the back door. No cars were parked in the back or in the rutted parking lot of the church next door. I expected to see the box from the delivery van on the back steps, but nothing was there. I tried the door, but it was locked. I even knocked again with no result.

Where had the box gone?

I walked along the narrow concrete sidewalk to the garage behind the house. The door was also locked. Standing up on tiptoes, I tried to see into the garage through a dusty cobweb-filled window. A weak stream of light showed garden tools and a lawn mower lined up against the far wall. Otherwise, the garage was empty.

In the alley, I heard the sound of a vehicle. It was coming toward the garage. Quickly, I backed away from the window and headed toward the front of the house. As I glanced behind me, I saw that the vehicle was a beige-colored utility van with no markings on it. The van pulled into the garage driveway. A high-pitched male voice was talking loudly, perhaps into a cell phone. I couldn't make out many of the words, but I did hear "shipment" and "get it tomorrow."

As the man came around the side of the garage, I ducked behind an overgrown shrub next to the side of the parish house. He was still talking as he walked up to the back of the house.

"No. We don't get more for a while. Things are a little messy here if you know what I mean."

I couldn't see his face, but I recognized the voice. I heard the sound of a key in the lock and the back door opening. It was all I could do not to jump out and brazenly walk in, demanding to know who was poisoning Jennifer.

Unfortunately, my cell phone rang just as the man let himself in. More unfortunately, it was in the bag slung over my shoulder. As I was digging through to shut it off, the man came out. I heard his footsteps.

"Who's out there?"

Quickly, I stepped out from behind the shrub and stood, cell phone in hand, as he came around the corner.

With a bright smile, I said, "Oh, good. Someone is home."

The man who faced me was the sour-faced usher who had handed out programs at the funeral and chanted "Amen" after Reverend Jennings's rant in church on Sunday. He did not look happy.

"I wanted to drop something off for the family to take to Jennifer." I started to dig in my bag. "She's still in the hospital, isn't she?"

He stared at me with his jaw clenched and his lips pressed into a thin line. I noted that his face was pockmarked from either a long-ago case of teenage acne or a bad case of chicken pox.

"It's in here somewhere." I continued to paw through the bag, even though I knew I had nothing to give him.

In his unusually high voice, he said, "No one is home. You should go."

"If I can find it," I tried to sound exasperated, "Perhaps you could leave it for them."

Finally, I looked at him with an embarrassed shrug. "I could have sworn I put it in my bag."

He scrutinized me with his dark, narrowed eyes. "You," he said. "I seen you before."

"Of course," I said brightly. "I went to the service last Sunday. Remember?

And before that, I met Jennifer at the funeral. You were there handing out programs. You looked so sad. Ramona must have been a friend of yours?"

He blinked but said nothing.

"By the way, do you know Ivan Rusov?"

He glowered. "Why you ask about Ivan?" The suspicion in his voice was palpable.

I shrugged. "I'd heard that he was on the church board, and I wanted to meet him. I'm so impressed with how the church welcomes people from all backgrounds."

I felt my nose grow longer by the second. What had gotten into me?

"No one home." The man pointed toward the front of the house. "You should go now."

On my way back to the car, I checked my cell phone. John Trapper left a message.

"Hi, this is John. I wanted to let you know that the lab came back with a report on the pills you gave me. Near as they can tell, the pills are generic multi-vitamins." He ended with, "Call me."

I sat in my car and hit redial on the phone. John answered on the third ring. I assured him that I was quite recovered from my panic attack. "Maybe it was a good thing because I slept like the dead last night."

He cleared his throat. "Glad to hear it."

I could tell he was skeptical.

Another delivery van pulled up to the parish house, and a man wearing brown shorts and a brown shirt pulled out a carton and took it around back.

"Excuse me," I said to John. "Can I call you back? I need to talk to this delivery person. I'll get right back to you."

I hurried to the delivery man before he got into his van. Waving at him, I called, "Wait. Can I ask you a question?"

He looked surprised.

"That carton you just brought to the parish house. Did you leave it on the back steps?"

"Yes, ma'am. That's what the delivery instructions say. Leave it on the back steps and ring the bell."

CHAPTER TWENTY-NINE

"So you don't wait."

"No, ma'am."

"Any idea what's in the box?"

He shook his head. "I just deliver. If I worried about what was in all those boxes," he pointed to the back of his van, "I'd probably have an ulcer."

He stepped into the van. "I do know that it's not drugs."

"Oh really? Because it's a parish house?"

He laughed. "No, because we have drug-sniffing dogs in the warehouse."

I considered following him to the back steps to see who answered when he rang the bell, but I didn't want to run into the pock-faced man again.

Back in the car, I tried John. It went immediately to voice mail. I left a message and said I'd call him when I got back to my apartment.

I stopped at a small local liquor store on the way home to stock up on beer and gin. After the last couple of days, I figured I needed a stash. Mark, the liquor store owner, greeted me.

"Hello, hello. Back so soon?"

I shrugged. "Interesting week."

Without asking, he went to the cooler, pulled out a six-pack of Summit Pale Ale, two bottles of cold Schweppes, and several fresh limes. From the gin selection, he chose Tanqueray.

"Anything else?"

I thought about it for a few moments and then said, "Your store isn't too far from the Welcome Congregation Church. Do you hear any scuttlebutt about it?"

The bell on his door rang, and a large man wearing cargo shorts and a T-shirt that read "Don't Ask Me" walked in.

Mark greeted him and said, "Westy here lives just down the street from that church. Maybe he can tell you something."

Westy lumbered over. I wondered, considering his shirt, whether I dared ask him. "Not much happening there in the last year or so. We used to have big parking problems on Sunday and some evenings because of stuff they were doing." He shrugged. "Not anymore. The wife says people stopped coming when the new minister showed up."

I handed Mark my debit card and commented. "I'm told they have a lot of deliveries."

Westy scratched his head. "Seems like the wife said something about hearing they get Bibles and send them somewhere." He grinned at Mark, the liquor man. "I always figured they were dealing drugs."

"What made you think that?"

"Oh, all those Russian types hanging around."

The bell over the door rang again, and a young woman walked in with an infant in her front pack. She waved at Mark and headed for the wine.

"New clientele in the neighborhood. Now I have to stock better wines."

Westy took this opportunity to move toward the back of the store.

I thanked Mark and took my package.

I made one more stop on the way home at Moon Palace Books on Minnehaha Avenue. It was a wonderful little independent bookstore that had new and used books. I had ordered a copy of John Grisham's *Calico Joe* because the clerk suggested it as a good baseball book. When I paid for it, I asked her if she knew anything about the Welcome Church. She shook her head with a frown, "I hear they aren't very welcome to the LGBTQ community. We stay away from toxic places like that."

As I drove back to my apartment, I mused about Russians and toxic places. What did this mean for Jennifer or Ramona?

Chapter Thirty

I sat with my freshly mixed gin and tonic and waited for John to call me back. The flip chart paper was still up on the wall, and I added the deliveries to the parish house to the known list. Then I added "Russians, drugs, and toxic places?" to the other list.

How did Ramona's involvement with Pastor Jacob relate to the arsenic poisoning of Jennifer and the hollowed-out Bible? I felt totally stupid not being able to connect the dots.

I was concentrating so hard on trying to put it together that I hardly noticed when Goldie jumped up on the couch and settled down next to me.

Without thinking, I stroked her, and she began to purr. "I just want you to know," I said to her. "This doesn't mean I like you."

The few minutes of rapport with the cat ended abruptly when Charlee's voice entered my head. Goldie took the opportunity to head to the bedroom to commune with my slipper.

"You interrupted my nice cat moment."

Charlee tittered, or at least that's what I thought I heard.

I pointed to the gin and tonic. "Drink?"

Ha.

"Why are you here?"

Invite him over. He can help.

"What are you talking about?"

The voice abruptly disappeared.

Scratching my head, I thought again about Charlee. Was she an auditory hallucination? At one point, that's what Dr. Slack called her. I remember

163

how the doctor sat in a long skirt and a white blazer with her ankles neatly crossed. She's kept her voice soft and neutral. "Liza, when someone has had a trauma like yours, sometimes they see or hear things because reality is too much to handle. I think Charlee is part of that."

I hadn't told her at the time that Charlee didn't just show up when Josiah attacked me. She'd come before when I was upset. I didn't want to challenge Dr. Slack's theories.

Goldie came back, but she settled near the doorway between the living room and the kitchen in case I decided to feed her early.

Before I could finish my drink, the phone rang.

"At last, we connect," John said in a pleasant voice.

Charlee's words came to me. *Invite him over.* How did she know? "Would you like to come to my place and stare at my wall?"

He hesitated. "Excuse me?"

After witnessing my breakdown, I wasn't surprised by his hesitation. I laughed and explained the flip charts on the wall to him. "Besides, I have tonic and limes."

He agreed to stop over after his clinic hours. In the meantime, he wanted to let me know that his sources at the hospital reported that Jennifer's condition was about the same.

"Has the family been up to see her?"

"They said the only visitors were a stepsister and a guy who said he was her cousin."

"Cousin?"

"He had an accent and acted nervous. They wouldn't let him in."

"Nicholas, I'll bet. He's part of the puzzle."

After we ended the phone call, I added Nicholas to the flip chart. "Who is he and why does he care about Jennifer?" I also added, "Where is the family when Jennifer is so ill?"

Before John arrived, I brewed a pot of coffee and was on my second cup when he knocked on the door.

Goldie welcomed John like a long-lost relative. She rubbed herself against his leg and purred so loudly I was sure Mrs. Wilkens would hear her upstairs.

"Animals love me. Babies—my own daughter excepted—do not." He sat down on the couch, and Goldie settled onto his lap.

"Sorry, she's usually not that friendly." At least to me.

"Wow," he said, looking at the flip chart wall. "It reminds me of last year when the clinic administrator decided we needed to have a mission and vision. We did this incredibly stupid brainstorm, and by the time the meeting was over, we'd come up with, 'Our mission is to save the world. We will do this by developing superhuman powers.'" He smiled sheepishly, "It was a pretty juvenile afternoon considering that the poor administrator—now long gone—was serious."

I poured him a cup of coffee. "I promise that I'm not roping you into a mission statement."

"Ah, yes," he agreed. "However, you do seem to be on a mission."

"Let me fill you in on the history of this project." I told him everything that had happened in the past week except the visits from Charlee. John stroked the cat and listened with a thoughtful expression, especially when I told him about the circumstances of Ramona's death.

When I finished, he carefully set Goldie on the floor and walked over to the flip charts on the wall.

"Here's what puzzles me. I know a lot about addiction and recovery. Sobriety is difficult, and most of us slip from time to time. I understand that. Every nerve in your body wants that drug or that drink, and it doesn't go away even after years of sobriety. You fight it every day and every hour. Some days, you simply want it over."

I nodded as if I knew, but in truth, I didn't. Just like I didn't know the pain and misery many of my fifth graders lived with every day.

He pointed to the bullet point that said Ramona's death was not a suicide. "Addicts commit suicide. Addicts also accidentally overdose. Especially with drugs—sometimes because they don't know how powerful the stuff is, sometimes because it's laced with something, sometimes because they're mixing it with other drugs."

I thought about all the recent opioid overdose deaths and how it was now considered an epidemic. I expected John to conclude it was likely Ramona died accidentally—no suicide and no murder. But he surprised me.

"This," again he pointed to the bullet point, "doesn't seem right."

"Why?"

"You told me she didn't do needles."

I shrugged. "That's what Mrs. Wilkens says her sister says. Who knows if it's true?"

John scratched the back of his head. "I don't think that someone who never used needles would suddenly inject herself. For one thing, there's a skill to finding a vein. For another, needles are scary."

I remembered how hard John and the paramedics had worked to start an IV on Jennifer. I also wondered if I could suddenly poke around for a vein in my own arm if I'd never done it before.

"IV drug users usually start with someone else shooting them up."

The conversation stopped when Mrs. Wilkens burst in without knocking. "Oh," she said. "You have company." She said it in a way that indicated this was unusual, which, of course, lately, it was.

I introduced them and filled her in on my visit to the parish house.

"No one answered the front door, but when I went around back, the deliveries were nowhere in sight."

"Well, I'd say someone must have been home." Mrs. Wilkens squinted at the flip chart.

I turned to John. "What else can you tell us about Jennifer?"

He shrugged. "My sources say the ICU staff is pretty upset with the family."

"It makes no sense to me that true Christians would abandon her."

"Unless," Mrs. Wilkens raised a finger. "Unless they're not really Christian at all.'"

I remembered how my friend Ed, the janitor, had said, "They are not people of God." I set my coffee cup down and thought about it for a moment. "You mean they are imposters?" I turned to John. "How would we find out?"

He shrugged. "I find it hard to believe that Hilda would be involved in deception. After all, she was my music teacher."

Sure, I thought. When you were in fourth grade. I pulled out my phone and Googled the Jennings once again. Nothing new popped up.

"We have to go back," I said. "We need to get into the parish house."

This time, John raised his hand. "Excuse me. Are you suggesting you break in?"

Mrs. Wilkens's eyes lit up. "Oh yes. Let's do that." She stood. "You can drive."

John shook his head. "No thanks. I have patients to see tomorrow, and I'd hate to have to call my ex-wife to have me bailed out of jail. It would only fuel her frenzy to get the child custody decree amended."

I touched Mrs. Wilkens's elbow. "I think we should wait."

Half-baked ideas began to swirl in my head. It occurred to me the best time to explore the parish house would be on Sunday during church services. Since it was Wednesday, we could use the time to plan.

I explained my thoughts to John and Mrs. Wilkens. He was still skeptical and finally agreed that his part in this would be to keep an eye on Jennifer. I said I'd try to get by the ICU receptionist tomorrow to visit.

John didn't look happy when I said I would go back to the hospital. "You sure that's a good idea?"

"I'll be fine."

Mrs. Wilkens watched the two of us with a puzzled expression. Maybe someday I would tell her about my panic attack, but not today.

We broke up the party when John's phone went off. He scowled as he looked at the phone. "The ex, again. I'd better go." He answered the call with an abrupt, "Hold on." Covering the phone with his hand, he whispered. "I'm not pretty when I talk with her."

After he left, Mrs. Wilkens raised her eyebrows, "So?"

"Nosy parker." I shooed her out the door, wondering where I'd gotten that phrase.

At 11:00 in the evening, Mother called. "Chester is in the hospital," she said without any greeting. "He has a blood clot on his lung. They say it isn't unusual, but could you check?"

I told her I'd talk with John tomorrow. She said he was comfortable and would probably come home in a day or two, and no, she didn't need me quite yet.

"What about Vincent? Is he still causing trouble?"

Mother was silent for a while. "Vincent is back in Oregon. Chester gave him some money for his new business, so I think everything is okay."

I didn't sense that everything was okay. I decided to take the plunge. "Mother, if you want to protect Chester, I think you need to get a lawyer and get married."

Poor Mother. I'm sure she was stunned at my directness.

"Oh," she stuttered. "Oh. I think I have to go now." Abruptly, she hung up. Once again, I'd shaken her world.

Goldie seemed to sense Mother's dismay because she jumped up on the couch and stared at me. If she could have talked, I'm sure she would have said, "Shame on you for upsetting your mother."

"It's none of your business," I said to the cat. I sighed and put the phone down. Too many voices and animals telling me what to do and what not to do.

Chapter Thirty-One

Once in bed, I found the pillow was too flat, my legs wouldn't stop kicking the sheets, and my mind was racing. It finally occurred to me I'd had four cups of coffee, and the caffeine had taken over. I was so restless Goldie abandoned her place on the pillow and retreated to the closet to sleep with my slippers.

"Sorry, cat." I got up, pulled on a pair of shorts and a T-shirt, and decided since it was plenty dark outside, I'd take a quick swing by the parish house to see if any lights were on. If they were, maybe I'd knock on the door and demand to know who poisoned Jennifer. Or maybe I'd just sit in the car and send them bad vibrations.

The Wednesday night streets were relatively quiet. I drove by a couple of little neighborhood bars where people were gathered in clumps outside smoking. I envied their conviviality and wondered when I'd last gone out and just had fun.

"Liza, you are sounding like an old lady who's given up on the world." Maybe I should stop, bum a cigarette and join the crowd.

The urge passed quickly when I noted a reeling patron throwing up in a patch of grass next to the bar.

Ah, yes, the bar crowd.

I slowed as I approached the church and parish house. The church looked dark and foreboding—no lighted cross, no illuminated signs, just dead space. Next door, the parish house looked equally dark. Both were a contrast to the other houses on the street that had porch lights on or little walkway solar lights.

I parked the car across from the church, rolled down the window, and sat watching for any activity. A couple of blocks away, a car without a muffler roared down Minnehaha Avenue. Otherwise, everything was quiet.

In the silence and the darkness, I started to wonder if I was crazy. What was I doing here after midnight spying on a church? What did I think I would find out? I pictured the flip charts on my wall and tried to come up with legitimate explanations for what I was seeing. I could come up with something for Ramona—she was an addict, and she'd relapsed. I could come up with the deliveries—Bibles for the third world. I could even rationalize that Nicholas, as unfriendly as he seemed, was simply shy and cared about Jennifer.

However, I couldn't fathom the arsenic and I couldn't fathom the family's indifference to Jennifer, and I couldn't come up with any reasonable explanation for the hollowed-out Bible.

While I was mulling all this over, I thought I detected a faint light behind the drapes of the parish house. I stared at it for a long time, wondering if my eyes were deceiving me. Finally, the caffeine that was still coursing through my body became unbearable. I couldn't sit still. Either I had to get out and investigate, or I had to start up the car and drive home.

Before I could rationalize driving home, I found myself crossing the street and angling toward the high bushes separating the parish house from its neighbor. The bushes, actually an out-of-control climbing rose, afforded a little camouflage as I crept toward the house. A car pulled out onto the street in front of the house and drove by at a slow speed. At first, I thought they might be casing the neighborhood until I saw the pizza sign on the side of the car. It stopped several houses down, and a delivery person got out.

I looked back at the parish house and was sure the drapes had been cracked open a little while I had been distracted by the food delivery.

Was that Pastor Jacob peeking out? If so, what was he looking for?

I didn't have to wait long for a dark sedan to pull up to the curb in front of the house. I pressed further into the rose bush. Thorns pricked the back of my neck.

The little yelp came out of my mouth before I could stop it. "Yipes!"

The person stepping out of the passenger side of the sedan stopped and surveyed the area.

"Did you hear something?" he called to the driver. I was sure the voice belonged to Reverend Jennings. I bit my lower lip and pressed myself further into the bramble as the thorns poked and scratched.

What was I doing here getting assaulted by a rose bush?

I held my breath while Reverend Jennings walked toward the house. If he looked carefully to his left, he'd see me. I knelt down, feeling the thorns dig and scratch through the thin fabric of my T-shirt and the bare skin of my legs.

The driver got out and came around the car.

Hilda. I almost said it out loud.

She talked to Reverend Jennings in a low voice, as I pushed myself further into the bush. I heard a few of the words.

"I tell you, one of the Bibles is missing. That girl must have taken it. We have to do something."

Jennings replied, "Leave her out of it. God will take care…"

Were they talking about Jennifer or about me?

The door to the parish house opened, and Pastor Jacob stepped out. In the dim light, I saw he was shirtless and wore a pair of boxer shorts. Somehow, this didn't fit with the image of the minister giving his boring sermon.

He was backlit by a weak light emanating from the parish house. He paced as Reverend Jennings and Hilda approached. I heard him talk to them in a hoarse whisper.

"Did you get it?"

Hilda stepped forward and grabbed him by the arm. "Get inside," she hissed. In her hand, she held a small bag. "It's in here, but I'm not getting any more."

She half-led, and half-pushed him into the house. Reverend Jennings trailed behind. As he approached the front stoop, a car turned the corner. For just a second, its headlights scraped across my crouched body. Reverend Jennings turned slightly to his left, and my gut told me he had seen me.

I took the opportunity to gather myself and will my legs to sprint. He hesitated, startled, before he called out, "You there. Stop!"

I hurtled myself around the side of the house and headed for the alley. I had the advantage of age, youth, and rusty athletic ability. I had the disadvantage of not knowing the terrain along the side of the house.

At the corner of the house, my foot caught the metal downspout drain, and I sprawled headfirst into the high grass in the backyard of the parish house. As the palms of my hands scraped the earth and slid through the grass, my fingers touched a small white box. I grabbed it and scrabbled to my feet.

Behind me, a voice called out in the darkness. "Hey. What are you doing there?"

The footsteps that followed the voice were slow and clumsy. Stuffing the box in the front pocket of my shorts, I sprinted the last 30 feet to the alley. I ran as fast as I could down the alley and to the next street. I kept running. A dog barked in a deep baritone woof as I passed a house on the next block.

Up until recently, I was used to running at least three miles a day. It helped clear my brain and kept me from ballooning up three sizes. I'd stopped six weeks ago when the school notified me that I'd been outbid on the summer program teaching position. Other than an occasional bicycle ride, I'd sat on my couch and watched reruns and let my butt turn to flab.

Now I cursed my laziness as my legs quivered and my lungs ached. Reverend Jennings was probably on the phone to report a prowler as I huffed my way down the street. I had two options. One, I could keep going and try to run all the way back to my little garden-level apartment, or two, I could circle around and sneak back to my car.

Considering that my chest was screaming, I didn't have running shoes, and I'd left my apartment key in the car, I decided on option number two. I spent the next ten minutes dodging through alleys, listening for the sound of a police siren. The neighborhood remained quiet except for an occasional car rumbling down the street. Directly across the street from the parish house, I noted the ever-changing bright lights of a television set behind a thin shade. As I skulked down the street toward my car, I kept as much in the shadows as possible.

Lights were on in the parish house, but I saw no one outside nor any evidence that the police had been called. As I reached my car, a voice called out.

"Hey Lady! What are you doing?"

I turned to see a teenager sitting on the front steps of his house smoking a cigarette. He wore earbuds, but I still heard the rumpa-dump of the music from his iPhone.

In the light from the street lamp, the kid looked familiar.

"Julio?"

His mouth opened in surprise. "Ms. Johnson?"

I stood staring at him for a moment. He'd grown since I knew him as a smart but wily ten-year-old.

"Did you ever conquer your multiplication tables?" I asked, relieved he wasn't about to call 911.

He grinned. "I got a calculator on my phone. What do I need with that stuff in my head?"

I approached him. "Can I sit?"

"What are you doing out here? I've been watching. I seen that you ran into the yard of those holy people."

I shrugged as I worked to catch my breath. "I couldn't sleep."

He laughed. Julio was one of my favorite kids eight years ago. He was sneaky and smart and a great storyteller. I hooked him up with the writer in residence back when the school district still supported arts in the schools.

"My Ma still talks about you. 'That lady, she don't give up on nobody.'"

Julio offered me a cigarette. I shook my head. "Bad stuff, kid."

"Yeah, I know."

I asked him how he was doing. He told me he just graduated from South High and was going to Minneapolis Community College in the fall. He worked a swing shift at a convenience store.

"Just got off my shift and thought I'd have a smoke when I seen you making a run behind the house of those church people." He took a drag on his cigarette. "You don't strike me as no robber."

"I'm not. I'm just too curious."

I thought he'd ask me more, but instead, he nodded. "Ma used to go to the church before that weird bunch moved in. She don't go no more."

I scratched at a mosquito bite on my arm. "I hear the congregation is dwindling."

"Ma said that minister and people who hang around there aren't nice—she especially don't like the Russians."

"Russians?"

"Yeah. When they started coming, everything went downhill. She said they was rude." He paused to mash out his cigarette. "I think they're dealing drugs."

"Really?"

He nodded. "People come and go all the time—day and night." He paused, and I saw a twinkle in his eyes. "Like you."

I looked at Julio. Here was a kid who was a survivor. I guessed he was undocumented, like many of my kids. His parents came here looking for a better life. I worried about all of them and about all the barriers they had to jump in order to reach the American dream. But Julio kept plugging and kept writing his stories.

I decided to tell him a little about my adventures to see if he could add to the story.

"Okay, Julio, I know you haven't asked, but here's why I'm out in the middle of the night spying on a parish house."

I told him about Jennifer, how she was in the hospital, and how no one from the family had visited. I told him I just wanted to see if anyone was home. I didn't tell him about Ramona, the arsenic, or the carved-out Bible.

He nodded. "I seen her out after they moved in. She planted some flowers in the front, but no one took care of them. She seemed nice. She always waved to me."

"Did you ever talk to her or Pastor Jacob?"

Julio was silent for a few moments. "One night when I was taking a break at the store, this guy walks in acting all nervous. My friend Berto was at the cash register. The guy come up to him and asked if he knew where he could get some Oxy to tide him over. He said something about the pharmacy being closed, and he'd used up his prescription. Berto sent him away. I come out just as he was leaving, and I'm sure it was that Pastor."

"Interesting. Is that why you think they've got some kind of drug dealing going on?"

Julio shrugged. "I don't know. I started to watch the place a little more after that. It pissed me off." He turned to me. "Pardon my language. He thinks that because me and Berto are brown that we know where the drugs are?"

Suddenly, I felt very tired. I was tired of the drama I'd gotten myself into, I was tired of the way kids like Julio were treated, and I was tired of the world in general.

I sighed. "I'm sorry about the prejudice, Julio. We're not all like that."

He nodded. "I know."

I stood up and held my hand out to him. "I think you've cured my insomnia. Thanks, and good luck. Remember, you're smart and a good writer. You're one of mine who is going places."

And I hoped "going places" didn't mean to a detention center and deportation.

He stood up and surprised me with a hug. "Ms. Johnson, you never give up."

Back in my car, I stared at the parish house. Drug dealing? That might explain the hollowed-out Bible and why Pastor Jacob was so interested in Ramona. Still, it didn't explain the arsenic or Jennifer's cryptic comments about saving the children. "Too much information," I sighed as I pulled onto the street. "Too much information."

Chapter Thirty-Two

Mrs. Wilkens woke me up from a dreamless sleep at eleven. I'd tumbled into bed without even washing my hands. I still had grass stains on them.

She stood in my bedroom doorway with a glint in her eyes. "You really should lock your door at night."

No kidding.

I wiped the sleepiness out of my eyes and kicked off the sheets without replying.

"Now hurry and take a shower and get dressed, dear. We need to be at IHOP by noon."

"What?"

She looked at me as if I had forgotten about the meeting. "We're having lunch with David Gray. You know, Ramona's drug counselor."

"Today?" I sat up and rubbed my eyes.

"I called him, and he can meet us at noon." She sounded a bit irked that I had no idea what she was talking about. "He's a busy man, you know."

After a few silent curses, I stood up and stretched. "You know I hate pancakes, don't you?"

"Tish," she said. "I'm going to fix a cup of tea while you take your shower."

Goldie sauntered out of the closet, arching her back and stretching. Apparently, she also slept in this morning. Of course, as a cat, she slept in every day.

Mrs. Wilkens stepped out of the bedroom before I had a chance to tell her the reason I hated pancakes. Mother, the queen of whole foods and fresh green vegetables, always put shredded broccoli and carrots in them. It wasn't until I was ten and stayed overnight with a friend that I discovered pancakes usually came with butter and syrup, not broccoli.

I showered off the grass stains on my knees and made myself presentable, wondering what we would say to David Gray. I imagined Mrs. Wilkens trying to convince him that Ramona was murdered. As a drug counselor, I guessed he had seen his share of overdose deaths. This wasn't going to go well for her.

Mrs. Wilkens was pacing between the kitchen and the living room when I walked in, toweling my hair. Today, she wore her neon orange tennis shoes, a T-shirt from the 2017 Women's March on Washington, and plaid shorts. At least I could pick her out easily in a horde of gray-haired ladies.

"You looked refreshed," she said. "Let's go."

Outside, the air was hazy and humid, another mosquito-smacking day. Maybe I would find out today whether the air conditioning worked on my Corolla. It would take us at least a half hour to get to the IHOP, located across from the Mall of America.

"So," she said, buckling herself in. "I think I know the poop on Pastor Jacob."

I interrupted her. "Is this why we are going to lunch with David Gray?"

Mrs. Wilkens ignored my question. "I checked with my sister about this support group that Ramona went to. She gave me David Gray's phone number. He's a drug counselor for the halfway house that Ramona was in last summer. She said he's a nice guy."

I vaguely remembered him from the funeral—friendly and kind of good-looking and in a heated discussion with Pastor Jacob after the funeral.

"I called him this morning and read to him a couple of entries from Ramona's journal. He said he'd like to meet me in person to talk."

I took Hiawatha to Highway 5 around the Minneapolis/St. Paul airport. I noted the airplanes taking off and felt a moment of wistfulness. I wanted to veer into the terminal, give my car keys to Mrs. Wilkens, and hop on a plane to somewhere. It didn't even need to be exotic. Maybe Sioux Falls, South Dakota, or Omaha, Nebraska—anywhere to get away from all this intrigue.

Mrs. Wilkens interrupted my musing. "We need to ask him about Rennie and Pastor Jacob."

"Rennie?"

"You remember. From her journal. Young man who didn't like Pastor Jacob."

Too many cast members in this play, I decided but said nothing.

IHOP was noontime busy when we arrived. I put my name on a waitlist and convinced Mrs. Wilkens to sit down. By now, it was 12:15.

"What if he was here at noon and left because we were late?"

The door opened, and the man I'd met at the funeral walked in.

I walked over to him and held out my hand. "Liza Johnson. I believe we're having lunch with you." I pointed to Mrs. Wilkens.

He smiled, and his teeth were luminous. Though he was clean-shaven, he had a shadow of a beard that added to the picture. He was handsome in a movie star kind of way. I noticed that two middle-aged women waiting behind us pointed at him and whispered to each other. They were probably wondering if he was a contestant on "The Bachelor."

My name was announced almost as soon as David had introduced himself to Mrs. Wilkens. Once we were seated, Mrs. Wilkens started right in.

"We want to know about Pastor Jacob and someone named Rennie. Ramona wrote about them in her journal."

The coffee arrived before David could respond. It was hot and strong, just the way I liked it. I watched as David dumped at least three packets of sugar in his. He saw me gazing at him and smiled that flashy smile once again.

"Sorry, it's a hold-over from the days I was using."

I would have asked him more, but Mrs. Wilkens interrupted. "Do you think Pastor Jacob might have had something to do with Ramona's death?"

David flinched and added yet another packet to his coffee before he answered. It looked to me as if he was choosing his words very carefully.

"I can't tell you much about Pastor Jacob, actually. He wasn't a member of the group. I only met him once."

I thought back to the two of them talking after Ramona's funeral. I was sure David Gray wasn't being entirely truthful. However, I let it go because our pancakes arrived. Mine had no hint of broccoli or carrots. I buttered them with gusto, thinking about how appalled Mother would be if she saw me pouring on the imitation maple syrup. I imagined her tsking about high fructose corn syrup.

"Well then," Mrs. Wilkens cut her pancakes into delicate little pieces, as if she was going to feed them to a toddler. "What about this Rennie?"

David set his fork down with a thoughtful expression. "My groups are anonymous, and I need to keep them that way. What's said in them stays with the group. I can't comment on Rennie."

Mrs. Wilkens turned to me. "See, there really was a Rennie."

I felt a wave of disappointment. I suspected we weren't going to learn anything from David.

He surprised me, however, as he resumed eating. "Pastor Jacob was not part of my group, so I can say this about him. I think he has a serious problem. Users sometimes hang around where groups are meeting. For them, it's a place where they can make contacts to get more drugs."

"Really?" I set my fork down, thinking about how little I knew about David Gray's or Ramona's world.

He nodded. "Sadly, not everyone who shows up is there to kick the habit. I'm usually able to ferret them out and send them on their way. In Jacob's case, he never joined my group."

Mrs. Wilkens picked at her pancakes, trying to sort all this out. "Is it possible Ramona was trying to help Pastor Jacob with his drug problem?"

"You mean supplying him?" I asked, confused.

David shrugged, but I noticed a wariness in his voice when he answered. "I can't speak about Ramona because I was her counselor. I'm sorry I can't tell you more."

We ate in careful silence for a minute or so. Mrs. Wilkens commented on the weather—usually a safe subject. However, she made the mistake of saying, "With all this climate change, Minnesota will be a desert in fifty years. Damn oil companies."

David cleared his throat. "I'm not sure about all the global warming talk. There's really no evidence to back it up."

179

Judging by the expression on Mrs. Wilkens's face, we were about to begin World War III. I thought about what John had said the other night about using needles and quickly interjected, "David, since you are a drug counselor, maybe you can tell me about how addicts start shooting up."

The concerned look on his face caused me to backpedal and lie. At this rate, I would have to check myself in the mirror to see how long my nose was growing. "Um, I had a friend. She got into the painkillers, and next thing I knew, she was shooting up. It happened so fast."

Over the last of the pancakes, he talked about how users were drawn into needles. "The high is quick and intense. It's an instant gratification."

"Did you shoot up?"

He smiled again. By now, I was less dazzled by his white teeth. "Among other things."

While the waitress cleared the table, he looked at his watch. "Oh damn. I have an appointment in fifteen minutes. I need to go."

Abruptly, he stood up. "Nice to meet you both. I'm so sorry about Ramona. I really thought she was on the right path."

He left without paying.

"That was rude," I said when the bill came.

Mrs. Wilkens pulled cash out of her purse. "Never mind. My treat."

On the way back to the apartment, the Corolla air conditioner blasted us with frigid air. I couldn't find a happy medium between ice-cold and lukewarm. When I noted that Mrs. Wilkens's knees were turning blue, I shut it off. By the time we reached the apartment, my back was soaked, and my shirt stuck to the upholstery of the seat when I stepped out. Ah, summer.

Mrs. Wilken, looking cool and comfortable, followed me into my apartment. She settled on the couch with her arms folded. "Well, that was interesting."

"He didn't tell us much."

"But now I know that Pastor Jacob is a drug addict."

While I wasn't ready to jump to conclusions, I decided to tell her about my strange encounter last night at the parish house. I described Hilda and the little bag and how she said she wouldn't get any more for him. I left out the part where I hid in the rose bushes, scratched up my neck, and was spotted by Reverend Jennings.

"See, that confirms it. Pastor Jacob, the swine, is a user. That's what David Gray said he suspected."

"So that's it? End of the mystery? Ramona was using and supplying the minister?"

Mrs. Wilkens's eyes narrowed. "Ramona wasn't using. Don't you remember what David Gray said about 'ferreting out' users?" Her face flushed. "I think Pastor Jacob tried to get her to steal for him, and when she wouldn't, he killed her."

She stood up and walked into the kitchen, her shoes squeaking on the vinyl flooring. Goldie sat by her food dish and watched. Occasionally, she called out a meow that Mrs. Wilkens ignored.

The only way I could get her to sit down again was to distract her. "Stop and sit down before you have a stroke. Let me tell you what else I learned in my walking after midnight." I pointed to the kitchen chair. "I won't tell you until you sit down."

Mrs. Wilkens sat down with her arms folded and an expression that said, you can't make me calm down.

"Now, about my late-night journey."

I told her about my conversation with Julio and how he saw people coming and going at all hours from the parish house. "He said his mother didn't like the Russians, and the church changed when they showed up." I also admitted that Reverend Jennings might have spotted me.

As I talked, I remembered the object I'd picked up from the grass in the back yard.

"Wait," I said. "I found something last night." I hopped up to check the shorts I'd left in a heap on the bedroom floor. I brought them out to the kitchen, and reached into the pocket and took out the little box.

"Look at that," Mrs. Wilkens said. "What was that doing in the yard?"

We both stared at a sealed pharmaceutical box labeled "Vivorna."

"John told me Vivorna was a prescription medication used for people who had HIV." I examined it to see if it had a prescription label but found none.

"Maybe we should open it up and see if that's what's inside." Mrs. Wilkens fingered the box. "It looks like the size of the box I get when I buy cold medicine. You know, the kind you have to sign for to keep kids from having meth labs in their basement."

"I don't know." I thought about my late-night trespassing and was suddenly embarrassed. What licensed, certified fifth-grade teacher goes sneaking around people's yards after midnight? On the other hand, what licensed fifth-grade teacher has a Charlee voice that comes and goes? "I think we should leave it alone—at least for now until I can ask John more about it."

We both stared at the package while Mrs. Wilkens' expression turned thoughtful, "Maybe it's got arsenic in it. Maybe that's how Jennifer was poisoned."

Oh, geez.

Chapter Thirty-Three

"I'm going to the hospital to visit Jennifer. If she's better, she can tell me about the pills. When I first sat with her, she gave me a blue pill wrapped in a tissue. Maybe she was trying to tell me something about these." I pointed to the box.

"Well, I'm going with Grace to the coroner's office to see if we can look at the autopsy report. It should tell us more."

"Remember," I warned her. "They might not have all the information. From what I've read, it can take up to six weeks or longer to get some of the lab tests back."

"Humph." Mrs. Wilkens folded her arms. "On television, they get them right away."

I laughed. "That's because the show is only forty-four minutes long."

Mrs. Wilkens did not appreciate my attempt at humor. As agitated as she was, I hoped Grace was driving.

I fed Goldie and wished her a fine afternoon of napping before I left for the hospital.

This time, I drove. On the way, I thought about how out-of-control I'd felt when the code blue had been broadcast. Should I risk having another panic attack?

After Josiah and my stay in the adolescent psych ward, Mother never mentioned it again. She referred to that summer as "the lost time" but never talked with me about what happened. As an adult, reminiscing about childhood, I realized this fit a pattern for her. She always looked forward, never back. Charlee had died as a four-year-old, and Mother dealt with the loss by never talking about it. At least I knew that Charlee existed. I knew nothing about my father other than they called him Vike, and he drowned sometime after Charlee died.

"No wonder you're so screwed up," I said as I pulled into the parking garage.

When I arrived at the ICU, the same receptionist was guarding the door. She looked at me without recognition. I told her the same story about being Jennifer's step-sister. She looked at her screen and said, "The family has requested no visitors other than her husband and in-laws. I'm sorry your name isn't on the list."

"I was here the other day." My voice dropped off.

The receptionist looked right through me and repeated, "I'm sorry."

I stared at her, wondering what was on her little screen. "Can you tell me how she's doing?"

Again, she said, "I'm sorry. You'll have to talk with her husband."

"Do you know when he'll be here?"

"I'm sorry."

I considered bolting through the door as soon as someone came out but thought better of it. The sick people in the ICU didn't need any more commotion than they already had. Sighing, I took the elevator down to the lobby and walked over to the coffee stand. I needed a caffeine boost while I figured out what to do next. I had the box with the alleged Vivorna in it tucked away in my bag. Maybe I could take it to the hospital pharmacist and ask about it.

While I was in line wondering how to approach the pharmacist, the nurse who had taken care of Jennifer when I last visited walked up behind me. Today, she wore her hair in a ponytail with little plastic rabbit barrettes.

"Ellen," I said, grateful for the name tag on a lanyard around her neck.

She looked at me for a moment, then smiled. "Hi." She said. "You brought the teddy bear."

"Can I buy you a cup of coffee?"

She shook her head. "I can't take gifts from families. It's a hospital rule."

Schools had the same kind of rules, but we were allowed gift cards if they were under five dollars. I had a drawer full of Starbucks cards at home but never one with me when I needed it.

I laughed. "It's not a gift. It's a bribe. I want to know how Jennifer is doing, and the receptionist upstairs wasn't very helpful."

"Well," she sounded reluctant. "I can't talk to you about a specific patient, but I could talk in general terms."

I bought her a soy latte, and we settled into a small table in the corner. I asked why, all of a sudden, I wasn't allowed in.

"Her husband came in today and requested no visitors."

"Did he say why?"

A look of concern crossed her face. I realized that she was beginning to wonder why I wasn't in the know about this.

I stirred my Americano. It was bitter enough that I added a packet of sugar, thinking about Nicholas and David Gray and how they doctored their coffee.

"Um, Jacob and I don't get along well." I leaned in closer to her. "We have some significant religious differences." At least I wasn't lying about that. "Can you tell me how she's doing?"

She looked around to see if anyone was listening. "I can't give you any details, but she's still listed as critical."

"Oh boy." I felt a stab of sadness for the frail girl who worried about the children. "Can someone who is critical like that communicate?"

"In cases like this, we have them in a drug-induced coma to allow the vital organs to recover."

I sipped my bittersweet coffee and pictured her in the ICU bed with all the tubes. For a second, I felt a little dizzy. I closed my eyes until it subsided.

Ellen regarded me for a moment. A little of the latte foam stuck to her upper lip. I realized as I talked with her that she was very young—maybe 24 or 25 years old. She was about the same age as Jennifer.

"It must be hard, in cases like this, when they are so young, to see them so sick."

Ellen's eyes moistened. "The teddy bear is the nicest thing anyone has done for her." She finished her coffee and absently wiped at the table. "I have to go."

"Jacob seems to genuinely care about her. I never really disliked him. I just disliked his preaching." I remarked as she stood to leave.

When she looked at me, though, her eyes said something else.

"What?" I kept my voice gentle.

Ellen sat down again and leaned close to me. "He's not my patient, so I can tell you this. When he came this morning, he had all kinds of questions about her pain medicine. He hardly looked at her. He wanted to know what we were giving her, how we were giving it to her, and he even asked where we kept the drugs."

I nodded, wondering where this was going.

"I've seen visitors like this before. They're drug seekers. I think he has a problem." At this point, she seemed to catch herself. "I could be wrong, so please don't say anything."

I smiled at her and said, "Take good care of Jennifer."

My phone rang as I finished my bitter yet too-sweet coffee. I don't like to talk on the phone in public places, and I probably would have let it go, but the caller ID said Mother.

"Hello, Mother." I kept my voice low.

"Oh? Liza?" As usual, she sounded surprised that I had answered. One day, when I was visiting her, I vowed to listen in when she called someone else. Was she always so surprised?

"Mother, can you hold on? I need to take this outside."

"Can't you talk in your apartment?"

Another thing about Mother—she still thought everyone had a landline. "I'm in a coffee shop at the hospital."

"Oh dear. Are you all right?"

"I'm fine. Do you want to hold on, or do you want me to call you back?"

I detected the hesitation in her voice. "Will it take long?"

"Thirty seconds." I gathered my bag and hurried out the door. As I went out the revolving door, Reverend Jennings and Hilda pushed their way in. I tucked my head down as if I was having a very private conversation on the phone and hoped they hadn't seen me. Hilda had such a grim look on her face that I wondered if something bad had just happened to Jennifer. Jacob was not with them.

I sat on the same bench in a little grassy area across the street from the hospital. The lady with the bags from the other day was nowhere in sight. Too bad, I wanted to assure her that I didn't have Ebola.

It was hard to hear Mother because of the cell connection and the noise of the traffic, but I could tell she was upset again. As Mother's voice faded in and out, I wondered for a second why, with all the development of gadgets on the phone, they couldn't fix the audio. You can take photos, watch a movie, and post to Instagram, but you can't hear your mother when she's in distress.

"Vincent again. Call from a social worker…"

"Mother," I interrupted. "I can't hear most of what you are saying. Could I call you back as soon as I get to my apartment? The reception is much better there."

I'm not sure she heard me because she kept talking. As I listened, I tried to piece together the fragments of conversation. It sounded like Vincent, the evil son, had reported to the county that Chester was being neglected and wasn't competent to take care of himself or make decisions.

"…Coming tomorrow. Can they take him away?"

Whoa, I was really out of my element with this one. I knew the rules on reporting for child protection, but I didn't know anything about elder protection.

"Listen." I found I was yelling into the phone because the connection was so bad. "I'll talk to Mrs. Wilkens. She's had some experience with this. Can you wait until I get home?"

"Oh dear, the dog just ran outside with Chester's new shoe. I have to go."

Maybe Mother's log house in the mountains wasn't a safe place for Chester. But it wouldn't be because she didn't take care of him.

I thought about taking the box labeled Vivorna to John's clinic in hopes he would be there, but I scratched that idea and headed back to the apartment. The steamy air fit my roiled mood.

As soon as I settled onto my couch, I called Mother. After seven rings, it switched to Mother's voice on a scratchy answering machine message. "We are either out or in a quiet space right now. Please leave a message and have peace in your heart."

I pictured her chasing the mop creature she calls a dog down her dusty road, trying to retrieve Chester's shoe.

"Mother, I'm home. Give me a call."

I sat in my own quiet space, thinking about Jennifer hitched up to all those tubes with only Hilda, Reverend Jennings, and Jacob to visit her. It sent a chill down my back.

Goldie joined me on the couch, and for the second time since she'd arrived at my house, I stroked her smooth fur and listened while she purred.

"Nope," I finally said. "I am not getting attached to you. Cat Haven is our next stop—one of these days." Goldie continued to purr.

I checked my watch. It was 3:30 pm—definitely late enough to have a gin and tonic.

While I mixed it, Mrs. Wilkens tapped on my door before sweeping in.

"Well," she said without any other greeting. "They say the autopsy report isn't complete yet. They need to get lab results."

I flashed her an I-told-you-so nod. "Do you want a drink?"

After I mixed it, I filled her in on my discussion with Ellen, the nurse. "She thinks Pastor Jacob has a drug problem, and they won't let anyone in to see Jennifer. It scares me that she's so isolated."

Mrs. Wilkens listened thoughtfully. "I think Pastor Jacob was trying to use Ramona to get to drugs. I think we should report him."

I shook my head. "Report him for what?"

"Murder."

Here we go again. Fortunately, I could distract her with questions from my garbled phone call with Mother. "Maybe you can help me with this. It sounds like Vincent called the county and reported that Chester was unable to care for himself."

Mrs. Wilkens nodded. "Ah, yes. I'm sure California, like Minnesota, has what they call 'adult protection.' It's generally a good thing. Some old folks are really vulnerable."

She went on to tell me about her elderly neighbor, Mr. Slater.

"This was when I still had my house in the Seward neighborhood. We talked over the fence from time to time. Not a very friendly old guy, but he kept the place up until the fall of 1991 when the Twins won the World Series. You know, when we had the Halloween blizzard."

I remembered people talking about the blizzard, but I was still a preschooler when it happened. Mother said she had to shovel several feet of snow to clear the sidewalk in front of the house. Maybe that's why she eventually fled to Northern California.

Mrs. Wilkens continued. "Well, after that nasty winter, he didn't come out much. I noticed one spring day he hadn't picked up his papers, so I went over and knocked. It took forever, but he finally answered the door. He looked awful—whiskery, hair greasy, and barefoot. I asked him if he was okay, and he told me to go away."

I wondered what was going to come next. Mrs. Wilkens did not like to be turned down.

"Well, I stuck my foot in the door, and I barged right in. The kitchen was a mess. It stunk to high heaven, and the only thing fresh around the place was a six-pack of beer. It took some pushing, but I finally found out that the neighbor on the other side had befriended him after the snowstorm. At first, she was nice and bought him groceries and took him to appointments. Then, in the winter, she started asking him for money. She said her car broke down, or she needed dental work."

I shook my head. "She weaseled the money out of him?"

"Yup. I called the police right then and there. I also called adult protection because I wasn't sure Mr. Slater could take care of himself."

"What happened?"

Mrs. Wilkens waved her hand in front of her face as if to push something away. "He wouldn't press charges against the neighbor, so she got away with it—over $100,000. It drained his bank account. He ended up in a nursing home and didn't last too long after that."

I could picture Vincent knocking on poor Mr. Slater's door with a six-pack of beer and a pen for writing checks.

The phone rang. It was Mother calling back. "Liza?"

"Did you get Chester's shoe?"

Mother laughed. Her laugh was high and musical and could bring joy to anyone. I relaxed my grip on the phone.

"It turned out it wasn't Chester's shoe. It was an old slipper. It's now safely buried in the woods."

"Okay, now tell me about Vincent and Chester."

"Vincent called yesterday, and one of the guests answered. She didn't speak English well, and I think she said something that made Vincent think that no one was looking after Chester."

Once again, Mother was trying to put the best face on Vincent. I guessed that he was looking for any excuse to get hold of more of his father's money.

"How is Chester?"

"He's fine. He's out golfing right now with one of those carts, of course."

"Then I don't think you have anything to worry about. Make sure Chester is there tomorrow when the social worker comes, and be truthful." I turned to Mrs. Wilkens. "Would you like to say hello to Mother?"

I found it interesting how well my mother and Mrs. Wilkens clicked. Mother was probably the daughter Mrs. Wilkens wished she'd had, which made me the granddaughter she was glad she hadn't. Or something like that.

While they spoke, I fed Goldie. Back in the living room, I heard Mrs. Wilkens telling Mother about Ramona. The last thing my poor, addled mother needed was to hear what we'd been up to. I waited impatiently for a break in the conversation. It was a long wait. By the time she was done, Mrs. Wilkens had told her about Ramona, Jennifer, and the Bible.

I finally grabbed the phone from Mrs. Wilkens. "Mother, we have to go now. My phone is almost out of battery."

"Oh?" Batteries and phones didn't mean much to Mother.

Before I ended the call, however, Mother said something interesting. "Liza, about that young girl, Jennifer. Wouldn't she be considered vulnerable? Couldn't you report her?"

Wow, I hadn't thought about that.

Chapter Thirty-Four

That night, the clouds rolled in, bringing cooler weather and rain. I woke up in the morning to the spit of raindrops against the bedroom window. An instant coffee in hand, I studied the flip charts on my wall. Outside, the rain tapered off into a gray mist.

Something niggled at me as I read through the charts. What was this Bible doing in my wrecked Toyota? How did it get there, and what did "fake" mean? Was the Bible itself fake? Was the organization that sponsored it fake? Did it contain some kind of secret spy code? I opened the book to Genesis and read, "In the beginning..."

I rifled through until I found the carved-out section. The scrap of paper with the word "fake" on it was still tucked in the hole.

"What do you think is fake?" I asked Goldie as she delicately lapped from her water dish. If nothing else, she was a neat cat.

I put the paper back in the Bible, closed it, and walked to the kitchen to make some toast. Because Mrs. Wilkens harassed me about my eating, I tended to buy whole-grain bread from the bakery and slice it myself. The problem with whole grain bread from the bakery was that it didn't keep. This loaf was no exception. When I pulled it out of its bag, it was already covered with spots of green fur.

Instead, I ate soda crackers and Cheez Whiz for breakfast. I was glad Mrs. Wilkens wasn't around to see me.

Goldie meowed, looking up at me from the floor as if I had some explaining to do.

"What?"

I felt Charlee's voice slide into my head.

"Does the cat know when you come? If so, that's kind of creepy."

I don't know what you mean.

I sighed and set down the box of crackers. "I know you're here to dispense a nugget of wisdom before you disappear again. I'm getting tired of this. I want someone I can sit down with and have a conversation."

Back in my teenage days, after Josiah, I went weekly to a therapy session with Dr. Slack. She always sat so still in an easy chair across from me, her dark hair pulled into a tight bun. She told me that Charlee wasn't real and the only way to be rid of her was to *think* her away.

"You have the control because she is part of your mind. Think that she's gone, and she will be."

She didn't know how little control I had over my twin. Today, I needed Charlee. So much was going on. "Okay, I'll be civil with you. Spit out your advice."

Things can fit neatly.

I accidentally knocked over the box of crackers. "See what you made me do with your cryptic remarks."

I righted the box, trying to figure out what she was talking about.

It fits in the Bible.

"Crackers?" I was even more confused. I felt a shimmer inside my head as if Charlee was giggling.

"Are you laughing?"

I am. Check the Bible.

Voices rose from the entry of the building as the front door scraped open. It was grocery day for some of the tenants. They carpooled to Byerly's, an upscale grocery store. Mrs. Wilkens was probably driving this week. I silently wished them a safe journey as I walked into the living room and picked up the Bible.

Sitting next to it on the coffee table was the package of Vivorna. I stared at the package, and suddenly it came to me.

"It fits inside the Bible, doesn't it? That's what you are talking about."

Charlee did not reply.

Sure enough, it fit snugly in the hollowed-out area of the Bible.

"This doesn't make any sense. Are they smuggling prescription medicine in giveaway Bibles?"

My head cleared to its regular chatter. She was gone once again. Someday, I thought, it would be nice to just have a cup of coffee with her and chat about the weather or the sad state of current politics. I pictured sitting by her gravestone in the cemetery with a thermos of coffee. The thought gave me the shivers. Maybe it was time to call Dr. Slack and tell her, "She's back."

Pushing those thoughts from my head, I sat down and punched in John's phone number. Of course, he didn't answer. I left a message saying it was very important that he call me. I paced. Goldie crept cautiously into the living room and watched me. I knew she wanted to say, "I'd prefer to live at Cat Haven than with a crazy lady who talks to the air."

I very nearly apologized to the cat.

I tried Mrs. Wilkens before I remembered that she was probably behind the wheel at this moment. I ended the call quickly. The last thing I wanted was to feel responsible if she crashed a car full of my neighbors.

Who else might know about the Bibles? I found the scrap of paper I'd written Reverend Martin Ellis's phone number on and called him.

He answered on the fifth ring with a hoarse, "Good morning, this is Martin." Before I could say anything, he started to cough. He wheezed into the phone, "Can you call back?" The call ended abruptly.

I needed to know who was behind the Bible operation. Did the Jennings have anything to do with it? Were they smuggling drugs somewhere in fake Bibles?

Goldie joined me as I sat on the couch with my laptop. She stared at the screen, mesmerized. I was reminded that Goldie, whether I wanted her or not, was a part of Ramona. Her presence reminded me every day that something wasn't right about Ramona's death.

Outside, the rain continued to patter. I stopped long enough to listen to it. The rhythm of the drops against the window should have lulled me. I needed to find what Mother would call a quiet space in my head to think this through. But I wasn't Mother. I was a schoolteacher, not an investigator.

I looked at the flip chart. In the bullet point about the Bibles I'd made the note, "Call Ivan Rusov."

I typed Ivan Rusov into a Google search and found a short article in the local Business Week magazine describing him as a developer and philanthropist. I also found listings for Ivan Rusov on a couple of charitable boards for several relief organizations. When I googled the organizations, however, I came up blank. Either they didn't have websites, or they didn't exist.

I called Martin Ellis again. He did not answer his phone after ten rings, and it didn't go to either voice mail or an answering machine. My next move would be a call to the church.

When I tapped in the number for the Welcome Congregation, it rang seven times, and then a mechanical voice replied that this number was out of service. Hadn't I called that number the day John sent Jennifer to the hospital? Was it now disconnected?

I tried again and got the same message. Perhaps they hadn't paid their phone bill.

Next, I looked through my cell phone until I found the number Jacob had called me from. I hit redial. After four rings, it went to a voice mail.

"This is Pastor Jacob. I'm unable to take your call. Please leave a message, and I will get back to you."

I hesitated and finally ended the call. I really didn't want to leave him a message.

Who else could I talk to?

While I was pondering all of this, John called me back. "You sounded desperate in your message. Where is the fire?"

"Sorry," I said, remembering the last time I'd called him in a panic. "No fire, but still an interesting development." I told him about the box of pills and how they fit into the Bible.

"Can you describe the box to me?"

I described the size of the box and the printing on it. "As Mrs. Wilkens noted, it looks like the kind of packaging you get with Sudafed or Benadryl."

I heard the tapping of keys. "Are you at your computer?" I asked.

"Yes. I'm hooked into the University Medical Library. I can get more accurate information on medication than what the drug companies provide in their package inserts and in the Physician's Desk Reference."

I waited, drumming my fingers on the coffee table. I heard a few murmurs and a "Now that's interesting" before he came back on the line.

"Something is amiss here. You are sure this is packaged in a sealed box?"

"I have it in my hand. It's sealed. It says it contains thirty capsules."

"Can you open it and tell me what the pills look like?"

I sighed. "I guess it's too late to take them back and drop them on the lawn."

Carefully, I pried the box open and pulled out the pills. Inside were three cards with ten bubble-packed pills in each. I described the bubble pack to John.

"Open one of the packs and take the pill out."

I opened it and slipped the blue pill into my hand. "It's blue and slightly oblong. One side has Novac stamped on it and the other the number 628."

"Huh." John's voice was puzzled. "The description of the pill is accurate, but the packaging is not. Vivorna comes in bottles of thirty pills with a desiccant inside. This doesn't make sense."

My head was swirling. "Can we get the pills tested to see if they are the real thing?"

"Let me talk to our pharmacist and see how we can get this done. Can you take a photo of the box and text it to me? I'll get back to you when I'm done seeing patients."

I didn't want to wait that long. The Jennings had some explaining to do. "I'm going to the parish house to see if they can shed some light on this. They might not even know about it."

"I'd offer to go with you, but I'm booked until six, and then I have to pick my daughter up. She's staying with me for a while." His voice dropped off.

"I'm sorry. It sounds like things are kind of shaky with your ex-wife."

"Yup." He paused, clearing his throat. "I'll let you know what the pharmacist says."

"No problem. Take care." I was about to press END when I thought of one other thing. "While you are checking things out, can you get a report on Jennifer? The family won't let anyone in to see her."

"I'll talk to my sources."

I took a photo of the box and the bubble pack. As I hit the send button, I silently wished him good luck with his ex-wife and daughter. A divorced friend of mine once told me that the split is ten times worse when children are involved.

Mrs. Wilkens called shortly after my conversation with John. I told her about the box and how it fits in the Bible. I also told her about my conversation with John about the pills.

"Well," she said. "It looks like we have to make a visit to the Jennings."

"We?"

"I'll be back in about an hour." Her voice took a commanding tone. "Now, you wait for me. Okay?"

"Yes, ma'am."

The room darkened as thicker clouds with more precipitation moved in. A gust of wind blew the rain so hard against the window that I was startled and spilled coffee on the carpet. We were having too many nasty storms these days.

"Mrs. Wilkens says this weather is the result of climate change, and the powers that be deny it because they are beholden to the oil companies." I looked at Goldie as I dabbed up the coffee. "What do you think?"

She offered no opinion.

I sat on the couch disgusted with the Jennings and wondered who they were beholden to.

Chapter Thirty-Five

The rain came down in sheets as I waited for Mrs. Wilkens. At least it wasn't accompanied by thunder and lightning. The way the past week had gone, I worried I would lose another car. On the other hand, my newest car did smell like cigarette smoke and something dead. Maybe another natural disaster wouldn't be such a bad thing. The hybrid SUV from the rental car company was looking pretty good right now. No cigarette smoke, no dead mouse in the heater, and a handy backup camera. Why hadn't I gone for a model like that?

"Because, as much as you see yourself as a modern, hip girl, you are an old fuddy-duddy, and you're cheap."

Mrs. Wilkens showed up at my door an hour later equipped for a siege. She wore a bright yellow slicker that was almost as neon as her orange shoes. She pulled a small flashlight and a Swiss army knife out of her pocket. "You can never be too prepared." I wondered if she had an assault rifle and fourteen rounds under her jacket, but knowing that she was a staunch peacenik, I shook the thought from my mind.

"Wait," I said as she stood impatiently in the doorway. "We need to talk this through."

"Nonsense, surprise is our greatest asset."

No, I thought, common sense was our greatest asset. "Come in and sit down."

Reluctantly, she took off her rain gear and sat next to me on the couch. I showed her the box of pills and how it fit into the Bible.

"I think someone is smuggling these pills either into or out of the country.

It might be a charitable endeavor. I checked, and one package like this would cost about $1400. It looks like two packages will fit in the Bible. People with HIV in Haiti or another third-world country wouldn't be able to afford the medication. Maybe this is a good thing, and we should close our eyes to it."

Mrs. Wilkens' mouth was set in a firm line. "Maybe, but it still doesn't explain Jennifer or Ramona."

I held my hands in surrender. "No. But maybe Jennifer and Ramona have nothing to do with this. And maybe we are jumping to conclusions about the smuggling."

Mrs. Wilkens's expression did not change. "It's all tied together. I've been around enough to trust my intuition, and my intuition says something is rotten."

I told her that while I waited for her, I found a website for "The Word International Foundation." It was listed as a 501C3 non-profit that distributed Bibles to third-world countries. Among the people on the board of directors was the mysterious Ivan Rusov. Neither Reverend Jennings nor Pastor Jacob were listed, and the site made no mention of the Welcome Congregation. Under "contact us," it listed an email address but no phone number. The site said that it had distributed over 10,000 Bibles in the last two years to 35 different countries.

"The website looked pretty basic but did include a way to make a contribution."

Mrs. Wilkens was on her phone before I could tell her the site had a photo of the Bible. It didn't look anything like the leather one I had on my coffee table.

"Hello, Gloria? This is Ruth Wilkens. Yes, it's been a while." They chatted for a few moments about the weather and a couple of mutual friends. Finally, Mrs. Wilkens asked, "Can you check out a charity called 'The Word International Foundation'?"

When she finished the call, she looked at me and said, "Gloria is a research librarian. She can find anything."

As we waited for Gloria to call back, the living room brightened with the sound of the rain letting up. By the time the phone rang, the sun shone and was burning the mists off the lawn. While Mrs. Wilkens talked, I retreated to the kitchen and washed up a few dishes. Goldie rubbed against my leg and meowed. I opened a can of fish-flavored cat food.

"Oh, this stinks."

Goldie didn't care. As I watched her eat, I thought again about the life of a cat. Sleep, eat, pee, poop, and purr. Would I be content with that?

I walked back into the living room just as Mrs. Wilkens clicked her phone off.

"Well," she said. "I didn't expect that call." She paced in front of the couch.

The light from outside highlighted the distressed expression on her face. Had Gloria, the research librarian, uncovered something sinister about the "The Word International Foundation" organization?

"Tell me." I sat on the couch and patted the cushion next to me. "But sit down first. You are making me dizzy."

Mrs. Wilkens sat down so heavily, the cushion emitted dust motes that hung in the air. I waited for her to talk.

"It wasn't Gloria. It was a hospice social worker. Remember Rennie?"

I could hardly forget him, considering that we'd grilled David Gray about him at IHOP.

"Well, Rennie is in a hospice and has asked to talk with someone in Ramona's family. My sister Grace told the social worker to call me. She doesn't want the girls involved."

"I wonder what it's all about?"

"He wants to tell the family something about Ramona, but he would only talk to one of her relatives. The social worker says he doesn't have much time."

She looked at me, her blue eyes moist behind her oversized glasses. "I'm afraid he'll tell us that Ramona was using again. I don't want the girls to see that as the last image of their mother."

As the sun brightened the day and lawns shimmered with the wet grass, we drove to a nursing home on the south side of downtown. It was an older brown brick building with an institutional look.

"This place was originally built by the YWCA to house single girls who came to work in Minneapolis. I had a few friends who stayed here back in the early fifties when the country girls came for factory jobs." Mrs. Wilkens looked wistful. "They came with hopes of education and independence, but most ended up getting married."

I knew Mrs. Wilkens grew up in a time when women were expected to stay home and raise a family. Few professional careers were open except teaching, nursing, and social work. She trained as a librarian, married her hometown sweetheart, and languished in rural Minnesota until her only son enlisted and came back from his army experience, as she said, "Broken." I worried that seeing Rennie might bring back memories of the lost son.

Mrs. Wilkens walked into the nursing home with her shoulders back and her head high. She still looked a little silly, wearing plaid shorts and a T-shirt that said "Pink" on it. At least she'd taken off the yellow rain slicker.

A cheery woman at the front desk directed us to the second floor. Once we stepped off the elevator, I expected to find crowded halls and drooping old people in wheelchairs. Instead, the halls were empty and quiet. The walls had been painted a subdued green and blue, accented by several large, beautifully crafted quilts.

At the nurse's station, a woman in a bright paisley top pointed down the hall. "He's awake. I'm glad you came. He doesn't get many visitors except for the hospice people."

I looked at her, puzzled. "But isn't this a hospice?"

She shook her head. "We are called a skilled nursing facility. Hospice staff come in to help us take care of our patients. He has a nurse, a chaplain, and a social worker who all visit. But he really loves his volunteer. She reads to him."

"Oh." I was certainly learning more about how we do health care than I expected in this summer of unintentional time off.

Rennie was in a bed by the window. The bed next to him was empty and neatly made. The blinds were partially closed. Enough light filtered through to show that he was extremely thin. His large brown eyes were clouded. I wondered if he was blind.

Mrs. Wilkens walked up to the head of the bed as if this was something she did every day. Gently, she said, "Rennie, I'm Ramona's aunt. You said you wanted to talk to me."

He blinked and pulled his skeletal hand out from under the covers. Mrs. Wilkens took it and sat down next to the bed. I stood at the foot of the bed, suddenly flooded with memories of my high school friend who died of AIDS. He had the same look.

Rennie stared up at the ceiling but did not let go of Mrs. Wilkens's hand. She sat quietly with him.

"The hospice social worker said you wanted to talk with me." Her voice had a soothing gentleness to it that caused Rennie to smile.

"Thank you for coming." He whispered, still holding her hand.

It looked to me like they had established a kind of sacred space in that small, curtained area in that small, cramped room. I pointed to the door, and Mrs. Wilkens waved me out of the room.

I found a sitting area across from the nurse's station and waited. Unlike the busy ICU area at the hospital, the room was quiet. I suspected this wing of the nursing home housed the most seriously ill—the terminal patients. I wondered if this was a place where indigents went for their final care on earth. On closer inspection of the hallway and the waiting area, I noted the shabbiness. The quilts on the wall had a layer of dust on the top border, and the colors were fading in the sunlight that came in through the nursing station window.

All the bleach and cleaning products couldn't mask the smell of bodily deterioration. I remembered Jennifer's bedroom in the parish house had a faint odor like this beneath the strong smell of garlic and rose air freshener. Was that the smell of neglect or the smell of death?

As I sat, a small tremulous voice called from down the hall, "Nurse. Nurse, come help me." I looked around, but the halls and the nurse's station were empty. The voice called again, "Help me! Help me!" I was about to check it out when Mrs. Wilkens came out of the room with an expression I couldn't read. She didn't look distraught, but she also didn't look at peace.

She nodded at the nurse, who hurried by as the woman's voice grew louder and louder. "Help me! Help me!"

Grabbing my arm, she whispered, "We need to find a bar. I could use a Bloody Mary."

Once in the car, she looked straight ahead and said, "Oh my, the plot does thicken."

Chapter Thirty-Six

I ordered my usual Summit Pale Ale from Joey, the bartender. Mrs. Wilkens had a Bloody Mary with a beer chaser. When Mrs. Wilkens drank a Bloody Mary, it usually meant she was extremely upset. It also meant I would have to watch her intake. Two drinks, and I'd have to carry her home.

I leaned in close to her over the scarred wooden table. "Okay. Tell me."

Mrs. Wilkens pulled the pickle out of her drink and took a bite. "Ramona wasn't using, but she was supplying."

"To Rennie?"

"Yes and no." She paused, taking another bite of her pickle. "Good pickles."

In the background, blurred music from a tape played an Eagles tune. I heard the phrase "Hotel California" and wished for a moment that I was there.

I waited for Mrs. Wilkens to say more. Meanwhile, the Eagles had morphed into the Doobie Brothers. Halfway through the next tune, I lost my patience with her. Before I leapt across the table to shake the story out of her, she finally loosened up and filled me in.

"Rennie has AIDS. He didn't tell me how long he's been HIV positive, but it turned into a full case of AIDS this spring."

I nodded. "He needed the oxycodone for pain or because he was an addict?"

Mrs. Wilkens took the toothpick with the green olives out of her drink and studied it. "He didn't need oxycodone. He needed the HIV medicine."

"What? Like Vivorna?" I pictured the box I'd found by the parish house. I was totally confused. "Ramona was getting Vivorna for Rennie?"

Mrs. Wilkens nodded. "Medicaid paid for the medicine, but he turned it around and sold it for rent money."

"There's a black market for HIV meds? Really?".

Mrs. Wilkens shrugged. "He didn't go into it, but someone was buying from him. I suspect there's a community out there of people who aren't hooked up to the healthcare system because they're transient or undocumented. They've tested positive for HIV and are looking for cheap pills on the black market. Or maybe the drugs go overseas. Who knows? Anyway, the poor young man. He asked to see me because he wanted the family to know that Ramona was clean." Her face in the dim light of the bar reflected sadness even though she shrugged and smiled. "At least I can tell the girls that her mother kept her promise."

"Ramona was getting Vivorna for Rennie? Where was she getting it?" I paused, letting this information settle in. "From her job? Or from the parish house?"

Mrs. Wilkens toyed with the empty shot glass in front of her. "Rennie wasn't good with details, and I didn't want to press him." Her blue eyes in the dim bar reflected a deep sadness. "He won't be with us much longer. So sad in someone so young."

We were both silent for a moment, thinking about the young man with the big brown eyes. I'd hardly noticed that I'd finished my beer. Joey came with fresh drinks for both of us. Since my breakfast had consisted of soda crackers and Cheez Whiz, I ordered a hamburger and French Fries. To my surprise, Mrs. Wilkens followed suit.

"Comfort food," she explained.

"What else did Rennie say?" I knew she was holding back.

"He told me that he was a prostitute."

"That's where he picked up the virus?"

Public health had worked long and hard on HIV prevention, but with AIDS out of the headlines and a new generation of kids who didn't know much about it, the numbers were rising once again.

"Rennie said men paid more if he didn't ask for a condom."

"He told you that?" I was having a hard time reconciling Mrs. Wilkens' grandmotherly appearance with a confession from a young man about not practicing safe sex.

Mrs. Wilkens waved me away. "He wanted to tell his story. I held his hand and let him know that he could tell me everything."

The burgers and fries arrived, and Mrs. Wilkens immediately took the patty out of the bun. "I'm watching my carbs."

"Well, I'm not, and if it takes 30 seconds off my life, so be it."

She dabbed at her second Bloody Mary. When she finished the pickle, she dropped the bombshell.

"What Rennie really wanted me to know was that one of his main Johns was from the Welcome Congregation. That's why he didn't want Jacob at the meetings, and that's why he didn't want to have the meetings at the church."

I stopped mid-fry with this revelation. "What? Was he sure?"

Mrs. Wilkens methodically cut her hamburger patty into bite-size pieces. "Liza, the boy is sick, and he's dying, and I don't think he would make it up. But am I sure? I don't know."

I thought about Reverend Jennings and the hate he preached from the pulpit. Was he addressing his son? And if Pastor Jacob was using unprotected boys, was he HIV positive? And what about Jennifer? Or maybe it was the deacon with the high-pitched voice. Or Nicholas?

My head was spinning as I pondered this. It didn't fit all together.

Mrs. Wilkens stood up and said, "Must use the facilities."

I stood up as well in case she needed help.

"I'm fine. I promise I won't break a hip in the ladies' room."

I watched her walk to the back of the bar. Her neon shoes squeaked against the floor. She walked with great confidence.

While she was in the bathroom, I thought through everything she had said. Ramona was supplying Vivorna. Rennie was sure one of his Johns was from the church and—I couldn't figure out the third thing. The second beer had gone directly to my brain. I checked Mrs. Wilkens's Bloody Mary and noted that she hadn't really touched the second one except to eat the olives and the pickles. I might need to turn the car keys over to her.

When Joey came by, I told him to add up the tab. I wasn't about to have

Mrs. Wilkens as my designated driver.

Mrs. Wilkens emerged from the bathroom with a frown on her face. When she sat down, she said, "If only we could find Ramona's last journal. I'm sure she would have written something about getting the drugs for Rennie."

Now I remembered the third thing—the bottle of oxycodone in her uniform pocket. "But what about the oxycodone? Was she supplying that, too?"

Mrs. Wilkens shrugged. "I don't know."

I tried to crawl into the head of Pastor Jacob. If he was HIV positive and trying to hide it from his father, and if he was addicted to oxycodone, would he trade his medications for it? Is that what Ramona found out? Was she supplying Jacob with pain drugs in exchange for HIV drugs for Rennie? If so, where was she getting them?

I shared my thoughts with Mrs. Wilkens, and we both agreed the answer was still in the parish house.

"We need to search that place." Her voice was emphatic.

I pictured us knocking on the door and saying, "Excuse me, we think a lot of illegal activity has gone on here, and we need to search your house."

Either Hilda or Reverend Jennings would have us arrested in minutes.

In my slightly beer-addled mind, I agreed, just like we'd talked before, that we needed to look further into the parish house.

Mrs. Wilkens must have read my mind. "So, let's go see what we can find."

I looked at my watch. It was nearly five o'clock.

"What day is it?" I asked. I'd found that in my idleness, I'd had a hard time keeping track of the days.

"Friday, of course. I missed my bridge club this afternoon."

At least Mrs. Wilkens had a life beyond binge-watching television programs.

"Remember when John came over, and we talked about searching the parish house? We decided Sunday would be a good time. We can sneak in, take a look around, and be out before the congregation sings the final hymn."

I'm not sure it was me or the beer talking at this point.

Mrs. Wilkens brightened. "Good idea."

Except on the way home, I thought about it more and decided it was a stupid idea. What did we think we were doing?

As I dumped food into Goldie's dish, I said, "Listen, if I get arrested, make sure you don't tell anyone that I hear voices. Okay?"

For a second, it really looked like the cat nodded.

Chapter Thirty-Seven

Mrs. Wilkens walked in that evening while I was feeding the cat. "I see you two are getting along better."

I shrugged. "If nothing else, she's a good listener as long as I'm holding the food."

Mrs. Wilkens nodded. "I think we need to strategize about our plan for Sunday."

I held my tongue. I wanted to tell her I thought we were getting in over our heads with all this intrigue. I knew the old lady would have none of that kind of talk.

Probably all good breaking-and-entering professionals planned it out ahead of time. I pictured us pouring over the blueprints from the parish house to determine the best entry and exit points and the precise timing.

Instead, we sat on the couch and came up with a vague plan that I would sneak into the parish house basement as soon as the service began. Mrs. Wilkens would attend the service and text me when it was time for me to leave. Very simple. I'd find more Bibles with drugs hidden in them, and then… Unfortunately, at that part in the planning, Mrs. Wilkens's head drooped, and I suggested it was time for her to turn in.

In bed that night, I stared at the ceiling, wondering what had come over me. I planned to break into the parish house and somehow prove something about illegal drugs. Closing my eyes tight, I willed Charlee to talk to me. I needed her to tell me this was a dumb idea. Nothing happened, and eventually, I dropped off to an uneasy sleep filled with dreams of being pursued by someone in a white robe wielding a Bible.

Sunday morning dawned humid and sticky. I think the gods of the summer weather were toying with us again. After the refreshing rain of Friday and a clear and mild Saturday, the weatherman promised a high in the nineties. I pointed to my air conditioner and warned it, "You'd better do your job today because I'm about to break into a house, and when I get home, I want it to be cool and comfortable in here."

Goldie looked up at me, shook her head, and wandered away. Apparently, she wasn't interested in my comments to the sputtering machine.

The fact that I was conversing with my air conditioner didn't bother me as much as the fact that I was having a hard time deciding what to wear to this break-in. At least on *NCIS*, they had bullet-proof vests with a logo. It was too late to get one monogrammed with "Nosy Schoolteacher."

Mrs. Wilkens appeared at my door in her Sunday best. She wore the same shirtwaist dress she'd worn to the funeral and a pair of white pumps. She looked to be in perfect disguise as my outside man.

"I'll send you a text if anything looks unusual." She pointed to her cell phone.

I should have backed out, then and there.

In the sunlight of a new day, without beer or gin and tonics in my system, the plan seemed even more shaky. Actually, it seemed downright stupid. It occurred to me that I would be putting my safety in the hands of an eighty-four-year-old and her phone. However, I was committed. Instead of telling her my misgivings, I filled her in on the research I'd done yesterday. First, I'd spoken with John. He'd given the photo I'd taken of the Vivorna tablet and the box to a pharmacist friend. The friend had compared the tablet with one in his stock. It looked genuine until they compared the colors. One was a deeper blue. His friend had called the drug representative to ask if they packaged Vivorna in boxes. The drug rep appeared to be quite upset by the question and said he'd get back to them.

"John said he found out a black market existed for certain drugs, although Vivorna was not known as one of them." I looked at Mrs. Wilkens. "He also said that there is current evidence of criminals manufacturing and selling fake malaria medication to African countries. Children are dying."

"Maybe someone is doing the same thing with Vivorna?"

"He didn't know."

Mrs. Wilkens was thoughtful. "It's hard to think a church would have anything to do with that. Especially something that could harm children."

I'd also called the ICU to check on Jennifer. My nose grew a quarter of an inch longer when I'd told them I was Jennifer's mother-in-law, Hilda. "They told me she was still on dialysis, and her vital signs were stable."

"Can she talk yet?" Mrs. Wilkens asked as she dug around in her purse.

"Still on a breathing machine."

She pulled out a small LED flashlight and a magnifying glass. "Here, these might come in handy."

I slipped them in the back pocket of my cargo shorts along with the business card for the lawyer who'd helped me with the paperwork for Ed, the janitor. She'd been compassionate and efficient, and I hoped I wouldn't have to call her from a jail cell after getting caught for breaking into the parish house and stealing Bibles.

We parked across the street and around the corner from the church under a Linden tree. The tree was just past blossoming, and a faint fragrance hung in the humid air. From my vantage point, I watched as the small congregation made its way to the church. It seemed like fewer people were attending than last week. Maybe Reverend Jennings's rant caused them to think twice about belonging to the church. Mournful organ music wafted out of the church every time the door was opened.

The man with the high-pitched voice stepped out of the driver's side of a black Lincoln MKX SUV and walked to the steps of the church. He wore a dark suit coat that looked far too heavy for the summer weather. Even at this distance I saw the oiled sheen of his hair.

Nicholas followed from the passenger side. He, too, was dressed in a dark suit coat. To me, they both looked like they'd come out of central casting for an organized crime movie. None of this made me any more enthusiastic about my break-in plan.

"I hope they aren't packing," I commented, then felt silly using the television cliché.

Mrs. Wilkens was busy writing something in a little notebook and did not answer.

About fifteen minutes before the service, we saw Pastor Jacob and Reverend Jennings walk out of the parish house. The Reverend appeared a little wobbly and leaned on his son for support.

"I'd better go." Butterflies fluttered in my stomach. In the light of the day, with the morning coolness slipping rapidly out of the air, this was looking more and more like a very bad idea.

I peered out the windshield to see Pastor Jacob stop at the back door of the church. He held on to his father with one hand and a book with the other. The book appeared to be the same size as the Bible on my coffee table. For a moment, he glanced around, looking directly at the corner where we were parked. I quickly bent down behind the steering wheel. Had he seen me?

"What are you doing?" Mrs. Wilkens asked.

"I think I've been made."

"Nonsense. Now, once I'm inside the church, if anything looks amiss, I will text you." She looked at her watch. "You'll have about forty-five minutes before you should get out."

She reached over and handed me a piece of paper. "Here's what you should look for." The paper listed:

- Ramona's journal
- Bibles with cutouts
- Boxes of Vivorna
- Arsenic

I folded the paper and slipped it into my pocket without comment. What do you say when you are about to break into a church parish house?

Chapter Thirty-Eight

Once Mrs. Wilkens was inside the church, I quickly slipped across the street and through the alley to the back of the parish house. The driveway by the garage was empty, and the parish house looked quiet.

From within the church, I heard the muffled swell of the organ and then the operatic soprano of Hilda Jennings. The congregation followed her in a muddy monotone. For a moment, the dreariness of the singing surrounded me. I should take this opportunity to go home.

As Hilda's voice rose, I sighed and tried the door. It was locked. "Damn it!" Somehow, my planning hadn't included the possibility that I couldn't get in. I scurried around the house to the front door. It, too, was locked.

On television, they either cleverly pick the lock or kick the door in. I pictured explaining to the Minneapolis Police why I was attacking the parish house door and decided to see if I could find another way in. Perhaps they kept a key under the mat or something. Meanwhile, the clock was ticking. Hilda's dirge continued inside the church.

Around back once again, I squatted down to search for a hidden key. I found nothing but leaves and debris. Near the backdoor, though, almost totally obscured by an overgrown shrub, was a basement window. I crab-walked over to it. The window was nearly opaque from years of dirt. It was the kind of older basement window that operated on two hinges and could be lifted on the inside to open. When I pushed on it, it gave a little. I knelt closer to the window for more leverage and pushed harder. The window had been painted shut from the inside, but it gave a little more. With a grunt,

I pushed as hard as I could.

"Amen," the congregation grumbled.

"Hallelujah!" I whispered as the window opened.

Fortunately, despite my slothful summer, I am slim, and the opening was large enough for me to wiggle through if I went feet first. I backed in, hoping I wouldn't land on something rat-infested. The shrubbery scratched my face and tangled in my hair as I inched through the open window. The basement floor was six feet below the window. I shimmied down, scraping my stomach on the rough cement walls of the basement. When I was in as far as I could go, I let go of the sill and landed between a pile of boxes and a wooden workbench. My knee banged against the workbench, and the pain shot up my leg and into my hip.

"This is not my idea of fun," I hissed, rubbing my knee.

A little crack of light came through the open window. Otherwise, the basement was inky black. I pulled Mrs. Wilkens's flashlight from my back pocket and clicked it on. The beam pierced the darkness. Somewhere, in the recesses of the room, a dehumidifier rattled like an old refrigerator. The air in the room was dusty but did not have that moldy subterranean smell of old basements.

From the small beam of the flashlight, I saw cardboard shipping boxes lining the walls. Bare light bulbs hung from the ceiling. The one closest to me had a pull cord. When I switched it on, the 100-watt bulb lit up this section of the basement.

"My god, it's like a warehouse," I said aloud as I surveyed box after box. On the box closest to me was a UPS shipping label that said, "The Word International Foundation," with the parish house address.

One of the boxes near the workbench was unsealed, with Styrofoam packing peanuts scattered around it. The dehumidifier clicked off, and the basement was suddenly encased in silence. I listened for the sound of footsteps overhead. Hearing nothing, I opened the lid of the box. Pushing through the peanuts, I found the first Bible. It had the same leather cover as the one from my car.

"So, what do we have here?" I opened the Bible, my heart pounding with

213

anticipation. The pages of the Bible were tissue-thin. I fanned them, looking for the carved-out hole.

The Bible was intact.

Grabbing another, I opened it only to find the same thing.

"This is not what I was looking for," I whispered. I was almost to the bottom of the box when my cell phone did its "blip" sound to tell me I had a text.

hannah left service did u find anything

I replied, **bibles in basement**

Before I could get my phone back into the pocket of my shorts, I heard the whisper of footsteps outside the basement window. They stopped for a moment, then went on. The back door above me opened.

I quickly pulled the cord and turned off the light. I couldn't imagine that Hannah would be coming into the basement, but I held my breath anyway. Even though her footsteps were light, I could follow them as she walked through the house. It seemed as if she was going into the bathroom. The sound stopped for a few seconds; then she walked back toward the door. It opened and, after a few moments, closed above me. When I felt like sufficient time had passed, I switched on the light again.

I examined another box. This time, I chose one that was still taped shut. I found a box cutter on the workbench and used it to cut through the cellophane packing tape. Styrofoam peanuts spilled onto the basement floor as I dug through the box for another Bible. It, too, was intact.

"This is stupid. Whatever was in my car was not from these." I put the Bible back in the box. Time was running out, and I needed to look for other things on my list. I switched off the light and walked to the stairs, using my flashlight as a guide.

The dehumidifier started with a rattle. Instinctively, I pointed the flashlight toward the sound. It came from a walled-off room next to the washing machine and dryer. A hose from the dehumidifier snaked into the floor drain by the washtubs. Something shiny caught my eye as I pointed the flashlight into the room.

In the dim light, I saw a captain's bed covered with a patchwork quilt. The shiny object that had caught my attention was a small mirror attached to the wall at the head of the neatly made bed. A single bulb hung from the ceiling with a switch near the doorway. I turned it on.

The room smelled slightly of roses, similar to the smell in Jennifer's room. It was furnished with a white plastic lawn chair and a small wooden table. On top of the table were toiletry items precisely lined up, including a hairbrush, comb, and several cosmetics.

"So, who have you been hiding in the basement?"

Two magazine photos were taped to the bare wall over the table. One was of Taylor Swift, and the other was of a band I didn't recognize. Nothing else in the room indicated who the occupant might be.

I pulled open one of the drawers under the bed. It contained the beige dress Hannah had worn the first day I saw her with Jennifer. Beneath it were two other dresses that were exactly alike. They were washed, ironed, and carefully folded.

A pile of books sat next to the plastic lawn chair. On top was an intermediate English as a Second Language textbook. Below, it appeared to be another leather-bound Bible. I picked up the Bible, and before I could page through it, it slipped from my hands. It landed on the floor with a "thud," opening enough to reveal the middle cut out.

"Whoa," I said, staring at the Bible with the Vivorna boxes jammed in. Before I could pick it up, I heard a soft voice.

"Who's down there?"

Quickly, I snapped off the light in the barren bedroom and held my breath.

Chapter Thirty-Nine

"**N**icholas, is that you?" The voice called again. "Pastor Jacob say you should go now."

I recognized the Haitian rhythm of Hannah's voice. I was tempted to step out and reveal myself, except I had no excuse for being in the basement.

Light footsteps descended the stairs. I looked around for someplace to hide. The room with the bed was windowless and pitch black. I pressed myself into the corner closest to the door, hoping that anyone who glanced in might miss me. The cement felt rough against the skin of my arm. Something brushed my cheek. I stifled a gasp as I realized it was a small spider dangling from its web.

Hannah's voice came from the bottom of the stairs. "You must go now." I could hear no movement. Either she was tiptoeing on the concrete floor, or she was simply standing and listening. I prayed that Mrs. Wilkens wouldn't text me at this moment.

We were surrounded by silence until the dehumidifier fan made its noise start again. I wasn't sure, but I thought I heard the stairs creak. I waited for a count of fifty, then came out.

Hannah was gone, and my little flashlight indicated that she'd shut the basement door behind her. I listened for sounds at the top of the stairs, but I heard nothing. I needed to get out, and the easiest way was up the stairs and through the backdoor. Cradling the Bible, I carefully walked up the steps. During my teenage years, I'd learned the quietest way to sneak out of a house with stairs was to step where the nails were. I made my way up the steps, creating only one or two creaking sounds. I didn't hear any noises near the basement door. At the top of the stairs, I checked my watch once again. My time was up. The service was probably over or nearly over. I turned the knob on the basement door as slowly and carefully as possible. When I pushed on the door, however, nothing happened. I tried again and again—nothing.

I was locked in.

For a few moments, escape possibilities raced through my brain. Maybe the basement door was simply jammed, and if I kicked it hard enough, it would open. However, kicking the door would raise too much noise.

Using the flashlight, I studied the door. Unfortunately, I remembered the deadbolt lock was on the kitchen side of the door. I doubted I could kick it hard enough to break it. I would have to leave the way I came—hoisting myself up and through the basement window. If I didn't show up soon, Mrs. Wilkens would be in a panic.

Sitting on the top of the basement steps, I texted her.

locked in basement DO NOT try to rescue

How long would I have to wait before I could try to escape? More importantly, how would Mrs. Wilkens handle my absence? I pictured her storming the parish house. Please, I thought, please remain cool.

With my luck, Mother would decide to call while I was hiding in the basement, alerting everybody to my whereabouts. Quickly, I reconfigured my phone to silence text and phone calls. Upstairs, the Jennings had returned. Their voices were muffled, but I thought I detected an urgency in the way they were talking. I pressed my ear against the door and caught a few words and phrases.

"They say she's waking up."

"She'll talk when she wakes…"

"No, not that…"

"Move stuff out today…"

The last voice was that of the high-pitched usher with a Lincoln SUV. The thought of him with his pock-marked face made me shiver. Something major was afoot, and it was clear I needed to get myself out of the basement.

Slowly, I moved down the stairs on my butt to more evenly distribute the weight. At the bottom, I considered my options. I could make a break for it right now through the basement window, or I could wait in hopes they would leave for a while.

Upstairs, a phone rang. After a few minutes, overhead footsteps moved toward the front door. I felt, more than heard, the door close. I listened for more sounds of people in the household but heard nothing.

My phone vibrated with a text from Mrs. Wilkens. **people leaving by front door. GO!**

I needed to take this opportunity to get out.

Quickly, I moved to the open basement window. This time, I didn't dare turn on a light. With the slim beam of the flashlight, I looked for something to step on. First, I tried moving one of the boxes, but it made such a loud grating sound against the cement floor that I stopped and listened. Still no sound overhead.

I studied the workbench. It was about two feet to the side of the window but three feet off the ground. I could climb up on it, lean over, and catch the window sill. Could I do this and still hold on to the Bible? If I'd truly taken time to plan this, I would have brought a backpack. Breaking and entering was clearly not one of my skills.

As I levered myself up onto the workbench, my foot caught something. Before I could do anything, a tool slipped off the bench with a metallic clang. Overhead, I thought I detected the sound of the floorboards creaking. It was time to make haste.

I scrambled the rest of the way onto the bench, stood up as far as I could, and reached over to the sill of the open window. The Bible was now jammed precariously between my upper arm and my ribcage. With one foot on the bench and another scraping the wall for purchase, I launched myself. The plan was to get my upper body as far out the window as possible.

Unfortunately, the plan did not account for my trying to hold on to the Bible. With my balance thrown off, I didn't notice how the corner of the open window jutted out. I cracked my forehead against it and instinctively let go, falling backwards. The Bible tumbled to the floor as my shoulder banged hard against the edge of the bench. My shoulder dislocated, and searing pain tore through my back and upper arm.

For a moment, I saw my ex-boyfriend, Terrence, at second base, reaching out to me. I had a feeling of great peace and serenity. Then everything faded. Before it all went dark, I heard a voice deep inside me.

I'm here. Listen to me.

Chapter Forty

Black blobs floated in front of my eyes as I propped myself up against the wall, cradling my dislocated right shoulder with my left arm. The room filled with a golden warmth as the endorphins, or whatever they were called, kicked in.

"Charlee?"

When I tried to straighten up, the blobs got worse, and nausea rose through my stomach and into my throat. I knew if I tried to climb the steps, I would either pass out again or throw up. I needed to get my shoulder back in place before I could do anything else.

"Can you help me?"

The voice embraced me. For a moment, I thought I would pass out again. *The bed.*

I couldn't process the words. What bed? For a few moments, I wasn't even sure where I was. Then the dehumidifier started with a squeak as the fan began to turn.

Go to the bed.

I was in no position to argue with Charlee. Squatting with my left arm cradling my right arm, I slowly lurched toward the room with the bed. Why the bed? Then I remembered how all those years ago, when I'd slammed into second base and dislocated my shoulder, the emergency room doctor who had pulled on my arm to put the arm back in the socket told me about how he once dislocated his shoulder at a remote cabin. "I climbed onto the kitchen table in the cabin and dangled my arm. The pull of gravity popped it back into place."

At the time, I hadn't appreciated his story. Now, I did. If I could get to the bed, it might be high enough off the floor so I could lie on my stomach and dangle my arm. I might be able to pop it back in. If I could get to the bed and get comfortable enough to see my phone, I could call for help.

My thighs seized up with every step, and sweat broke out on my forehead. A myriad of thoughts drifted through my brain. I made bargains. If I could get to the staircase, I promised never to meddle in other people's affairs. If I could get through the door to the room with the bed, I promised to say nice things about the cat. If I could get to the bed...

I didn't finish the third promise because I heard voices upstairs once again. I needed to hurry. Somebody, perhaps the high-pitched usher, would soon be down here.

You can do it.

"Easy for you to say," I gasped.

With one giant effort that left me damp and shivering, I made it to the bed. I climbed onto it and sat on my knees, panting. In my pain, I'd forgotten what to do now that I was on the bed. "Now what?"

Dangle your arm. It will hurt.

Gingerly, I let go of my right arm and lowered myself with my good arm. Clamping my teeth to keep from screaming, I swung my right arm over the side of the bed. White hot pain shot through me, and I saw lights exploding in front of my eyes. Then, once again, everything faded.

I saw a bright light in front of me and was enveloped in a cocoon of warmth. If this is what it felt like to die, I was all for it. To heck with binge-watching *NCIS*. Bring on the pallbearers! And if Pastor Jacob wanted to do a funeral service for dummies—which I clearly was—then so be it. The feeling faded quickly when something vibrated against my hip. My phone was ringing.

Instinctively, I reached for it with my right hand. To my surprise, it worked. I had popped my shoulder back in place. The ache was still present, but the lightning-hot pain was gone. With great care, I turned on my side and pulled the phone out. Mrs. Wilkens had texted me.

where are you

I thought about texting her back, but suddenly I was exhausted. I needed to rest for a bit and then try the stairs. Perhaps someone had unlocked the door.

A little light filtered through from the bulb at the bottom of the stairs. Hannah must have left it on. I patted my back pocket and found that I still had the flashlight and Mrs. Wilkens's magnifying glass. I would spend ten minutes letting my shoulder settle back into the joint. Then, I would tackle the stairs.

Before I could close my eyes, the phone vibrated once again. I was tempted to shut it off but worried that I had so little battery turning it back on would drain it. Mrs. Wilkens wrote in all caps:

CALLING 911 IF YOU DON'T REPLY

I replied.

found bible trying to get out

Ramona had indeed uncovered a hornet's nest. I needed to get the book to the police.

When I stood up, I found I could walk without either passing out or throwing up. This was a good sign.

At the bottom of the stairs, I stopped and listened for household sounds. I heard some noises in the distance, but they appeared to come from outside. I prayed that I could open the door. I needed to get out of this hell hole and to a police station. I spied the dropped Bible on the floor beneath the window. I was within three steps of it when the door opened. Hannah stood holding a box.

"Psst."

She motioned me to the steps. I reached for the Bible and yelped at the pain it caused my shoulder. Ironically, I thought, what I really needed right now was some oxycodone.

Hannah walked carefully down the stairs. Her eyes were wide, and she turned often as if to listen for sounds upstairs.

"Why are you here?" I whispered.

"Voice inside my head say to come."

Charlee? But I didn't have the energy to ask, and this wasn't the time for a discussion about woo-woo stuff.

She pointed to the door. "When they go, you can go."

I nodded. At the bottom of the stairs, I sat down and patted the step. "Hannah, sit down and tell me what's going on." My voice was a mere whisper and had a tremor to it. "Did you put a Bible in my car?"

Her eyes widened. "Don't want no trouble. Mrs. Jennifer ask me to." Shuffling noises came from overhead. She glanced up. "I must go upstairs, or they will miss me."

"Are you being held here when you don't want to be?"

I thought about Mrs. Wilkens and her nattering on about human trafficking. Perhaps this was part of the puzzle that added to the evil of the parish house.

"Oh no, Missy. The Jennings are good to me. I help for two years, then they send me to school, and I get card to work here."

My god, I thought. Mrs. Wilkens was onto something.

"How did you get here?"

She smiled. "I help the church in Haiti, and Pastor Jacob and Mrs. Jennifer, they bring me as a student. They say I can finish school here. But they tell me to be very quiet for now."

"In two years?" I couldn't see Jennifer using Hannah like that, but I also didn't know any of the Jennings that well.

Overhead, it sounded like someone had entered the backdoor. Hannah looked up quickly. "I go." She handed the box to me. "I think this is bad. I think this is what makes Mrs. Jennifer sick."

I took the box and opened it in the weak light. Inside were packets of a powdery substance. "What is this?"

"Medicine from farmer's market. Mrs. Hilda buys it and tells me to put in the tea and water for Mrs. Jennifer. I think it's bad medicine." She whispered as she hurried back up the steps.

I thought back to our 911 call for the ambulance and how panicked Hilda had looked. I heard Jennifer's voice in my head, the whisper, *is it safe*? Was Hilda poisoning her daughter-in-law?

Chapter Forty-One

I needed to get out as quickly as possible. I moved up the stairs, hugging both the Bible and the small box. At the top, I stopped to listen. It sounded like voices in the backyard. Damn.

Charlee spoke to me, *Front door.*

"Thanks." I stepped into the kitchen. "Really, I mean it."

In the kitchen, a tea kettle boiled on the stove, making little burping noises. I needed to get through to the front door before it started to whistle. I walked softly on the linoleum floor, hoping to make as little noise as possible. I heard no other sounds besides the tea kettle. Maybe I was home free.

Then, as I rounded the corner from the kitchen into the living room, the high-pitched usher walked in the front door, studying his phone. Should I turn around and try the back door? I was ready to back slowly into the kitchen when the small box that Hannah had given me fell out of my grasp and tumbled to the floor with a soft thud.

He looked up, his mouth open in surprise. "What you doing here?" His eyes zeroed in on the Bible. His slicked-back, dark hair shone in the light of the living room. Even from across the room, I smelled the scent of hair gel.

Sometimes, the best defense is a good offense. I decided to attack.

"What are *you* doing here?" I countered as I stooped to pick up the small box. Instinctively, I pulled the Bible closer to my chest. "I don't recall letting you in."

For a moment, he blinked in confusion. I took it as my cue to move around him.

I almost made it. I was close enough to him to know that his deodorant wasn't working well underneath the heavy suit. I was almost by him when he pointed to the Bible. "Who give you that?"

I had to think quickly. My head pounded, and my whole upper torso ached from the injury to my shoulder. My brain fogged, and I hesitated a second too long in replying.

"Stop!" He took a step toward me with his arm outreached. "You steal. That Bible not yours!"

Overhead, I heard footsteps. Someone was upstairs.

I kept moving toward the door.

"Give me that!" He made a grab for the Bible.

I spun away, and the movement caused an intense pain to shoot down my side. I cried out as his hand brushed my injured shoulder. Don't pass out now, I pleaded with my body.

"Give me that!" he demanded again.

I clutched the Bible even tighter. "It's mine." In the back of my brain, I thought, this is playing out like a schoolyard squabble. I needed a teacher to intervene.

Tell him it's for Jennifer.

I took a deep breath and willed myself to relax and look calm. I said, "It's for Jennifer. She asked me to bring it to her in the hospital, and you are in my way." Then I added. "She's very sick, you know, and the Bible will be a great comfort to her."

He stood still. "Jennifer talk to you? What she say?"

I should have used his momentary hesitation to run. Instead, I took a couple of slow steps closer to the door as anger welled up in me. I pictured Jennifer trussed up with all the tubes and machines because of this stupid book.

"She says bad people are using it." I glared at him, finally realizing it was time to make a break for it. "What do you suppose that means?"

He stared at me for a moment. I quickly sensed that I wasn't doing a great job of going on the offensive.

Go!

I remembered how I used to play touch football with a group of kids in the neighborhood. The wiry little kid from down the street had a way of lowering his head, tucking the ball under his arm, and running it into the end zone. I put my head down and pointed myself toward the front door.

Go!

Charlee urged me on. I glanced up for a second to see the boys in the photos on the wall watching. They were my audience. I hoped they were cheering for me and not for the greasy-haired man who tried to grab the Bible from me.

"Give me that!" He lunged, and I jumped away, jarring my shoulder. White hot pain shot up my arm and into my neck, but I kept moving.

I almost made it to the front door. I would have, except that my foot caught on a throw rug in the entryway. At the same time that I tripped, the tea kettle burst out into its sonorous whistle.

The high-pitched usher was on me in seconds as I staggered forward. He grabbed my bad shoulder, and the pain was like someone kicking the air out of my lungs. My knees buckled, and the annoying black blobs floated through my vision. After all this, I was going to fail my mission.

This time, it was Hannah to the rescue. She came running in from the kitchen. When she saw me stumbling, she yelled, "Pastor Jacob! Pastor Jacob! Someone is hurt!"

I heard footsteps coming down the upstairs staircase. Jacob called out. "What's going on here?"

I didn't wait to hear an answer. The usher let go for a moment, and I thrust myself forward, ripping open the door. To my astonishment, I nearly tackled Julio on my way out.

He stood on the steps, looking startled. "Your friend told me to come and ask for you."

The usher came out the door, his face reddened with rage. Julio, to his credit, planted himself between the angered Russian and me.

"Stop!" Julio commanded, then launched into a stream of Spanish that so startled my pursuer that he pulled up on the front step landing.

Without looking back, I walked with as much dignity as I could muster toward Mrs. Wilkens, who stood on the corner waving like the queen.

Behind me, I heard a shrill voice. "She has Bible! She has Bible!"

A lower, calmer voice of Pastor Jacob replied, "Let her go. There's nothing in that Bible."

Under other circumstances, I would have questioned a Christian minister, claiming there was nothing in the Bible. Today, I was happy for his declaration.

Julio quickly turned and joined me.

"Holy crap, Ms. Johnson. What was that all about?"

Silently, I thanked Charlee once again.

Chapter Forty-Two

Mrs. Wilkens wasn't smiling when I approached her.

"Where have you been? I called the police, but they haven't come yet." She looked at Julio. "Fortunately, this nice young man was out on his steps and volunteered to go fetch you."

Fetch me? I didn't need fetching. I needed rescuing.

I looked back at the parish house. The usher had disappeared inside. While we stood watching, he hurried back out carrying a carton to a van parked in front of the house.

"They're taking the evidence," I gasped. "We need to do something."

A patrol car turned the corner just as the usher loaded the carton into the van.

I headed toward the patrol car, still clutching the Bible and the little box. Mrs. Wilkens stepped in front of me.

"Wait."

"What?"

"Let them discover whatever it is to discover on their own."

"But?" I couldn't find the words.

Mrs. Wilkens cleared her throat. "My friend Julio here, and I consulted before I called." She beamed at him. "He suggested that an anonymous call might be best."

I stared at both of them.

Julio nodded. "Ms. Johnson, you see. You broke into that house. We didn't want you to have to go downtown to explain."

Mrs. Wilkens shrugged sheepishly. "I was so worried this morning that I

228

brought two phones. This one belonged to Ramona. I was going to give it to one of the girls."

I felt like the heat and humidity were closing in on me. My forehead broke out in a cold sweat, and I shivered in the warm air. A car rumbled down the street, slowing to gawk at the police as they spoke to the usher by his van.

"What did you tell them?" I asked weakly.

Mrs. Wilkens' eyes sparkled with mischief. "Oh, something about drug dealing and maybe kidnapping."

"Kidnapping?"

She pointed to me. "Well, we weren't sure you would get out."

"My god," I whispered to myself. "The police received a call from a dead woman about kidnapping and drugs in Bibles. Whoa."

Mrs. Wilkens was no dummy. If my arm hadn't hurt so much, and my brain didn't feel like it was packed with cotton, I would have laughed.

I grimaced and pointed to my back pocket. "Take my keys and get me to the emergency room. My shoulder is killing me."

We should have stayed, of course, but all I wanted right now was a painkiller, a gin and tonic, and a nice nap.

We bid Julio goodbye, and Mrs. Wilkens drove me like a wild woman to the hospital emergency room after I told her how I'd dislocated my shoulder in the basement.

"It doesn't look dislocated."

"I relocated it." I closed my eyes and prayed we wouldn't crash.

The X-ray showed that my shoulder was back in its regular spot. I probably had some soft tissue damage that would take a while to heal. The doctor told me to see a physical therapist and an orthopedic surgeon. He gave me oxycodone, an immobilizer, and sent me on my way.

Two pills later, I lay on the couch in my apartment with a cold pack on my shoulder and a general dull ache. Mrs. Wilkens wouldn't let me have a gin a tonic.

"You know it can be lethal."

Thinking back on the bright light and warm cocoon that had surrounded me in the parish basement, lethal didn't sound so bad.

She sat next to me and randomly rubbed my feet as I filled her in on my parish house adventure. Goldie purred beside her.

"You found a Bible with drugs." Her eyes sparkled as she patted the Bible, now sitting side-by-side with the other one.

"Yes, but not in one of the cartons. I found it in the little room where I think Hannah sleeps. It's more like a cell, you know."

"See, human trafficking." She made a tsking sound.

I told her how I fell trying to hold onto the Bible and pull myself out the window. "Charlee guided me into the room with the bed and coached me on getting my shoulder back in place."

"Who's Charlee?"

"My twin," I smiled, thinking about how my twin had helped me. "She's part of me, you know. Mother told me so."

Mrs. Wilkens patted my foot, smiling and furrowing her brow at the same time. "How nice." I could tell, even in my opioid-induced state, she had no idea what I was talking about.

"She also got Hannah to bring me the box with the powder inside it that Hilda has been giving to Jennifer."

"Uh-huh."

The small box from Hannah sat on my coffee table next to the Bibles.

"We need to get it to someone to have those packets tested." My voice sounded like it came from someone else as my eyelids drooped shut. Next thing I knew, it was evening. I must have slept for a couple of hours. The living room was bathed in an orange-colored light. The ache in my arm had subsided, but I still had a throbbing headache.

Mrs. Wilkens looked down at me with a Cheshire cat smile. She waved a notebook in front of me.

"Look what I found!"

"Huh?" The room spun a little as I lifted my head.

"Ramona's last journal! I found it in the bag of her clothing we took from the dumpster."

I tried to sort out what she was saying.

"Remember, once we found the pills in her smock, we stopped looking

230

in the bag. While you were sleeping, I finished going through it. And guess what?" She waved the notebook in front of me.

I blinked hard to clear my head. "No one stole it?"

"No," said Mrs. Wilkens. "It turns out the girls had arranged for someone to pick up the rest of the stuff. It was all legitimate."

"Oh." I sat up with a groan. "Could you get me a glass of water?"

While she puttered in the kitchen, I urged my brain to work. It felt like bicycling up a steep hill in the wrong gear.

Mrs. Wilkens set down a plate of crackers and a glass of orange juice. "You need something in your stomach."

What I really needed was for her to go away so I could take more pills and crawl into bed. Instead of leaving, she sat down beside me with the latest Ramona journal and read, "At church today. Volunteered to clean with Jennifer. Jennifer crying and sez she found out they are using Bibles to smuggle drugs from Asia. She sez they're fake. Can't believe a church would do this. Will ask Pastor Jacob."

I pushed my way to a sitting position. My head pounded. "I need a pain pill and lots of water before I can take this all in."

Mrs. Wilkens brought me a large glass of ice water and my bottle of ibuprofen. I took two more oxycodone to go with the ibuprofen. In ten minutes, the pounding subsided enough that I could get my brain cells moving again.

"Fake HIV medicine?" I thought about how the packages of pills didn't match the description John gave me.

"Here's more," she squinted as she read. "Pastor Jacob sez Jennifer misunderstood. Welcome brings in pills for charity in poor countries. Pastor Jacob sez the pills are tested and they're fine. Feeling better now except that I can't keep taking stuff from patients. Soon will get caught. He needs different supplier."

I rubbed my eyes. "Jennifer was trying to tell me something was fake."

Mrs. Wilkens read the last entry. "Sorry I got into this. Rennie way sick. Jennifer pretty sick now too. Jacob won't leave me alone. Can I get more? Can I get more? Finally confessed to DG. He's going to meet with Jacob.

Worried I might lose my job."

I took the words in and nodded. "Okay, I think I've got this. She was stealing Oxycodone from work in exchange for the HIV medication from Jacob, which she then gave to Rennie."

Mrs. Wilkens bowed her head. "I think so."

"And then she told David Gray all about it?"

"Maybe that's why he was so careful when he talked with us."

I wasn't interested in David Gray, though. I was interested in the supposed drug smuggling, and I was interested in Hannah. She said Hilda was poisoning Jennifer. Why would she want to hurt her daughter-in-law?

"We have to talk with Hilda and Reverend Jennings. I don't know if they would tell the truth, but I need to ask them some questions."

Mrs. Wilkens nodded, "Good, I'll get my purse."

I sighed heavily. The oxycodone was going to my head, and I was getting sleepy again. "I was thinking tomorrow. Or even next week. Or maybe next month…"

Mrs. Wilkens was emphatic. "We have to talk to them now. While you were resting, I drove by the parish house. They had a big U-Haul in front, and that nasty usher was carrying boxes out to it."

"But…"

Goldie jumped up on the couch and stared at me at the same time Charlee entered my head.

They're leaving. Go.

"I don't wanna." My voice had turned into a four-year-old's whine.

Go.

"Did you say something?" Mrs. Wilkens busied herself, gathering up all our evidence as well as my car keys.

"Wait." Even though my brain was fogged over and I was being directed by an auditory hallucination, I realized it didn't make sense to take the Bible back to the parish house. I could see Hilda grabbing it from Mrs. Wilkens and destroying it. "Use my phone and take a picture of the Bible. We'll show them the photo."

Mrs. Wilkens gazed at me. "Ah, smart girl. But I'll drive. You are in no condition to get behind the wheel of a car."

I was in no condition to do anything but go to bed as I allowed the old lady to guide me out the door. Goldie watched us with an expression that said, you'd better come back. I need to be fed, you know.

Chapter Forty-Three

It was dark by the time we careened to a stop in front of the parish house. Mrs. Wilkens's driving had been like three shots of espresso. I was wide awake and gripping the door handle with my left hand.

The U-Haul Mrs. Wilkens had seen earlier was gone, replaced by the Jennings' sedan. I looked hopefully for two things: yellow police crime scene tape and a completely darkened house. I figured with either of these, we could turn around and go home. I saw no evidence of tape, and the house was ablaze in light, both upstairs and downstairs.

"Remember," I turned to Mrs. Wilkens. "If no one answers and you want to get inside, you are welcome to go through the basement window. I'll stay in the car."

She was focused on making sure she had the photos of the Bible and the little box with the powder in it. "We'll get to the bottom of this."

"Or go to jail trying."

She walked around to the passenger side and opened the door. "I need you to back me up."

"Sure." I was in great shape to back her up as I staggered behind her to the front door. Hilda answered after the second knock. Her expression changed from greeting to bewilderment to anger.

Hilda's face floated in front of me, her hair flying wildly out of its bun. She looked like a cartoon witch to me. I'd taken another oxycodone and a muscle relaxant before we left the apartment and wondered now if I'd overdone it.

"You." She pointed her finger at me and said something that sounded like "devilish fawn." I started to giggle. Me, a devilish fawn?

Mrs. Wilkens spoke in a loud, firm tone, "She is no devil's spawn. She's a good person who has uncovered your evil doings, and we need to talk." Her voice was steely enough that the giggle died in my throat.

Hilda did not move. I watched this standoff like a spectator at a boxing match. Someone was going to get knocked out. My money was on Mrs. Wilkens to win the fight, especially when I noted how she squared her shoulders, clenched her jaw, and hissed, "We will talk. Now. We can either do it inside or in front of the police."

Leaving the door open, Hilda disappeared inside. I followed Mrs. Wilkens. As soon as I saw the living room, butterflies launched themselves in my stomach. I fought the urge to abandon my elderly neighbor and head back to the car. I hated this house.

Hilda stood, blocking us from going further than the living room. Several packing boxes stood in the middle of the floor. All the artwork, including the creepy ones with the boys, had been taken down.

I took a couple of deep breaths and regrouped. I let the painkillers relax me. The photos of the boys were leaning against the wall. I stared at them long enough that their eyes seemed to come alive. I saw fear and resentment in their faces, not joy.

"Somebody is hurting those boys," I pointed to the photo. To my surprise, Hilda winced. Quickly, though, she pressed her lips together in a stern expression.

"What do you want?" Her voice was high-pitched and strained. "Haven't you done enough damage?"

Mrs. Wilkens motioned Hilda to the couch and commanded. "Sit."

Hilda didn't move. Behind her, I heard shuffling. Reverend Jennings emerged from one of the bedrooms wearing slippers, pajama bottoms, and a long-sleeved white shirt. His clerical collar was still buttoned around his neck. As soon as he saw us, his brow wrinkled in annoyance.

"What are they doing here?" His voice had the whiney quality of a tired child. Where was the man who commanded from the altar?

Again, Mrs. Wilkens pointed to the couch. "Both of you. Please sit." She reached into her large bag and pulled out the phone, swiping to open up the photos. "I want to know about this." Marching to the couch, she held the phone in front of them.

Reverend Jennings wheezed as he studied the photos. He looked like an old, sick man. I wondered what was wrong.

Hilda glanced at her husband, and he nodded. "If we explain, will you please leave us alone?"

The additional oxycodone permeated my brain. I felt woozy and very unsteady, so I slipped into the easy chair while Mrs. Wilkens paced in front of the Jennings.

"You were smuggling prescription drugs, weren't you?"

Hilda looked at her husband as he glowered at Mrs. Wilkens. "We were doing the Lord's work. We were bringing in low-cost drugs to help save the children."

Mrs. Wilkens pulled the Vivorna package out of her bag. "These?"

Why hadn't she left the box at home?

Hilda continued talking. "We were doing a good thing. Now people who can't afford these expensive medicines can get them." She assumed a pious look that did not fool Mrs. Wilkens.

"Who supplies you?" Mrs. Wilkens demanded.

They were both silent.

I decided to chime in. "I think it's your usher with the soprano voice and the greasy hair. He's part of the Russian Mafia, isn't he?" It sounded so silly I started to giggle.

Mrs. Wilkens glared at me the same way the assistant principal had when I was in junior high. I expected her to tell me to wipe the smile off my face. In fact, I was so addled, I wasn't sure if I was smiling or frowning.

Hilda scowled. "What's wrong with her?"

"I'm a little stoned." I tittered. Then I added, "Your drugs are fake. Fake." Oh, what a devilish fawn I was.

"No," Hilda was emphatic. "They're not fake. They've been tested."

Were they really so naïve?

Reverend Jennings started to cough. He brought out a white handkerchief and pressed it to his mouth. When he pulled it away, it had a spot of blood on it.

Somewhere in the back of my brain, the part that wasn't floating in opioids, a puzzle piece fell into place as I watched him. For the first time, I noticed the small, dark growth on the edge of his thin hairline. I'd seen this before, years ago, with my high school friend who eventually died of AIDS.

I felt calm and completely peaceful as I uttered, "It was you, wasn't it? You who wanted Rennie. You who railed against the evil inside you." I peered at him. "Ironic, huh?"

Mrs. Wilkens stopped pacing and stared at me. "What are you talking about?"

I pointed to the Reverend. "The drugs were for him, too." I remembered how Jennifer had said they didn't have health insurance. I guessed that the Reverend would never lower himself to go to a public clinic. To do so would be to admit he had the disease.

Hilda let out a sob as the color drained from her face. "How could you say such a thing about this righteous man of God."

"He likes young boys, doesn't he?" I really felt like I was floating benignly around the room. How many of those pills had I taken? "By the way, would you have some coffee? Without the arsenic."

Hilda stood up. "That's enough. Get out of my house!" If she'd had a weapon, she would have tried to kill me. I saw in her a mixture of rage, desperation, and guilt. She *knew* about her husband's pedophilia, and yet she protected him.

As I looked at her, I felt something boiling in me also. The giddiness, the silliness of the painkillers disappeared. I pointed to Reverend Jennings. "He's dying because the drugs are fake. And that's why Rennie is so sick."

Reverend Jennings stood up to join his wife. His voice cracked. "Leave this house!"

To both of them, I said, "Is that why you poisoned Jennifer? Because she figured out what you were doing? Is that why you killed Ramona?"

Mrs. Wilkens swiped the phone until the photo of the little box with the packets of powder came up.

Hilda's face turned the color of the white walls in the living room. She opened her mouth, closed it, and opened it again. "I didn't know it was bad. You can't accuse me of trying to poison that pathetic little girl. She made herself sick all the time. I was trying to help!" Her voice rose.

I wanted to slap her face and pull the rest of her hair out of her rat's nest bun. I wanted to pop Hilda in the nose, but when I stood up, the room spun.

Reverend Jennings started to cough. As the coughs wracked his body, his legs buckled. Hilda caught him and lowered him to the floor. "See what you did? See what you did?"

Calmly, Mrs. Wilkens called 911. "Yes, someone has collapsed and is having trouble breathing. I think he's having chest pains, too. Please send an ambulance." She gave the address, ignored the dispatcher's plea to stay on the line, and motioned me to the door.

"This is an ugly place. Let's get out of here."

We were pulling away from the curb when the ambulance, fire department, and Pastor Jacob arrived at the same time. I looked back to see him rush from the passenger side of a sporty car. Where had I seen it before? My head swam.

I sat back as Mrs. Wilkens squealed away from the curb and thought, "Who cares.?" I was asleep before she came to the first stop light.

Chapter Forty-Four

I don't remember much about Mrs. Wilkens bundling me into my apartment and onto the couch. I woke up in the near-dawn hours completely dressed and an Afghan tucked around me. My mouth was dry and sticky, and I had a dull headache that wasn't quite a hangover. Goldie sat on the floor, staring at me as if I was an alien. She meowed in a demanding tone and pointed her nose toward the kitchen.

I sighed, rubbed my eyes to help focus them, and sat up. "Breakfast for the queen, I suppose."

The smell of the cat food as I poured a scoopful into the dish made me nauseous. "Another reason to send you off to Cat Haven."

Goldie ignored me, jumping at the dish as soon as I moved away.

My shoulder still ached, but after last night, I wasn't interested in taking more opioids. I'd have to live with the ibuprofen for the time being.

Mrs. Wilkens walked in as I was trying to put on the immobilizer over my T-shirt. I wasn't having much success. The child in me wanted to whine and throw a tantrum. The adult wanted to curse like teenagers in the schoolyard.

She rescued me by deftly adjusting the Velcro. "Better?"

"You're good at that."

"Of course."

I didn't ask her to elaborate.

She brought fresh coffee and decent bagels. I had two bagels and coffee with lots of cream and sugar before I said anything.

While I was devouring breakfast, Mrs. Wilkens scanned through the *Star Tribune* for news about the Welcome Parish House. "I don't see anything," she said with disgust. "It seems like we gave them enough clues."

"We should go down to the police station and file a report." I spoke without enthusiasm. I knew that we had to stop the drug smuggling, but I didn't want to end up in the headlines. I guessed the Bibles with the drugs were probably long gone by now. At least we had one of them to use for evidence.

At times like this, I was very good at rationalization. I was surprised Charlee didn't show up to chide me about having a responsibility to step forward and do the right thing, but my head stayed clear of her chatter. However, the hot coffee did go down the wrong tube, and I coughed and sputtered until tears came to my eyes. Maybe that was Charlee's revenge.

"Do you think Hilda was telling the truth about Jennifer's poisoning?" I rasped when I could speak again. "Hannah said she got the powder at the farmer's market. I read a couple of weeks ago they closed down a booth because it was selling folk medicine that was poisonous."

Mrs. Wilkens continued to scrutinize the paper. She was now in the sports section, where it was noted that the Twins were on a two-game winning streak. "You'd think there would be something in the paper."

"Probably not in with news of another Twins pitcher being brought up from the Saints. If you want the latest, you go to the internet."

I booted up my laptop and checked the local news sites. One article of interest popped up.

Local Philanthropist Detained

Ivan Rusov, a real estate developer, and his nephew Nicholas Rusov were detained at the airport for questioning by DEA agents. Rusov, a Russian immigrant who has lived in the Twin Cities for seventeen years, is known for his charitable work. (Developing story.)

I smiled. I would bet another two bagels the high-pitched usher was Rusov. For a moment, though, I felt bad about Nicholas. At least he had shown some humanity in his concern for Jennifer.

"It's not enough." Mrs. Wilkens sat with her arms folded and her lips pressed into a fine line.

"What do you mean?"

"We still don't know who killed Ramona."

Outside, the lawn mower roared to life. I felt like we'd just spent the last few days running in a circle, and were back to the beginning.

John called midmorning. I'd finally convinced Mrs. Wilkens that she needed to get back to her routine. On Mondays, she volunteered at a senior daycare center. She helped out a local poet who worked with people with advanced Alzheimer's. When I said I couldn't see the demented writing poems, she'd told me, "You would be amazed at what's tucked into the depths of those old brains." I still preferred to work with kids, but it reminded me I was wasting my talents in front of the television.

I was in the midst of taking down all the flip charts on my wall while I waited for the orthopedic surgeon's office to call back when the phone rang.

"Hey," I said to John.

"I hope you haven't been breaking and entering."

I laughed. "If I have, you'll never know."

He wanted to fill me in on what he'd learned.

"The drug rep told my pharmacy friend the company was concerned knockoff drugs were getting into the country from Asia. He said the photo of the package you found was similar to ones that showed up in Indiana. The rep would very much like you to turn it in for testing."

Taking down the information on where to send it, I confessed. "I apologize to everyone involved, but this has to be an anonymous tip. I, um, didn't exactly get the medicine by honest means."

I wasn't sure if I detected a note of disapproval in his voice. "The other thing to let you know is that Jennifer is improving. My contacts say that she has asked to talk with the police. I'm not sure it has to do with the drugs or with the arsenic."

The information flooded me with guilt. Jennifer was braver than me.

I wasn't sure where to go in the conversation at this point. Would I ever see John again? I remembered how good it felt when I panicked to have his arms around me.

He helped, however. "I'm free tomorrow evening. Would you like to go to dinner?"

"Who is paying?"

I heard the laughter on the line. "You are, of course. It's tradition."

"Sure, the unemployed schoolteacher," I mumbled to myself when I ended the call.

By afternoon, I knew I also needed to get back to a routine—something that didn't involve crime, watching crime on television, or committing crime. I drove to Ed's house a bit erratically because my shoulder was in its brace.

When he opened the door, he immediately pointed to the brace. "So?"

In the stillness of his backyard, with lemonade and Oreo cookies, I told him about the Bibles and the drugs. He sat in his chair, looking straight ahead as if he wasn't listening.

When I was done, he grunted and cleared his throat. "Not God people at all." Two crows landed on the electric wires going to his house. They scolded him until he threw them a piece of the cookie.

He reached for another cookie, broke it up, and tossed it to the birds. He wrinkled his brow, "Why would they kill that drug lady?"

"I don't think they did." By now, several more crows had joined the first two. If Ed didn't stop, I was afraid his yard would end up with a swarm of them. "I think she was despondent over everything and overdosed."

Ed shook his head. "No. Someone else did it. You need to keep looking."

I waited for him to say more, but he stayed silent. The conviction in his voice sent a chill down my back. I remembered how he had predicted the unexpected winner of last year's World Series. I'd asked him how he knew. He'd shrugged his shoulders and said, "I just knew. That's all." He had an uncanny ability to read situations.

We settled into the next chapter in *The Iowa Baseball Confederacy*. I relaxed to the singsong of his voice and put Ramona out of my mind. It was good to listen to the story of an eternal baseball game going on in Iowa. Before I left, he handed me an Oreo to take with me.

"That Charlee, she's good. I'm glad she's back."

Now, I really did feel chilled. It was hard to convince myself that Charlee was imagined when Ed knew about her.

Just before I slid into the driver's seat of my smelly Toyota, I sensed her arrival.

Listen to him.

And then the voice was gone.

The next morning, I curled up on my couch with a cup of coffee to finally finish watching the next episode of *NCIS*. I'd decided this would be the end of my binge-watching. I'd find something to do for the betterment of mankind as soon as this episode was over.

Goldie and I had come to an arrangement. She could snooze undisturbed beside me on the couch while I watched television, and I would resist the urge to throw her off if she started to snore. We were India and Pakistan living in harmony.

At the end of the episode, they revealed the grieving sister was actually the murderer. Who would have guessed?

Charlee swept into my head. *You have work to do.*

"You're interrupting my program."

Pay attention to the formula.

"What? Can you clarify that remark?" My voice rose in either anger or frustration.

Help Ramona.

Really, this was getting tiresome. "She's dead, you know."

You can find the answer.

I sat up, groaning with the sharp pain in my shoulder. "She overdosed. End of story."

Goldie, apparently tired of this argument, leapt off the couch and headed to the bedroom.

Sometimes, you speak before you think.

A hallucination, insulting me. Really? I was readying a retort when the voice disappeared. "Hey, not fair. I didn't get a chance to tell you what I think about your cryptic messages and your audacious way of showing up. I'm going to apologize to the cat for talking with you. She must think I'm crazy."

As I walked back to the bedroom, I wondered why this visitation had made me so angry. It came to me as I squatted by the closet door and talked softly to Goldie. "It's okay. You can come out now. I'm done shouting."

I was angry because she was right, and Ed was right. We'd missed something. I thought again about the formula for the television series. It's always a minor character introduced in the beginning. What had I seen that didn't quite fit?

Pastor Jacob and a sports car, that's what.

"Okay, Charlee, you win."

Chapter Forty-Five

I spent a busy early afternoon on the phone. I even had a short but relatively civil cell phone conversation with Jacob Jennings. He was at the hospital with Jennifer on one floor and his father on another. I didn't ask how the Reverend was doing.

What he told me added to my suspicions. I did not share what I knew with Mrs. Wilkens. I wanted confirmation first.

When John arrived at my door that evening, I told him about my plan.

"Just a quick informational visit. Then we can eat. Your choice of restaurants, and it's on me."

He looked skeptical. "This better not be illegal."

Perhaps a little dangerous, I thought, but I didn't tell him.

He drove. I noted his car was older than mine.

"I used to have a shiny new SUV." He explained. "Now it belongs to the ex. Too bad, because I could haul a canoe and all my camping equipment in it."

I couldn't think of anything to say other than some clichés about the difficulty of marriage breakups. I'd certainly seen plenty with my teacher colleagues.

He pulled away from the curb. "Where is it we're going?"

I directed him to the house just off Lake and Pleasant. It was a neighborhood of large two-story houses. For many years, absentee landlords had carved up the old homes and turned them into rentals. More recently, young families had moved in and revitalized the neighborhood. One of the leftovers from the years of absentee landlords was a proliferation of halfway houses.

We pulled up in front of a once majestic, old white clapboard house with a large open front porch. Paint peeled from the porch pillars, and one of the gutters sagged beneath the eaves. The house had not been well cared for.

Several people were lounging on the porch, smoking cigarettes and drinking canned soda.

"You can stay in the car if you'd like. I will just be a moment." I fumbled with my left hand to open the door.

Without replying, John got out of the car and came around to help me open the door. He half-smiled as we walked up the sidewalk. "This better not result in another 911 call."

I approached a man who could have been thirty or sixty. His face was worn, and he had meth teeth. The front uppers were missing, and the rest looked like they would be gone soon.

"Hi," I said. "I'm looking for David Gray."

He glanced at his companions on the porch and back at me. "And who should I say is calling?" I sensed the four people on the porch pulling together to protect their counselor. Did he think I was a cop? Really, would a cop show up with her arm strapped to her chest in a shoulder brace?

"He helped a friend of mine, and she wanted me to give him a gift." I pointed at my bag. "Maybe you knew her? Ramona?"

Three out of the four loungers shrugged. Meth man looked interested. "What did she want him to have?"

I didn't like the way he asked the question. I backed up a little.

John interrupted. "Is he here?" He pointed to his watch. "We're running a little late, dear." I was pleased at how well he read the situation.

As if to answer the question, a red BMW pulled into the narrow driveway of the house. David Gray stepped out.

I waved to him like we were old friends. His hair was again a perfect advertisement for a pricey blow-dry shampoo. He had on a pair of cargo shorts and a polo shirt with a Ralph Lauren logo. He wore expensive loafers without socks. His car and outfit contrasted with the state of the house and the motley crew on the porch.

"Hi," I said. "I'm here with something from Ramona."

At first, he looked puzzled, as if the name Ramona didn't mean anything. Then he nodded. "Please come in."

"No, that's okay. I'll stay right here."

The four on the porch were suddenly very interested.

"She kept a journal, you know. It had lots of good things in it." I patted my bag and moved a little closer to John.

David joined the man with the bad teeth on the front steps. "She was a good, but very troubled, person," he said. He smiled, and I almost winced at the brilliance of his teeth.

I focused on the four halfway house residents and asked them, "Did you ever wonder how a halfway house drug counselor could afford a BMW?"

David continued to smile in a friendly but puzzled way. "What is this all about?"

I didn't answer the question. I pulled out a spiral notebook and made to open it. "Ramona was quite specific when it came to you."

He shrugged and said, "We all know that addicts are the best liars in the world." He looked for confirmation with the gathering on the porch. "Don't we?"

They nodded, and one of them grinned, "Damn straight."

I brought the attention back to the notebook. "Shall I read what she said?"

David took a step toward me and pointed his finger at the notebook. "If she accused me of dealing, she was wrong." He motioned to one of the residents, a woman in her mid-thirties with a snake tattoo wrapped around her throat. "I teach the Twelve Steps. The BMW belonged to my father."

The woman nodded. "David is the real thing."

I turned to John, who looked as confused as most of the people on the porch. "That's all I needed. Thank you. We can go."

I turned, and David called out, "Wait a minute. I'd like to see that journal. It's probably full of lies." He leapt off the porch and caught up with me. "What are you trying to do?"

I shrugged. "I just wanted to know, and now I do."

"I'd like to see it, please." He made a move to take it from me. I let go of it and watched as it fell to the ground.

While he stooped to pick it up, I hissed to John. "Let's go. Now!" And shoved him toward the car.

We were safely locked into the car and halfway down the block by the time David had paged through the journal. In the sideview mirror, I saw his expression change from bewilderment to anger.

It wasn't until we were seated at the Greek restaurant and I'd had a shot of ouzo that I finally explained what I had done.

"You see," I said. "Ramona's last entry was about how she planned to talk with David about Pastor Jacob and the oxycodone. The night we left the parish house, I saw Jacob get out of a sports car. I'd seen the car at the funeral and thought it was out of place in the neighborhood."

John sipped his iced tea and continued to look puzzled.

"I put the two together and did some checking. First, I talked with the caretaker in Ramona's building. Had she seen a red BMW around the time Ramona died? Yes, she remembered it because the man who drove it had such beautiful hair. She wasn't sure she could place him on the day she died, though."

An appetizer platter with Greek phyllo wrapped around cheese arrived. For the first time since Ramona died, I felt like eating decent food.

I brushed away a crumb and continued. "I called Jacob and asked him point blank if Gray was dealing in oxycodone. To my surprise, he broke down over the phone and admitted that once Ramona stopped supplying him, Gray offered to help. He also admitted that he told Gray Ramona was making noises about turning him in."

John put down the pastry. "He told you all of that? Why?"

"Guilt, I guess."

The lamb kebabs arrived sizzling hot. I ordered a glass of Retsina to go with it. As I toasted John, I said, "Never underestimate the joy of drinking something that tastes like Pine-Sol."

"I doubt the Greeks drink the stuff."

He sat back in his chair with his arms folded. "So, what was our 'informational visit' all about, and why did you let him have the journal?"

"Ah," I said. The ouzo and Retsina were making me happier than I should have been under the circumstances. "I wanted to see if he said anything about being a dealer. You might not have noticed, but all I said was that Ramona had written some interesting things about him. He was the one who used the word 'dealer.'"

John shook his head. "Hmmm."

"And," I grinned, "The notebook I left for him was empty." I didn't add that I'd come up with the ruse from one of the television episodes I'd watched this summer. I wanted him to think I was smarter than I really was.

John put his elbows on the table and leaned forward. "All my professional instincts tell me that was pretty dumb."

I should have been offended by his reaction, but instead, I thought it was funny. "Of course, it was dumb. But he's now going to be on the run."

For dessert, we ordered baklava. While it wasn't as light and flaky as some I've tasted, it was a fine ending for the meal.

We finished with coffee.

"After I fill Mrs. Wilkens in, I plan to report this to the police. Honest, I won't be anonymous."

He nodded in approval.

Back at my apartment, he walked me to the door. I invited him in, and for a moment, it appeared that he was thinking about it. In the end, though, we had a short but promising kiss.

"Sorry," he apologized. "I really like you, but I'm still too close to my divorce."

Once in the door, I allowed myself a heavy sigh. John was the most appealing nurse I'd ever met.

Over a glass of twenty-five dollar Pinot Grigio I'd brought back from my last trip to California, I filled Mrs. Wilkens in on my suspicions about David.

"I think he saw her as a threat to his business and visited her."

"Wait," Mrs. Wilkens pulled the cell phone out of her purse. "It never occurred to me to see what kind of calls she had."

As we flipped through the list of calls on Ramona's cell phone, we found what we were looking for. On the day she died, she received a call from an unidentified number. I dialed it, and when a man answered, I simply said, "David?" He replied, "Who is this?"

I hung up. "I recognized the voice. It was him."

After that, it was all I could do to keep her from calling 911 with the information. By the second glass of wine, we decided to put everything we knew together in an email and send it through the Crimestoppers website with a copy to Detective Peterson. Neither of us thought David was going to run.

We clanked our glasses together in honor of Ramona and said goodnight. Little did we know that the chapter wasn't quite finished.

Chapter Forty-Six

The glass shattered in my living room window at 2:37 a.m. I had been in a troubled sleep. At first, I thought it was part of a dream in which I was using the leather-bound Bible as a drink tray. A bottle of red wine tipped off the tray and shattered at my feet. In the dream, I stared at it while gasoline and smoke fumes wafted out of the shards.

Goldie woke me up meowing and scratching at my face. In my half-sleep, I batted at her, but she stayed on the bed with me. "What? Stop that!" She jumped onto the floor as soon as I sat up.

Follow the cat.

In the hallway, the smoke detector started bleating. My shoulder ached as I ripped the covers off and pulled on a thin cotton robe. Goldie stayed by my feet as if guarding me. Already, smoke seeped into my bedroom under the door. My first instinct was disbelief. This can't be happening. Except Goldie's cat voice grew into an unnatural howl as she ran for the bedroom door.

I heard crackling like a campfire coming from the living room. Grabbing my phone, I dialed 911 as I opened the bedroom door and found thick tarry smoke in the hallway. Goldie ran ahead of me, her tail straight up.

Stay with the cat.

I followed her.

A tinny voice on my phone repeated, "Ma'am, are you alright? Ma'am, can you talk to me?"

"Fire! I have to get out," was all I could gasp. Then I thought about all the others in the building, many far too old to get out quickly.

251

"Lots of old people in this building. Please hurry." For a moment, in my panic, I couldn't remember my address. I stuttered and finally got it out.

"Stay on the line," the tinny voice pleaded. "Help is on the way."

Outside my apartment, I heard thumping noises and shouts. The smoke detector kept up its shrill bleating. It felt like the noise was inside my head, behind my eyes. Goldie and I had now made it to the kitchen. Through the suffocating smoke, I saw how the flames shot out of my couch. Like my old Toyota, the couch had been with me for a long time. I felt an irrational urge to somehow save it.

Get out!

I watched in horror as the flames spread to the coffee table with the Bible and all the other evidence we'd gathered.

Where were the firemen? What was taking so long? I looked at my phone. The tinny voice was still there.

I made a move to the apartment door, but the heat drove me back. Goldie was still at my feet.

"Trapped. Can't get to the door." I'm not sure if I said it or thought it. The sirens weren't coming. Where were they?

Follow the cat. She's a survivor.

With the clouds of smoke and the confusion of the noise, I lost sight of Goldie. Above the crackling of the fire, I finally heard the sound of sirens. By the time they got here, I'd be overcome. I had no choice. I needed to crawl back to the bedroom and hope that I could close the door to keep the smoke out.

"Goldie! We have to go back to the bedroom." But I couldn't see her. I turned toward the hallway when I heard her "meow."

"Where are you?" The heat was growing more intense. I'd have to leave the cat and pray that she would be okay.

Look for the cat.

"I'm trying," I coughed and gasped in the horrid, contaminated air.

The smoke was so thick now that I could hardly see the living room from where I stood in the kitchen. Once again, I heard a "meow." It sounded urgent. I turned toward the sound and caught a glimpse of the straggly tail on the kitchen counter by the window over the sink.

If I could get to the window, I could crawl out. "I'm coming, Goldie," I croaked, dashing for the sink.

In my youth, I had gotten pretty good at climbing out windows. I willed some of that muscle memory as I scrambled onto the sink. My shoulder howled as I used both arms to lever my way up.

The window was latched, and I had to push Goldie away to get at it. Her eyes told me she was as panicked as I was. I could barely hear her over the noise from the now-roaring fire in my living room. It took several tries before I got the latch open. By then, the flames were licking at the doorway between the living room and the kitchen.

Above the din, I heard shouts. I thought I heard Mrs. Wilkens' voice, but I couldn't be sure. I willed her to be safe.

The window was a slider with a screen. I needed both arms to pull it open, and I knew when I opened it, the fresh air could draw the smoke and the fire. I had a very short time to get it open and get it out before I'd either collapse from the smoke inhalation or be burned to a crisp.

My right shoulder screamed at me as I pulled on the window with every ounce of strength I had. I fought back the pain and nausea and asked all the deities I could think of, plus Charlee, to save me. The fresh air flooded in with a whoosh. Only the screen blocked me from shimmying out. I tried butting it out with my head. It didn't move.

Outside, red lights flashed, and people shouted.

"Help!" I yelled. "I'm here." My voice was drowned out by the roar of the fire. How could something like this happen so quickly?

My brain was fogging, and the pain in my shoulder now overtook the entire right side of my body.

Pull, don't push.

Oh god, yes, the screen came out from the inside. I needed to pull it out, not push it. With my last ounce of rational being, I fumbled with a latch on the screen and pulled it away. It went crashing into the sink. I grabbed the cat and torpedoed us through the open window.

My right shoulder caught on the frame, and, for a moment, I saw the floating black blobs. In that insane moment, the thought crossed my mind: I'd forgotten to follow up on making the appointment with the orthopedic surgeon. Now, I'd never get it fixed.

The flames spread into the kitchen. I felt the searing heat on my backside as I scrambled through the window. Helping hands reached out and grabbed me, pulling me out. My shoulder dislocated once again. My last thought before I blacked out was, "You were right about the cat, Charlee. She saved me. Thank you."

Chapter Forty-Seven

Sitting in the ambulance with the oxygen mask on, I insisted they couldn't take me anywhere until I knew everyone had gotten out of the building.

"Where is Mrs. Wilkens? I need to know she's okay. And the cat? She saved my life. Is she okay?"

They finally led Mrs. Wilkens to me. She was wrapped in a blanket, cradling Goldie in her arms. Her gray hair was disheveled, and she smelled of smoke. She had on her neon tennis shoes.

"I was worried sick about you," she said. "But everyone got out. Mr. Diaz was amazing in getting us all up and out of the building."

A good caretaker is hard to find, I thought. I hoped they wouldn't check for his green card.

I pointed to Goldie. "Is she okay?"

"She's a little singed, but I'll have her checked out in the morning."

I explained to the firemen and then to the police that I woke up to something being thrown through my window. I thought about David and his ragtag group of people. Could they have done this?

The EMTs insisted I needed to go to the hospital. In a moment of panic and pain and exhaustion, I told them, "Not Hennepin County, please." The thought of being in the same emergency room as Josiah had been all those years ago nearly sent me into a full anxiety attack.

They took me to Fairview instead. I don't remember much about the next several hours except that in the noisy curtained cubicle, I finally drifted off to sleep. Who knows what they'd given me? And who cared at that point?

I woke up to the sound of Mrs. Wilkens haranguing a nurse down the hall. "Of course, I'm family. Just point me to where she is!"

The poor nurse didn't have a fighting chance against my neighbor.

Mrs. Wilkens swept in, her hair still tangled. At least she wore a clean T-shirt. She stood at the foot of the bed with her arms folded. "Well, this is a fine mess."

I squeezed my eyes shut a couple of times, trying to piece together what happened. My mouth was dry, and my head was filled with cotton. "What happened? Did my apartment blow up?"

"Humph, that damned counselor happened."

Before I could ask her to clarify, Detective Pete Peterson, dapper as ever, walked in. "So, Liza Johnson, you've created quite a storm."

This would have been the time for Charlee to chatter inside my addled brain, but she stayed quiet.

Detective Peterson pulled up a chair. "I got your email and discovered your apartment had been torched."

Mrs. Wilkens jumped in, "I've had a chat with this nice detective, and we have it all straightened out."

Straightened out?

"A neighbor down the street from your apartment reported a strange man hiding in his garden shed." Detective Peterson explained. "Turned out he smelled like he'd been doused with gasoline."

My brain wasn't taking this in. "A man in a shed smelling like gasoline? What?"

Mrs. Wilkens interrupted with an impatient tap of her foot. "It was someone from that halfway house. You know, where David Gray 'counseled?'"

"He was quite a talker," Detective Peterson added.

For the next ten minutes, they explained how David had directed him to "scare" me. He decided the best way was to hurl a Molotov cocktail through my window. He confessed almost immediately, and David was now at the precinct station being questioned.

"Oh. That's nice. Can I go home now?" I drifted back to sleep.

Two weeks later, Mrs. Wilkens and I sat on Mother's deck in Northern California. We were her only guests. Her mop creature, she claimed was a dog, had fallen in love with Goldie. I watched him sniff at her and try to lick her ear. She responded with a resounding hiss.

Okay, the cat was kind of growing on me. After all, she had led the way out of the burning apartment. With the help of a strong tranquilizer, one for her and one for me, we were able to take her on the airplane to California. The mop creature had decided he'd found his long-lost mate and followed her wherever she went. For the most part, Goldie ignored him.

It was a perfect afternoon, with bright sunshine and a cool breeze. I sipped the organic juice concoction Mother made for me. It was the color of mud but tasted of fresh blueberries. Chester sat in a lounge chair drinking the same stuff, and Mother sat beside him. She had a youthful glow to her that I envied. I felt old and cranky. I wasn't looking forward to more police interviews, lawyers, and shoulder surgery when I returned home.

"I still don't understand," Mother said, popping a fresh strawberry into her mouth. "Why did someone try to burn down your building? And who was smuggling drugs?"

For the umpteenth time, I told my story. The first several times, it was to police and investigators.

"It's complicated."

"I'll say," Mrs. Wilkens added as she fed little bits of cracker to the mop creature whose name was Riley.

"Here's the condensed version." I had it almost down to an elevator pitch. "Ramona was drugged and injected by her counselor, David Gray after she confronted him with his sideline of drug dealing. She learned about it from Pastor Jacob when Gray became his supplier after Ramona wouldn't get him more drugs."

Mrs. Wilkens jumped in. "You see, Ramona was trying to do the right thing. She was getting drugs for Jacob in exchange for Vivorna for Rennie. Ramona was a good person, just not a very wise one."

Poor Mother looked totally bewildered. "But what has that got to do with poisoning and Bibles?"

"And human trafficking," Mrs. Wilkens added with emphasis.

I sighed. At this rate, we'd be explaining all afternoon. "Ivan Rusov was smuggling fake HIV drugs into the country in Bibles. He then turned around and sold them through a shell company to charitable organizations that were supplying free drugs to third-world countries like Haiti. The Jennings didn't know the drugs were fake."

"Or so they claim," Mrs. Wilkens interjected.

Mother looked distressed. "But that's immoral."

"But very lucrative, I'm told."

Chester repositioned himself on the lounge chair and took Mother's hand. "So, the church was a front?"

I needed a gin and tonic to get through the explanation. Unfortunately, Mother didn't believe in alcohol. I was stuck with my mud concoction, and unless it fermented quickly, I would stay sober except for the pain pills.

"No, the church was legitimate. Rusov met the Jennings in Haiti and discovered Reverend Jennings's little secret about his need for boys and his HIV status. He decided he could use this information. He promised the drugs for Jennings and sold them on the idea they were doing God's work by supplying cheap HIV prescription medications to needy people."

Riley, the mop creature, yawned and settled next to Goldie, who was sunning herself on the deck. Oh, I thought, to live The Life of Riley.

"They were duped," I added. "But I don't have any sympathy for them. The Reverend is a predator with HIV, and his son is addicted to prescription pain pills. Meanwhile, the mother is just plain nuts." I pictured Hilda Jennings singing her dirge-like aria in the church and shuddered.

"Oh my." Mother stood up. "Can I get you more to drink?"

Mother tended to leave a conversation when things either got too complicated or shed light on the frailness of humanity—especially if the villain was a mother. She had never completely recovered from the trauma of Josiah's Household.

After she closed the screen door to the deck and disappeared inside, Chester asked, "So, what was it about the daughter-in-law? The one who was poisoned?"

I closed m eyes picturing the frail Jennifer telling me how much she liked teaching the children.

Mrs. Wilkens jumped in to explain. "They think the poisoning was accidental. Hilda was fed up with what she thought were Jennifer's fake illnesses and decided some folk medicine would help. Unfortunately, it was laced with arsenic. On the plus side, the arsenic really broke the case." She flashed a grin at me.

"In talking with my friend John, who is a nurse, he suspects that Jennifer hasn't been faking periodic illness all these years. He thinks she has some kind of an autoimmune disorder that flares up. It flared again when she began suspecting that the HIV drugs were a scam. When Ramona told her that Rennie wasn't getting any better, she put two and two together."

Mother came back out with a tray of sliced fruit. This was my third day at her house, and I was craving potato chips and dip, not fruit and yogurt. Mrs. Wilkens, on the other hand, was perfectly happy with the food. So was the mop creature. Goldie, on the other hand, demanded canned liver or some such awful meat daily. The vet had told us that she needed it to help recover from the singeing and the smoke.

"Nice weather," Mother commented. It was clear that she wasn't interested in the rest of the story—like how my shoulder got dislocated twice and how my apartment burned up. "We are in for a lovely fall if it doesn't get too dry. I'd hate to see forest fires again."

Mrs. Wilkens's phone rang. She took the call in the house. Riley trailed behind her. I sat enjoying the sun on my face and tried to push all the "to-do's" out of my brain. I would need at least six months of temporary housing until my apartment was redone. Fortunately, the firemen arrived in time to save the building, so most of the damage was confined to my apartment.

The Northern California air and the aura of peace at Mother's lulled me. I was just dropping off to sleep when Mrs. Wilkens came back out.

"Well," she said. "That was my sister Grace. They are reopening Ramona's file. The drug tests came back from the autopsy, and it looks like she was full of sedatives before she died."

I opened my eyes to her expression, which said, "Didn't I tell you?"

"Besides that," she added, "Grace is going to take Hannah in, so she can finish her schooling. Grace won't expect her to be the household slave."

All's well that ends well, I thought, as long as the immigration people don't meddle.

Mother, Mrs. Wilkens, and the mop creature retired to the house to talk about the menu for supper. Goldie stayed with me.

"I think a nice vegan nut loaf with a quinoa salad would be good." Mother's voice from the kitchen was downright joyful as she talked.

Chester looked at me with a rueful expression. "She's driving me crazy with all this health-food stuff. What I'd really like is a rare steak and a good baked potato with all the works."

"I know just the place. Should we sneak out?"

I drove Mother's ancient van to a steak house in Grass Valley. The van ran smoother than my Corolla, even though Mother hardly ever changed the oil or did any maintenance on it. She believed that cars responded to Karma. Who knew?

Chester ordered a scotch on the rocks, and I had my usual gin and tonic. We sat in comfortable silence, waiting for the good old-fashioned white flour dinner rolls to arrive.

Charlee, who had been silent since after the fire entered my head. *They should get married.*

I coughed, sputtered, and thought about a retort, like "mind your own business." Except Charlee was gone before I could get my voice back.

I studied Chester for a few moments before I leaned toward him, "Isn't it time for you to get married?"

He thought about it. "Vincent would not be happy about it."

"Then don't tell him."

He proposed the next day. Mother accepted and moved immediately into high gear. The next couple of days were abuzz with hasty email and telephone invitations, menu planning, and wedding arrangements. Five days later, they were married on the deck of Mother's log house. Riley, the mop creature, wore a collar of daisies, but Goldie would have none of it. She spent the wedding in my mother's closet. The wedding cake was gluten-free and, yet, surprisingly edible.

After the ceremony, Mrs. Wilkens and I looked at each other and said, "Time to go home." I had school to prepare for, and Mrs. Wilkens needed to settle into a temporary apartment down the street from our building.

Two days later, just before we left to catch our plane, Mother came out with a gift bag. "I want you to have this."

Inside, wrapped in pink tissue paper, was a framed photo. "That's you and your sister. She was such a calm, sweet little baby."

I studied it. Mother sat in a chair with two babies wrapped in blankets. Father stood behind her with one hand on her shoulder. Mother had a serene expression, while Father's eyes appeared to be lit with amusement. In Mother's arms, one baby slept peacefully, and the other had her face scrunched up like she was about to wail. "Which one was Charlee?"

Mrs. Wilkens peeked at the photo and chortled. "That one. You're the one who has your mouth open." She looked at Mother. "Am I right?"

Mother nodded, her eyes shiny with tears. "She was never very strong. I think that's why she was so calm."

Mrs. Wilkens patted Mother on the shoulder and gave her a long hug while I murmured, "Thank you."

Once on the plane with Goldie tucked in her carrier under the seat, Mrs. Wilkens said, "That must have been hard for your mother to lose a child."

"She never talked about her, just like she never talked about my father. She's had some terrible losses in her life, I guess."

"Poor dear."

We chatted about the weather back in Minnesota, about how nice the wedding was, and how uncomfortable the airplane seats were. Finally, Mrs. Wilkens asked, "Where will you live?"

"Oh, I found a place on Craig's List." I kept my comment vague because I needed some space from the old gal. Who knew what intrigue she might otherwise drag me into?

I settled into my seat and closed my eyes. As the airplane climbed above the clouds, I thought about Charlee. Would she continue to come to me as a voice in my head? Would I ever see John again? The plane's engines roared,

and a brilliant sun poured through the window.
The adventure has just begun, sis.
I fell asleep without responding.

A Note from the Author

A number of effective medications exist both for the prevention of AIDS and the treatment for those who are HIV positive. The medication featured in this book, however, is a product of the author's imagination.

Acknowledgements

Thank you to the late Dawn Dowdle, my agent, who saw something in my writing and took me into her fold. To Shawn Reilly Simmons, my Level Best editor, who has helped me refine the characters and the story. Both have been great supporters and advocates. To my writer's group, Jan Kerman, Carol Williams, and Randy Kasten, who are honest and astute in their critiques. To Jerome, who has been with me through all the iterations of Liza and this story.

About the Author

Linda Norlander is the author of A Cabin by the Lake mystery series set in Northern Minnesota. Books in the series include *Death of an Editor, Death of a Starling, Death of a Snow Ghost,* and *Death of a Fox.* Norlander has published award-winning short stories, op-ed pieces, and short humor featured in regional and national publications. Before taking up the pen to write murder mysteries, she worked in public health and end-of-life care. Norlander resides in Tacoma, Washington, with her spouse.

SOCIAL MEDIA HANDLES:
  facebook.com/authorlindanorlander

AUTHOR WEBSITE:
  www.lindanorlander.com

Also by Linda Norlander

A Cabin by the Lake Mysteries:
Death of an Editor
Death of a Starling
Death of a Snow Ghost
Death of a Fox

www.ingramcontent.com/pod-product-compliance
Lightning Source LLC
Chambersburg PA
CBHW050152120726
47903CB00002B/590